Just Between Us

**Center Point
Large Print**

**This Large Print Book carries the
Seal of Approval of N.A.V.H.**

Just Between Us

DEBORAH BEDFORD

CENTER POINT PUBLISHING
THORNDIKE, MAINE

This Center Point Large Print edition
is published in the year 2005 by arrangement with
Steeple Hill Books, a division of Harlequin Enterprises Ltd.

Copyright © 2002 by Deborah Pigg Bedford.

The text of this Large Print edition is unabridged. In other
aspects, this book may vary from the original edition. Printed in
Thailand. Set in 16-point Times New Roman type.

ISBN 1-58547-587-4

Cataloging-in-Publication data is available from the Library of Congress.

Evergreen is a little village in the Colorado foothills. It does have a lovely old museum and a gathering place called Hiwan Homestead, run by the Jefferson County Historical Society. Monica's antique toy store is a fictitious addition to what already exists there. I trust my friends in Evergreen will forgive me for taking such poetic license with their town.

Just
        between
                us,
it was easy, once,
to say we'd be sisters and mean every word . . .
We drew hearts on our hands and
vowed
never
                to wash them
                off . . .
                                I
                        look
                                now
                and see a woman's hand,
                my own,
                a mother's hand, a wife's hand,
                and in my mind
I still see the drawing there,
a tiny heart that promises we *belong* . . .
                        Sisters
                        who teased
                        who grieved
                        who tried
                                to laugh,
                                to comfort,
                                and who cried.

We led each other to a stronger place,
learned to live within God's grace.
       Sisters.
       It didn't happen when we were nine.
       It took a life
              and love
                    and time.

—Deborah Bedford

This book is dedicated to my Heavenly Father,
in whom all things are possible.

Chapter One

February 17
Dear Diary,
I know you are wondering why I ripped out all the January pages and all the rest of February and just started on today. I did it because I filled January up with dumb stuff. Little girl stuff. And now I'm not a little girl anymore.

I ripped everything out so I can just open this book and start all over on this day.

This is going to be a very important book. I am going to write my thoughts and feelings in here so when I get old and I have a daughter who is fourteen, I can remember about some of the things I was thinking and feeling. I really think I'll remember everything. But I decided to write it down in case I don't. Because I wonder if my mind might change when I get old. Like when I get to be thirty.

The first thing I have to write about is being a teenager. When I grow up I am always going to love my daughter. I won't care if she talks back or if she says the wrong thing or if she isn't very pretty or if she wears too much purple eyeshadow or even if she screams at me. I don't mean to scream at Dad. But sometimes it seems like everything aches inside me all at once and I don't know why. I need him to be my friend and he's too busy worrying about the trains and I just want to die.

That's when I scream. I want him to grab me and shake me and make me stop. And then I want him to hug me and tell me he's going to make me feel better inside. But Dad never will. He just stands there looking at me like I'm a real goof, and his arms just dangle there. He just stands there and looks at me like everything is wrong with me. And maybe it is.

I'm not going to do that when I have a kid. A baby.

Diary, maybe you are thinking, why is she writing all this stuff and talking about her own kid? I'll tell you why. This is kind of hard to write. I'll probably look at this page next week and laugh. (I hope I can laugh.) Anyway, here it comes.

I am going to have a baby. Me. Ann.

I think.

I skipped school today and walked over to that Planned Parenthood place. And I'm supposed to call them back later and they'll tell me. But I'm already pretty sure. And I'm scared, I think.

I thought to have a baby you had to do it all the time like you do when you're married or when you're in the movies. I asked Pam, a girl at school I hang around with, what she knew about it and she said that it's common knowledge to everybody that it could happen any time. But nobody told me that.

My dad is going to die, I mean not funny die or even mad die. I think this is going to hurt him so much he will die. But no matter what he does, I am

*going to get a little baby that belongs to me. And
that will be okay, I think. I hope the baby will love
me.*

*I'd better go,
Love,
Ann Leidy Small
(Age 14)*

The pretty dark-haired teenager lay down her pen and
stared out the window of the tiny town house she
shared with her father. It was snowing outside again,
great, huge flakes that covered everything like sugar
frosting. *I've got to call that place and really find out,*
she prodded herself. But she didn't want to call yet,
didn't want to know for sure that everything was
changing. She wanted to sit on her bed and pretend
everything was going to stay the same. *But,* she
reminded herself, *I don't really want anything to stay
the same, either.*

Ann stuffed her diary beneath a pillow and then
flopped across the unmade bed to reach for her purse.
She rummaged around in it until she found the business
card. A nurse had written the number she needed on it.
She carried it into the kitchen, where the phone was,
and dialed. And the nurse at the other end gave her the
answer she was half hoping, half dreading to hear.

"Your test came back positive, Ann. You *are* pregnant. If you need anything, counseling or advice, please
come . . ." But Ann didn't hear the rest of it. The words
hummed in her ears, but never made it to her brain.

She had to tell her father.

He's not gonna understand. He never understands anything anymore.

She was scared, but she had no other choice—she had to tell him. She went into the den and curled her legs under her on the ancient olive-green sofa. It would be a long wait; he was never home from work before nine anymore. But if she made herself sit here, made herself not move until her legs ached, she knew she could make herself brave enough.

Sure enough, it was hours before he came home, looking tired and angry. She could tell when he came in the door that he had had a horrible day.

"What are you doing up? Isn't your homework done yet?"

She shook her head at him. She had never even thought to finish it.

"What's going on then?"

"I need to talk to you, Daddy."

The little-girl word she so seldom used with him anymore tugged on his heart. And it made him realize more than ever how grown up she had become. He couldn't believe it was little Annie sitting there. Where had the kid he had known so well gone? She had turned into a woman who was a stranger to him.

It had seemed like only months before but, really, it had been years since he had yanked her dark curls to tease her when he came home from his brakeman's job on the train. He had worked for Union Pacific then, and every time he walked in the door, he'd teased her and told her she was ornery before he squeezed her to him.

"I'm not ornery. I'm *Ann*." She'd danced around him

as if he hadn't even looked at her yet, flailing her arms against his knees as he tried to hug her momma. "Did the train go fast? Did you get the coal to California? Did you bring me anything?"

He always whipped a pack of gum out of his pocket and stuck it behind her ear. "I love you, Pip-squeak. Here's your present. Go away for a minute so your mother and I can smooch."

Now she stood before him and he didn't even know who she was. He and his daughter had stopped telling each other "I love you" a long time ago. He couldn't remember when or why—it had been a slow process, eroding over days, months, even years. He looked at her now and saw a girl he didn't know, a dainty, emotional beauty whose developing, compact body shouted a beware signal to him every time he thought about hugging her or teasing her or telling her he still cared.

"I need to tell you something." She was clutching a sofa pillow with both hands, holding it in front as if it was a shield. "It isn't an easy thing to say. And you aren't going to like it."

There was something about her expression that made Richard feel as if he had deserted her and, really, there were times he knew that he had. He didn't even know what to say to Ann anymore. It made him ache just to look at her. He diverted his eyes from her and searched for the day's *Rocky Mountain News*. He couldn't remember where he had dropped it.

"You have to look at me. This is important."

He found the newspaper beside the TV set. And then he made himself meet her eyes again. It was the first time he realized how scared she was. "Maybe you'd better go ahead, Ann."

"I had this *test* today."

He had no idea where she was coming from. "Did you do good on it or did you flunk it or what?"

"No." She reddened. "Not that kind of test. Not the kind you flunk. The nurse gave it to me. At a clinic."

"Out with it then. Stop fooling. What sort of test?"

Ann couldn't look at him when she said the words. She didn't want to see the anger or the pain or even worse, the indifference in his eyes. She focused on the gray, scuffed toes of her sneakers. "It was a pregnancy test." A little louder. "It came back positive." She couldn't make herself sound quite as penitent as she thought she should sound for him. She had been so lonely for so long. Maybe this would make it better. She touched her stomach. "A baby, Dad."

He stared at the top of her head. The head with the curls he used to tousle.

She wouldn't raise it.

He felt as if the stranger standing before him had dealt the daughter he loved one final, fatal blow. Despite their differences, he had wanted her to have everything. "Ann. No. *You can't be.*"

"But I am."

"But you're too young—" his voice sounded unfamiliar even in his own ears, staccato, grinding in his throat like gravel "—too young and too smart for this."

"No." Her voice was louder now. "No on both counts."

He wanted to shake her but he didn't; he hadn't

touched her in years. "Oh, Ann, didn't you know? Couldn't you see . . . ?"

But she was shaking her head. And now she was crying. "No, Daddy. I really didn't know."

She had called him daddy again. The word itself and the knowledge of what she had done twisted inside of him and then, like a fist, hauled off and flattened his guts. He wanted to rip into something. A boy had touched her. Seen her. *Used* her. "Who did this to you?" He would kill the kid.

"Don't you know?"

Her question threw him off guard. He had been home so seldom with her that he really didn't know. But then he remembered one boy from the high school. Ann had talked about him some, and since she had met him, she'd seemed happier. Richard couldn't remember his name. "I don't . . ."

"Danny Lovell." It was the first time he had seen her smile since he walked in the front door.

"How could you let him do this to you?" The pain in his guts was turning to fury.

"I love him. That's the only reason . . . I . . ."

For one horrible moment, Richard wanted to thrash out at her, to wound her the way she was wounding him. "You don't love that boy. You're only fourteen years old! You don't know anything about love!"

"I do so!" She was shrieking at him. "Danny's taught me everything about it."

"He's a kid. He can't know anything about it."

"He cares about me. And he's sixteen. And he wants to be with me. He makes me feel special."

"He's *using* you," he shouted at her.

"Well, at least he's *around*," she shouted back, and, when she did, he realized everything she was accusing him of. "At least he's *here*. Not like you. Not like you who doesn't even care. I don't know why you're acting so mad. You don't even want me!"

Oh, man. I didn't know. I didn't know it was doing this to her.

"You just stay at the station all day and all night long worrying about your stupid trains. That's all that matters to you and I know it."

He had come here to Denver for her sake. After her mother died, he had wanted the two of them to live a civilized life without him racing after the freight trains and the big money. He had saved just enough out of that long-ago freight-train money to give her a start in college. But now, he reminded himself furiously, it didn't matter. She had blown it in a big way.

"You can't say that," he growled at her. "I am a father and my duty is to work hard and bring home money so we can *eat*." For the past five years, he had been a mother to her as well, and he supposed he hadn't been a good one. But, try as he might, he couldn't do everything.

Ann's words came back to him then. *No, Daddy. I really didn't know.* The words tormented him as they echoed over and over again inside his head.

This is my fault, he thought. *And it has been all along. I was so afraid to reach out to her . . . so afraid to tell her what it means to grow up. Perhaps Ann's right to blame me.* He struggled to shore up his emotions. And his voice, when it came, was certain and strong. "What would your mother do if she was here?"

"I don't know," Ann said.

"I thank God she isn't. I thank God she can't see what you've done." *And what we've done to each other.*

"Maybe . . . if she was. . . ." Ann trailed off. But Richard finished her sentence in his mind. *Maybe it wouldn't have happened. Carolyn would have helped Ann. Or me.* But Carolyn was gone and he was alone now, always alone, except for his daughter.

Ann was standing close to him, and for a moment he felt a strange beckoning, as if her thoughts were so penetrating they were reaching out to him. He imagined she wanted him to be her daddy again, to cuddle her, to tell her everything was going to be okay. But he couldn't do that, couldn't tell her because, now, things wouldn't be.

He faced her. "Are you going to have the baby?"

She flinched. "Yes."

"Will you keep it?"

"Yes."

"There are other things you can do, you know. Adoption. There are couples all over the country searching for an available baby. You can see them on the Internet." She had been his baby girl once. So tiny and innocent and beautiful. He remembered the first time he had ever seen her, lying in Carolyn's arms, wrapped in everything pink they could find. She'd been bald as a balloon, with eyes open, alert, surveying him.

"I want to keep it."

He couldn't soften toward her now. "I'm not supporting another kid, Ann. I've already paid my dues."

She sighed. "I know that. I wouldn't ask it of you." It was what she had expected him to say. But still his words made her cringe. *He wasn't happy taking care of me. He was biding his time, paying his dues. And that doesn't have anything to do with loving me.*

"If you stick with this decision, you've got to find a job. You won't have time for school. And you won't have any time with the baby, either, because you'll be working so hard." *Like me. Like what I did with you.*

"You don't think I can take care of it? You don't think I'm even good enough for that?"

He knew he had to tell her what he was feeling. He knew she deserved his honesty. He wasn't trying to be cruel. "I used to think *I* was good enough for that. But I wasn't. Bringing up a kid by yourself will be the hardest thing you've ever done, Ann. Maybe the hardest thing you'll ever do."

He didn't want her to be idealistic about a baby. And this time when he spoke to her, it was the first tender thing he'd said to her all evening. "Ann. A real baby isn't like a doll. You can't put it up on a shelf when you are tired of it or when you are finished playing."

"I know that," she said.

Maybe in her mind she knew it, but in her heart she didn't. He could read it in her eyes. "Babies never sleep and they eat every two hours and the diapers cost ten bucks for a bag that lasts only a few days."

Ann looked shattered. "Was I that horrible?"

No. You weren't horrible. But Carolyn wasn't four-teen when she had you. "You were a big job, Ann." The

20

moment he said it, he knew it was the wrong thing. He was alienating her again. It happened every time he forgot how careful he had to be and started being honest with her instead.

She looked as if he had just punched her. "I hate you," she whispered. "I hate you."

"Fine," he said, giving up, knowing he was defeated. "It's a free country. Hate me." Ann exhausted him. Carolyn's death exhausted him. His job exhausted him. "Feel whatever you want to feel about me." He was grieving for her now. He knew he had lost her. And his next words wrenched out of him, tearing loose a part of him as they did so. But they were words he knew he had to say. "I haven't been a good father to you, Ann. And I won't be a good grandfather to a baby. You mustn't count on me for anything."

"I won't," she said bitterly. "I never have."

He turned and walked away from his daughter. Her last words were a final knife plunge into his heart. He was beaten. He stalked into his bedroom, the pain he felt making his movements disjointed and awkward. *Oh, Carolyn, I can't go through this alone.* He could hear Ann sobbing as he shoved the bedroom door shut and kicked a pile of dirty clothes out of his way. *How could she do this? How could I have let her do this?*

Richard surveyed his reflection in the mirror. Then he looked down at his hand and watched his own fingers ball into a huge fist. Without further ado he swung his arm back and, almost gleefully, using the power of his emotions, slammed his fist through the plasterboard wall.

Ann jumped at the sound of the wall shattering in the other room. "Oh, please," she wailed into her hands. "Oh, please . . . I don't know what . . . to do! Daddy, Daddy . . ." She sobbed heartbrokenly. *I knew he was going to be mad. Maybe I hoped he was going to be mad.* And, as she thought about Richard's reaction, she began to feel better.

Richard couldn't know it but his anger had been a victory of sorts to Ann. She had been almost afraid he wouldn't care. But maybe . . . if he cared enough to get that furious . . . maybe he still cared about her.

Ann buried her face in her hands again. It seemed as if she had been sitting here for hours but it was all over now. Or maybe it was just beginning. She wasn't certain. And this time she didn't cry, she only whispered it, as the clock beside her ticked away the minutes. "Maybe," she said softly, "maybe he'll stay at home more. . . ." And then she was sobbing again, great racking cries that came from somewhere deep within her. "Maybe . . . he'll start caring about me . . . more than he cares . . . about the *trains*. . . ."

Monica Albright gave the miniature locomotive one more tweak with the tiny screwdriver before she held it up and studied it. She had acquired the turn-of-the-century steam engine for the antique toy museum. It was a lovely addition to the collection. But it would be even nicer if she could get the thing to run.

"Okay." She spoke as if the little train could hear her. "We're going to try this one more time." She carried it into the exhibit room and placed it on the track. "Here you go."

Carefully she took her hands off it and switched on the power. The model engine lurched forward. "Sylvia!" she hollered to her assistant. "It runs!" And then, for a while, she was lost, a child again as she coaxed the steam engine around a corner and across a bridge.

"Monica, don't forget your appointment." Sylvia entered the exhibit room and pointed at her watch. "It'll take you at least forty minutes to get down to Denver. And the traffic might be bad this time of day."

"Okay. I'll go." She glanced distractedly back at the train display. She couldn't believe she'd been fiddling with it for almost half an hour.

She gathered her things and hurried to her Cherokee. This appointment was an important one. She didn't want Joy Martin to think she wasn't punctual. Forty minutes later she turned the Jeep off of I-25 onto Clarkson and parked in front of the square red-brick building.

Monica rushed to the third floor, pausing momentarily outside the door marked "Colorado Big Brothers/Big Sisters Agency." She shifted her briefcase to the other hand, pulled the door open and entered.

"Hi." The receptionist greeted her immediately. "Are you Monica?"

"Yes."

"I'm Gwen." She extended a hand and Monica clasped it. "Joy will be with you in a minute. I'll let her know you're here."

When Gwen left the room, Monica took the chance to look around the office. It was basic and drab, typical of a nonprofit service agency. The carpet was threadbare and she guessed the couch along the far wall had been donated years ago. But the pictures, plaques and letters scattered around the room attested to happy Little Sisters.

Monica gave a small smile of pleasure. For a long time now, Monica had been praying, asking the Father to show her a place where her faith could make a difference to someone else. In her busy life, she felt like she didn't have much chance to touch others with love. Her pastor had mentioned Big Brothers and Big Sisters in a sermon last month, and she had researched the organization on the Internet. Standing at this desk now, it felt like the perfect fit.

She thumbed through the brochures lying on the table. *Making Life Choices. How to be a Friend. Boys in Love.* Her smile broadened. Important topics, all of them.

"Joy's ready for you." Gwen led Monica up a long, narrow hallway. "Right in here."

"Thank you." Monica turned her attention to the woman waiting behind the desk. "Joy. Hello."

"Are you ready for this?"

"Very." Monica was still grinning. "And very excited."

Joy stood from her chair. "It is an exciting day. So many Big Sisters look back to the day they were matched with their Littles and see it as a real milestone." She pulled a manila folder from the pile on her desk and flipped it open. "Before I tell you about your match, I want to go over your file with you just to be certain I'm current." She pulled her chair closer and sat down.

"Fine." Monica crossed her ankles and leaned forward in one refined, fluid motion.

"Correct me if I've got anything wrong here. You are single. Thirty-two years of age. Willing to serve as a Big Sister because you have lots of positive energy to share."

"Yes." *And You Father,* she thought. *I want to share Your love.*

"You are curator of the antique toy museum at Hiwan Homestead in Evergreen."

"Yes."

"An interesting job. How did you get started?"

"I used to play with an old train collection of my father's." She hesitated and then realized Joy was waiting for more. "My sister always played with dolls. I was always more interested in Dad's trains. He taught me about his own collection. And when the Jefferson County Historical Society needed someone to put together an antique train display for Hiwan Homestead, I offered my services. And my father offered his trains."

"It began as a single exhibit?"

"Toy trains started coming in from everywhere. And then other toys, too. Wooden wagons. Kewpee dolls. Wrought iron fire trucks. It grew into quite an assortment. And, finally, the historical society voted to give the exhibit its own space and make it a permanent thing."

"I like that," Joy said. "You take a small idea and turn it into something much larger."

Monica nodded, still smiling. "That's a particular character trait of mine." One she was proud of sometimes but one that often gave her trouble.

Joy paused over an item in the file. "I had forgotten you were adopted."

"I am."

"How do you feel about that?"

"I'm human. I've questioned it at times." Monica did her best to answer Joy candidly. "I did search out my biological mother several years ago. But my true parents are the ones who raised me." She stopped when she saw the worried look on Joy Martin's face. "Is that going to be a problem?"

"Only if you perceive it as one. We wanted to match you with a pregnant teenager."

"Is she going to put the baby up for adoption?"

"At this point, we don't know," Joy told her. "She wants to keep the baby. But she's very young, very insecure. . . ."

"I can't see her decision affecting me one way or the other," Monica answered truthfully.

"You might have to help her make it."

"I could do that."

Joy thumbed through another stack of portfolios and selected one. The caseworker slid a school photograph across the desk toward her. "Here she is. Ann Small. She's fourteen, a ninth-grader in middle school."

"And she's pregnant?" Monica was astonished.

"She's having a tough time."

"Is she staying in school?" Monica asked.

"Not unless someone close to her starts giving her some support."

Monica held the photo between two finely manicured hands, framing it with her thumbs. Even in the picture, Ann Small looked sad. Her eyes were huge, round and melancholy. Monica felt her heart go out to the girl. "She's a pretty young lady. But she doesn't look happy."

"Ann isn't happy. She has a very low self-esteem," Joy explained. "Her school counselor referred her to us just last week. The counselor approached her because the girl was despondent, not because she knew about the pregnancy."

"The counselor? What about her parents?"

"Her mother is deceased. She died five years ago in Wyoming. You will meet Richard Small when we go to meet Ann. I have to warn you, Monica, that the father did not instigate any of this. From our interviews with Ann, it sounds as if their relationship is abysmal."

"What does she say?"

"She's a very lonely child and we believe her problems stem from her relationship with her father. He works long hours. She isn't just another latchkey kid. He leaves in the morning before she wakes up and usually isn't home until she's in bed. And sometimes it's seven days a week."

"Poor kid."

"She needs a lot of companionship and love, Monica."

"It's love I'm prepared to give." She studied the photograph again.

"So the situation sounds . . . acceptable to you?"

Monica didn't answer for a moment. She wasn't questioning her own decision to become a Big Sister. She was mesmerized by the sadness on Ann Small's face. A scripture from Genesis was running through her head. "This is how you can show your love to me— Everywhere we go, say of me 'He is my brother.' "

Chapter Two

Monica stood behind Joy Martin as Joy rapped on the door of the tiny town house in south Denver. The door opened a crack and a girl with huge dark eyes and a pixie face greeted the caseworker. "Hi, Mrs. Martin."

"Ann," Joy said gently. "I'd like you to meet Monica Albright. She's going to be your Big Sister."

"Hello, Ann." Monica extended her hand. "I've been excited about meeting you." Ann was pretty, but not in the conventional way of most teenagers. Her nose was angular, her lips were full and there was something slightly off center about her. She sported a head of unruly curls that tangled wildly about her neck.

"Me, too," Ann said, taking Monica's hand. Her dark eyes were not quite as pensive as in the photo, but they were filled with reserve, as if she were afraid to allow herself to be happy.

I'm betting she doesn't know how pretty she is.

Monica stepped forward, forgetting her nervousness. She was intrigued by the young girl who was about to become an integral part of her life. "Were you as scared as I was about this meeting?" she asked.

"Yes," Ann replied. And then, more softly, "I really wanted you to like me."

When I was fourteen, I thought I was awful and ugly and awkward. But Mom and Dad always told me I was wrong. I wonder if her father's told her how lovely, how special, she'll grow up to be one day.

As if on cue, Ann remembered her manners. "You'd better come on in. My dad's here. He wanted to come to . . . this thing." Monica saw the spark of hope in her expression as she stepped back to allow them inside. "This is my father, Richard Small."

He was standing in the middle of the room holding a bag from the local bakery. "Hi," he said, smiling uncomfortably. He saluted them with the sack. Monica could see the sugar soaking through it.

"I'm glad you're here," Joy told him with professional warmth. "Ann has been telling me how difficult it is for you to get away from work."

"She told you right." He offered them no other information. He didn't tell them he had begged Tyler Hill to stand in as station manager for him tonight. It was something he hadn't done in years. But he had decided it was time for something to change between him and Ann, although he didn't know how to start it.

Besides, he had a hundred and one reservations about letting some woman he didn't know come in and take over with Ann when he had failed her.

"I'm Monica Albright," she said to him. She had been ready to extend her hand to him, too, but just

29

before she spoke Monica saw something akin to sorrow rear up in his eyes, only for a flash and then it was gone. She didn't reach out to him.

"Nice to know you." His face was stoic again. His features could have been etched in granite. "Here." He held up the bakery bag for the third time. "I stopped for these doughnuts so we could have some. I didn't know how formal this was supposed to be or anything."

"Thank you," Joy said politely. "We didn't need anything but it's certainly nice of you."

It was uncanny how much he and his daughter favored one another, Monica decided. Richard Small had the same cognac-colored hair, the same unruly curls, the same basalt-dark eyes. And actually, she decided, he would be handsome if not for the glacial coldness in his eyes.

"Thank you for entrusting me with your daughter once a week," she said in a desperate attempt to begin conversation with him. "I hope we'll become good friends, Ann and I."

"I'll just see to these doughnuts," he said, waving the bag at her one more time. Then he disappeared into the kitchen, and Monica suppressed the urge to giggle as she heard what sounded like hundreds of pans clattering to the floor. He returned carrying a cookie sheet with a half dozen chocolate-covered doughnuts and cinnamon rolls on it.

"We don't often have company," Ann said, and Monica got the feeling she was both embarrassed by her father and at the same time proud of him.

"May I write down your schedule, Mr. Small?"

Monica asked him. "I need to know when Ann and I can plan our outings."

Richard didn't answer her immediately. He was eating his cinnamon roll, unrolling it from the circle and chomping off little bites. For some reason, his little-boy way of eating pastry endeared him to her and she felt her heart going out to him.

Maybe my being here isn't right, she reasoned. *Maybe he feels as if I'm trying to take over his daughter.* But that wasn't what she wanted to do at all. When she added the rest of it, she spoke so softly he could hardly hear what she was saying. "I'm just here to help. That's all. If you don't want me, maybe Mrs. Martin can find somebody else. . . ."

He almost visibly jerked when he realized she had read his thoughts. It wasn't that he didn't want *her.* He didn't think he wanted *anybody.* This time, when the wariness lifted from his eyes, Monica was startled by the intensity of sadness there. She wondered for a moment if he was aware he had even let her see it. "Anytime, Miss Albright. You may come for her anytime."

Monica felt the need to continue. "I want specifics, though. I don't want to take her away from time she might spend with you."

She saw the loss he was feeling before the distrust came down again, like a shield, to protect him. He might as well have spoken aloud: *You are here because they don't think I'm doing such a good job of it by myself.*

"Dad's never home," Ann said. "You don't have to

31

worry about taking me away. He's never here."

"What about weekends?"

"I generally work seven days a week, Miss Albright," he told her almost angrily.

Who was he protecting? His daughter? Or himself?

"Fine," she said lightly. "We'll just have a . . . good time . . . whenever. . . ."

"Yes," he said. The anger—forceful and sheer—was barely veiled.

She realized she shouldn't push him. Suddenly she wondered what they were doing, tiptoeing around an indignant father when the child needed so much help. Something about Ann made her ache inside. She yearned to make Ann laugh—not the laughter of a woman, but the full bellyache giggling she and her own sister, Sarah, had shared as children.

It isn't something Sarah and I do much anymore. It's a shame, I suppose. It's a shame you have to lose something to figure out it was valuable once.

"We should be going," Joy said, touching her arm.

"I suppose we should," Monica echoed, looking around for her purse. When she found it, she took out a little notebook. "What do you think we should do for our first outing, Ann? Maybe window-shopping? Or we could go up in the mountains for a snow picnic. . . ."

"Window-shopping sounds the best," the girl said. "Maybe we could look at baby things."

"Sure." They set a time and Monica slipped the notebook back inside her purse. Then she turned to Richard once more. "Thank you . . . for trusting me enough . . . for this. . . ."

He was surprised by her comment. He almost said, "I didn't have any other choice." But he didn't. He eyed her for a minute. *She'd better not underestimate me. She thinks she can use tact to make me trust her.*

"We'll see you again, I'm sure," Monica was saying. She smiled at him, looking perfectly poised, and he couldn't help noticing how pretty she was.

He took her hand, his expression guarded. "I'm sure."

I won't trust her with Ann. I don't trust myself with Ann, much less someone the school counselors and a social agency have forced on me.

As he watched them walk away, the helplessness swallowed him again. They were strangers and they thought they could give Ann more than he could give.

"Don't be mad, Dad." His daughter stepped up beside him. "I think it'll be fun. And I think it'll be good." She was holding the cookie sheet, still covered with the pastries. "Thanks for getting doughnuts. They liked them, I think."

"Yeah, sure. You're welcome."

As he said it, he couldn't help thinking of the way Monica Albright had eaten hers, holding it delicately, her little finger pointed outward. She held the chocolate doughnut the same way he had seen English ladies hold teacups on television shows.

He glanced out the doorway at the two women climbing into separate vehicles. Monica Albright's honey-colored hair caught the sunlight and, as it glinted, he found himself thinking of Carolyn. Carolyn's hair had been like that once, all shiny and smooth, before she had gotten sick. When the thought came, Richard had no idea he was saying it aloud.

"We were so happy then."

"Were we?" Ann asked.

Monica and Ann paused beside the lavishly appointed window at Precious Cargo.

"You sure you don't want to go in?" Monica asked.

Ann shook her head. "I know you think I'm dumb. I mean I said I wanted to come here and everything. But looking in there, I just wouldn't know what to do, you know? I'd feel weird."

"You shouldn't feel weird. You're as entitled to go in there as anybody. But whatever you feel is okay."

They were window-shopping at Southwest Plaza—their first planned outing together.

"I don't want to go in because all the salespeople will look at me funny when they find out about the baby."

"Why would you think that?"

"Because they'll think I'm too young and too dumb," Ann answered frankly.

It was the umpteenth time Monica felt her heart go out to her Little Sister. It was the umpteenth time Ann had belittled herself.

"It doesn't matter what they think," Monica told her. "I know it seems important right now. And I know it's hard to believe. But when I was in high school, I used to agonize over the fact that my sister, Sarah, had more friends than I did. And when I grew up, it wasn't

34

so bad anymore. It was just me, who I was, how God made me."

It was the first time she had seen Ann really grin. "Okay. Okay. Point taken. Is this what a Big Sister is supposed to do? Tell me I'm going to be all right someday?"

"Yeah." Monica grinned back. "Something like that."

"I think you're just telling me all this stuff so I'll go in with you and look at baby things."

"If it really matters to you, I could tell them I'm the one having the baby," Monica offered.

"Let's just look in the window," Ann said, turning somber.

"Okay." Monica conceded. "That's fine with me."

They stood there gazing for at least five minutes. In the end, it was difficult for both of them to pull away from the lovely display of bonnets and blankets and ruffled booties. Even though it was still February, the shop was already gearing up for Easter. Assorted Easter bunnies peered out from behind the expensive baby items.

"Look at all these precious, tiny things," Ann sighed.

"It makes *me* want to have a baby," Monica sighed in turn.

"Look at all those little shoes. They're so *teeny*. It's amazing to think I'm going to have to get some of this stuff."

"You will need a lot of this stuff, I think," Monica said. She started laughing. "But I'm really no expert."

"Look at that rabbit there. He's so cute."

"You're going to need things like diapers and little

sleepers and receiving blankets," Monica reminded the girl jokingly. "Stuffed animals aren't so essential." But it was a lovely, funny big bunny with wrinkled plaid pants and elastic suspenders striped in every pastel color imaginable. It had tall yellow ears lined with satin. "Baxter Bunny for Babies," the tag read. "Safe for children of all ages. 40."

"Maybe I'll save up for him," Ann whispered.

"For the baby?" Monica asked. "Or for yourself?" She was half teasing, half serious.

"For both of us, I guess. We could share it. And whenever one of us needed a hug the most . . ." She cast her eyes up toward Monica, eyes that were forlorn again, an expression that wrenched Monica's heart.

Ann is so lovable. It's a shame she doesn't know it. If only her father would tell her. . . .

"Guess what," Monica said, laughing again as she extended her arms to the girl. "This is what Big Sisters are for, too. Hugging. I give great hugs."

Ann's eyes widened. It had been forever since her father had hugged her. For the longest time she had thought maybe she was just too old for hugs. "Really?"

"Really," Monica reassured her emphatically. With that, she gathered the teenager into her arms.

During their second outing together, Ann and Monica went for a snow picnic in Bergen Park near Evergreen. As they spread the plastic tablecloth over a huge flat-topped rock, the big wet snowflakes of March began to fall.

"Oh, *no*," Monica wailed as she gripped her hot pink

ski parka tighter around her. "Having a crazy winter picnic on *top* of the snow is one thing—"

"But . . ." Ann finished her sentence for her ". . . having it dump down on top of you is another."

"Right," Monica nodded. She was doing her best to hide her disappointment. "The weatherman said it was supposed to be sunny today."

"He's never right," Ann teased her, sounding surprisingly mature. "Haven't you figured that out yet? Dad watches, too, because of the trains. He says you listen to the weather and then you figure on it being opposite of what the guy on TV says. He says the odds of you knowing what's going to happen are better that way."

Monica looked at Ann. "Your dad doesn't trust many people, does he?" Maybe it wasn't a fair judgment to make. They were talking about the weatherman, after all. But Monica hadn't seen Richard since their first meeting, when she had sensed she was hurting him, even undermining him, by being there.

"I don't know," Ann told her. "He never tells me."

She was certain Joy Martin wouldn't have forced the Big Sister-Little Sister program on him. Richard could have told them no. The program had so much merit, so much to offer a teenager like Ann who wasn't certain how she should feel about herself.

"Does he ever talk about being mad because you have a Big Sister?" she asked Ann.

Ann shook her head. "He doesn't talk about that either. I don't know. Sometimes I want him to get mad about things. At least I know he cares about them then."

"He doesn't get angry at things?"

"Not usually. But he did when I told him I was pregnant. He told me he was glad my mother wasn't here to see me. And then he went into his room and he made this big hole in the wall. I heard him do it. And I found it later when I went in there for the laundry. That must have hurt his hand."

Monica asked the next question carefully. She asked it because she wanted to know Ann, wanted to understand what the girl must be feeling. "Is that why you got pregnant, Ann? So he would be angry? So you would know where you stood with him?"

Ann couldn't stop the tears that welled up in her eyes. She shook her head vehemently. "No. That isn't it. I didn't get pregnant on purpose. I just didn't know some things about it."

"Your dad didn't tell you how a girl can become pregnant?"

Ann shook her head. "No. Sometimes I think that's why he got so mad. I think maybe he's mad at himself."

"Those things must be hard for a father to talk about." She didn't know why, but she was remembering the sadness on Richard Small's face. She caught herself feeling almost sorry for him. She hadn't stopped to think how difficult it must have been for him, raising a teenage daughter on his own.

The snow was coming down harder now. Ann studied the ominous sky above them. "It doesn't look like it's going to stop."

"So maybe it's time for Plan B," Monica suggested amiably. "I know this great little pizza place about a mile from here."

38

"I didn't bring much money."

"It's okay," Monica told her. "It's my treat."

During their third outing together, Ann and Monica skipped the snow picnic altogether and headed straight for BeauJo's Pizza in Idaho Springs. They were going Dutch this time. Monica didn't mind paying for Ann's pizza, too. But Ann had saved some of her allowance and Monica didn't want to insult her.

"See that girl over there?" Ann asked as they sat across the table from each other, munching the thick crust and honey BeauJo's was so famous for. "She's really pretty. I bet she's a cheerleader at her school."

"Did you want to be a cheerleader?" Monica slathered more honey on her crust and then licked the side of her hand where it had dripped down.

"Oh, everybody does," Ann answered nonchalantly. "They're the ones everybody likes."

"I guess you're right," Monica told her lightheartedly. "Everybody does. I wanted to be one, too. I even tried out. But I didn't make it. Evergreen High was pretty big even then. I couldn't do the tumbling routines well enough to make people vote for me. But my sister made it."

"You guys tried out at the same time?"

"We were in the same grade at school. We did everything at the same time."

"Did you get mad when your sister made it and you didn't?" Ann asked.

Monica chortled. "I'd like to say no. But I have to be honest. It bothered me a lot. But now I look back on things and I can't complain. We're exactly the same age and we were best friends. Everybody liked her and she liked me. In the end, that's what mattered. That we loved each other. . . ."

Ann didn't understand the twinge of regret that registered in Monica's expression. "How can you be the same age? Are you twins?"

"I'm adopted. My parents adopted me and then they found out my mom was pregnant. It's pretty funny. Sarah's almost nine months younger than I am."

"So did you do lots of stuff together?"

"Always." A wistful expression crossed her face as Monica spoke. "We were tomboys, Sarah and me. Mom and Dad kept horses for us to ride and we'd go out into the trees and play. We'd take turns tracking and capturing each other and then we'd torture each other."

Ann wrinkled up her nose. "How did you torture each other?"

"Oh, just crazy things," Monica chuckled. "We'd make each other hang upside down in a tree, or say the name of a boy we didn't like, or sneak cookies out of the kitchen. That was a great way to get killed, let me tell you. It was all very daring."

Ann was snickering. "Sounds like you had lots of fun."

"We drove Mom and Dad crazy."

"Sounds like you drove them bananas."

Monica was giggling, too. "I guess that's what kids are for."

They looked at each other and then Ann looked down at her stomach. "Oh, *no!*"

"You just wait!" Monica said, teasing her. Suddenly both of them were giggling so hard they had to set down their pizza crusts and hold onto their stomachs. Monica felt as if she was fourteen again. The people sitting around them glanced in their direction and smiled.

Ann was the first to stop giggling. "What," she asked breathlessly "are we laughing at?"

"I . . . can't really remember," Monica blurted out.

"Me, neither!" Ann admitted. She reached across the table and tentatively touched Monica's hand, her expression sobering. "You know what?"

"What?"

Ann leaned toward her, as if they were conspirators. "I like you, Monica," she told her. "I really do."

"I feel the same way," Monica said fervently. "I'm awfully glad we found each other."

March 2
Dear Diary,
Today I am writing you and I feel sort of different because I have a new friend. I'm sure I'll be writing a lot about her for a while. (I hope forever because she's so nice!) Her name is Monica Albright. She's grown up but when we talk, she looks me right in the eyes and listens like she really cares what I have to say and I think she really does. She told me just this week that she's GLAD we found each other.

I was scared about getting to know Monica. I was scared she would just be another adult like Dad who wouldn't know how I feel and who wouldn't really care, but she's a girl so maybe that's what makes it different. Today we talked about when she wanted to be a cheerleader and she tried out and her sister made it but she didn't. I think that might be terrible, to have somebody you love and be hurt by them and be sad and happy at the same time. And I think about it and I think maybe I've felt that way sometimes, too.

   Is that just a girl thing?

   I'd better go. I'll write more about her later. We've done lots of things together. It's really nice to have Monica to talk to even though she's old. I don't know how old. I think maybe at least thirty.

Hugs,
Ann Leidy Small

Chapter Three

With an earsplitting screech of metal on metal, the third train of the afternoon pulled out of Denver Union Terminal. "You've got to admit—" Tyler Hill shouted across fifteen boxes of freight toward Richard "—the gal is going to take pressure off you. She'll be good for Ann. You just can't let your pride get in the way."

"I know all that. I'm ungrateful. I'm a fool. I oughtta take all the help I can get." Richard tossed a heavy crate up and over several others. Even so, the action didn't ease the pressure building inside of him. "But I can't see it that way, Ty."

"Well, it doesn't hurt to *try*."

Richard grinned wryly at his best friend. "So you think I'm stubborn, too."

"Yes," Tyler stated emphatically.

"At least you're honest, buddy. These ladies come to my house and sit on my sofa and I see their minds working. They're looking at my daughter, thinking, 'We're going to play this little-girl game now and make everything turn out all right for this poor child.'"

Tyler picked his words carefully. "So maybe that's what Ann needs for a while. Little-girl games. That's what she is, after all. And from what I understand about Big Sisters, that's how they work. They don't want to take a parent's place. They only want to offer a positive influence. I read about it in the newspaper once. It sounds like a fair deal to me, maybe a fair deal that Ann deserves."

"I think she deserves so much," Richard said strongly. "Much more than I've been able to give her." He doubled up both fists and slammed them down against the crate. He had been doing that so often lately his hands were sore. "If you could have seen them all." Then he couldn't help himself, he had to smile again even though he was still angry. "If you could have seen the Big Sister. All dressed up in a fancy skirt, carrying this purse that probably costs more than my grocery budget for a month. She didn't have a hair out of place, Ty."

"You thinking she's better than you are?"

"I'm thinking maybe Ann'll think so."

"Listen to me." Tyler moved around the boxes and took his friend's shoulders. "Ann is going through one of the most intense experiences a woman can go through. It's not gonna hurt her any to have a woman by her side guiding her a little."

"You think so?"

"How long has it been since you've talked to me about Ann? Two years? Three? I know how hard you've tried, Rich. It's a tough job to do alone. Nobody's going to take your daughter away from you. Maybe all of this, the pregnancy, the Big Sister stuff, will be good. Just make sure Ann knows how much you love her."

But Richard was shaking his head. "I haven't told her in a long time."

"Why not?" Tyler asked. "You do, don't you?"

"Yeah. I do. But making her understand is a whole different story. She's a long way past hopscotch and jump rope, old friend. It's too late for that. She's gone and made certain of it."

"I think you're avoiding the issue here."

"I am not. I had so many dreams for her. I haven't saved up enough for college for her, but I started. I always thought maybe she could live at home and drive to Boulder and learn to be a teacher. . . ."

Tyler jumped right in. "So maybe this Big Sister arrangement could help her there. Maybe this Big Sister is a teacher—"

"No." Richard raked his hair back off his forehead. "I got this paper about her. She takes care of a toy museum. In Evergreen."

Even Tyler was taken aback. "What? And it's a *job*?"

"Yeah."

Tyler let out a long, low whistle. "Evergreen. That's big bucks. Does she live there?"

"It's where she grew up. She's even got a house."

"She married?"

"No." Richard wished he could say it was because she was unattractive and old. But that would not be the truth. Actually she was quite pretty, with straight blond hair that hung down like a bell around her head, and a mouth that seemed to smile most of the time. "She probably doesn't have a husband because of the way she eats doughnuts. Holds 'em with four fingers and sticks the fifth one out like a gun pointed at you." He shot Tyler a devilish grin. He was grasping at straws and he knew it. But everybody kept telling him how wonderful this Big Sister stuff was supposed to be. He was desperate to find something wrong with this woman. "I'd never marry a woman who ate doughnuts like that."

"Ah," Ty grinned. "Marriage. It's about time you mentioned that word again. A new mother might be what Ann needs, too. You'd have control over that situation." He eyed his best friend pointedly. He knew Richard Small pretty well. Richard had lost control of so many things when Carolyn died. He guessed that's why the Big Sister situation was bothering him now. He wasn't in control of it. "You could actually pick the woman."

"When," Richard shot back "do I have time to pick a woman? I don't have time to spend with my own daughter."

"It was just a thought. I wasn't worrying about the details."

That afternoon, after rerouting a train around a derailment in western Nebraska, Richard lay his pen down on his desk and started worrying about the details. He couldn't picture himself ever marrying again. He couldn't picture himself ever loving anyone but Carolyn.

When Ann was little, Carolyn had kept order in their lives even though he had been gone forty-eight or even sixty hours at a time. When the bone disease began to destroy his wife, it began to destroy him and Ann, too. When Carolyn finally died, she took part of them along with her.

Richard missed train after train while she was sick. He wasn't earning anything. United Bank waited until Carolyn was gone to foreclose on the house. That's when he knew, for his own sake and Ann's, they had to get out of Rock Springs: Tyler got him the job in Denver—the station manager's position. It was a compromise for anyone who loved traveling the rails the way he did. But it looked like an accomplishment to others. And, despite the long hours he knew he was going to have to devote to it, Ann would have order in her life again. He wanted a lot for her. School. Friends. A future.

The passenger-train industry didn't pay anything like freight trains did, even with the hours he put in. He worried about heating bills, grocery bills, the phone and the rent for the little town house. It was a struggle he was never sure of winning. Still, he never felt as inept as he did sitting across the room from his daughter after he got home from the station, just before she went to bed, wanting to share closeness with her and not knowing how to begin.

He wanted to know what she cared about and why she felt the way she did about things. Yet it seemed as if some horrible force took over their conversation and bent it each time. The words were different, of course. But the sparring between them remained the same.

"You in your room, Ann?"

"Yeah." A pause. "Do you need me?"

"No." He always wondered what else to say. "Yes. Maybe."

She came out then. "What?"

"Tell me what you did today."

"Went to six classes."

"Were they good classes?"

"No. Boring. Why?"

He didn't become angry. But he always lost hope at this point. "No reason why. I wanted to know."

"Why?"

"I'm your father. That's enough of a reason."

"I'm fourteen years old. You want to know what all I did today? I went to school. I came home. I wrote in my diary. I watched *The Flintstones*."

"Don't smart mouth me, Ann."

He had no idea how Carolyn would have handled the situation. All he knew was that when he looked at Ann he was filled with confusion. He loved her and he wanted to treat her as he had when she was little, but she lived in a body that was all of a sudden sprouting womanly parts. Sometimes he wanted to throttle her. Other times he wanted to hold her. He wanted to tell her he was sorry she had him for a father, that he never knew exactly what to do and, often instead of merely muddling through, he just quit trying.

"I'm going to bed, Ann," he'd always say. "I'll see you tomorrow night."

And always, always after he left, he could hear her crying.

For some reason, he found his mind wandering back to Monica Albright. Maybe . . . maybe she really could help Ann. Maybe Tyler was right. Maybe the only thing he could hold against her was the fact she was one more circumstance in his life over which he had absolutely no control.

Ann's reflection stretched across the front car window, following the curve of the glass as Monica watched her. "Do you know you are pretty, Ann?" Monica asked.

Ann looked first at her Big Sister and then at her image in the window. It was as if she was seeing it for the first time. "Am I really?"

Monica nodded. "Yes."

"I've been hoping so. But I didn't really know."

"Nobody has told you before?"

"No."

"You're going to be beautiful when you get a little older." Monica glanced in her direction once more. She could see Ann blushing. She reached across the front seat and patted her knee. "I didn't mean to embarrass you. I just thought you should know."

"Thanks," Ann whispered. She was smiling. She turned toward the window to look out. A moment later, she added, "Maybe Danny thinks I'm pretty. I can't wait for you to meet Danny."

They were driving to the Humane Society to look at kittens and puppies. It was something Monica had always loved to do. One of these days, when it got warmer, she planned to take Ann to the zoo.

"I hope I can meet him," Monica told her. "I'd like that."

"He's the baby's father."

"I thought maybe he was." Ann talked of him often during their times together. "How does he feel about that?"

Ann didn't answer. Monica glanced across the front seat at her. She was staring out the window, concentrating on scenery she must have seen a thousand times before. "You can't blame him if he's unhappy about it, Ann. That's a pretty normal reaction."

"I guess I haven't given him much of a chance to be unhappy, Monica," she said softly. "He doesn't know yet. I haven't told him."

Monica swallowed her surprised, judgmental words. She knew she had to be careful not to give Ann her opinions unless she asked for them. "Why not?"

"Everything's been happening so fast. We don't go to the high school until we're in tenth grade so I don't see him every day."

"Ann. It's been a *month*." As she said it, Monica felt a flash of recognition. Avoidance. From what Ann told her, it was exactly the same way her father handled situations. Ann had told her she and her father never talked about anything.

"He's been asking if he can come over but I don't know what I'm going to say. I'm really scared he'll be mad at me."

"How can he be, Ann? It isn't just your fault."

"I'm in love with him, Monica. I can't lose him."

Monica raised her eyebrows. It was big talk coming from a small teenager. Monica had already told Ann about her own emotions, how intense everything had seemed when she was fourteen and in school, how important small details seemed back then when her hormones were rampaging through her body for the first time. "So tell me what you're going to do about this."

"I don't know."

"Does Danny make you feel special?" Monica suspected Ann saw herself through Danny's eyes. It was a scary way for the girl to be measuring her self-esteem. Maybe it was the only yardstick Ann could find.

"Yeah. He does. And he could have anybody, Monica."

"If you don't go to the same school, how did you meet him?"

"At Roller City at a skating party last year. He ran into me because he couldn't skate very well, and then he was really worried he had hurt me, so we sat down and talked for a long time. His mom and dad are divorced and I told him about my dad always being at the station. And I couldn't help it—for some reason I just started crying. And the next day Danny called me."

"He sounds like he does care about you."

"When he called he told me he thought it was neat that I would cry like that about my dad not being here. He liked the way I didn't giggle or say stupid stuff, that I just told him the truth."

"He just didn't catch you on one of your better giggle days—" Monica broke in with a smile "—the way I did last week."

"Yeah." Ann grinned, too. "I guess you're right."

"So what did he say then?"

"That he and his mom had learned a long time ago how to take care of each other. That he thought it sounded like I needed somebody to take care of me, too. He said he wanted to do that after he heard me talking about Dad."

She found Danny the same way she is finding me. I hear about her father and I want so badly to make things better for her.

"You weren't worried he just felt sorry for you?"

Ann thought about the question. "No. Because it wasn't like that. It's like he needed me, too."

Comprehension rushed in. "Needing each other is an important part of love. But there are other parts, too." Monica had learned that a long time ago with her parents and Sarah. "Everyday things like knowing you can depend on each other and that you can disagree with each other and still belong."

As she said it, she thought of Richard Small and she wondered if Ann had any experience, any way to know about loving. Certainly a father had to love his daughter, didn't he?

• • •

March 19
Dear Diary,
This can't be long because I'm supposed to be in here doing my geography homework. We're learning about Indonesia. Fun stuff, huh? Sometimes I get discouraged. I wish we'd quit learning about places and start learning about life here.

I've had my Big Sister, Monica, for a month now. We've done lots of things together. Yesterday we went to the Humane Society and played with kittens. Last week we ate pizza. The week before we had this snow picnic that was supposed to be fun only it was pretty goofy. She even went to Southwest Plaza with me one day.

Monica says I'm pretty. Can you believe it? Somebody really thinks that about me? And you know what? I looked at myself for a long time in the mirror tonight and I think maybe she's right. Isn't it funny? I might buy a magazine at the grocery store that says how to put on makeup and stuff. Or maybe Monica can help me. She wears eye shadow. I think she's pretty.

Monica and I talk a lot about Danny and the baby. I haven't told Danny about the baby. I'm really scared. I guess I'm going to have to tell him. I don't know what he'll say. Maybe he'll do what Dad did and make a hole in the wall.

Monica and I are going to some nutrition classes together soon. Joy Martin told me about them. I guess I need to learn how to eat. From the chart

Joy Martin gave me, I have to drink about three gallons of milk a day. (Not really. But it seems like it.) I have my doctor's appointment next Wednesday afternoon. That sounds scary and fun at the same time.

I'd better go. I have to locate all the major cultural centers in Indonesia. I'll write more later, I promise.

Love,
Ann Leidy Small
(Age 14)

P.S. When I have a little girl, when she starts to grow up, I'm going to tell her she's pretty. And if she isn't, I guess I'll just have to help her get that way. I like being pretty.

Danny Lovell leaned against the chalk-colored brick wall, his pile of books balanced precariously on one jutting hip. "I'm glad you wanted me to come over, Ann." He peered up at her while his blond hair blew in little wisps around his temples. "I got the feeling you've been avoiding me or something."

She was sitting above him, atop the brick wall.

"I thought you were mad at me."

"No," she told him softly, trying to sound calm, even though her legs were shaking. "That isn't it at all."

He plopped his books on the chunks of ice that covered the grass. They made a horrible crunching sound. He pulled himself up to sit beside Ann. He jostled her with his elbow to see what she would do. He was going to put his arm around her and kiss her but suddenly it felt wrong. She was sitting very, very still. "Ann? What is it?"

"There's something happening." She spoke softly, but her voice seemed to ring out like a tiny chime in the cold late-winter air. "Danny, I'm pregnant."

It was Danny's turn to sit very still. *It couldn't be.* Ann was only fourteen, after all. She was just a ninth-grader.

He thought back to the day he had met her, how hearing her talk about her father had made him remember how horrible it had been when his own father had gone away.

He had wanted to show Ann he was a man, too, that he could always take care of her.

Things like this happened to kids on TV. It didn't happen to real people like him and Ann.

"Well, say something," she said, and this time he could tell her voice was trembling. She must have been very, very scared. "I've known for a while. I went to the doctor today." She smiled, just a touch of a smile. "I saw the baby on the ultrasound."

"Is that why you've got this new Big Sister lady?"

"Yeah. It is."

"I thought you were avoiding me because you wanted to spend all your time with her," he said slowly. "I had no idea about the . . . the . . ." He couldn't make himself say it.

"The baby?"

"Yeah." He just looked at her for a minute. "Oh, boy, Ann. I don't know what to say."

"I know." She was doing her best to help him along. "I can't believe this."

"I know." She gazed down at her hands, because she couldn't stand the expression of bewilderment on his face. "I couldn't believe it, either. I didn't think . . . it could happen. . . ."

Danny said the first thing that came to mind. "My mom's going to die. Don't tell her, Ann. Maybe she never has to know."

"I told my dad." She gazed up at him again, and when she saw the frightened look on his face, she wanted to cry for him. "You don't have to tell her if you don't want to. But she might want to know she's going to be a grandma."

The reality of it hit Danny at the exact same time the anger hit him. His awe at what they'd done was gone; they were in real trouble. "Ann. There's things you could have done. You could have used birth control or something. Didn't you know that?"

"No," she snapped right back at him. "I didn't know it. I don't have a mom to tell me stuff like that. You know what? I'm sick of everybody telling me things I should have known. What about you? Why didn't you do something?"

"I guess I didn't think about it."

"Why didn't you tell me? Why didn't you think about *me?*" she asked. Why was he pointing fingers at her when they were both to blame? It made her angry. "Monica Albright is the only one who cares enough about me to tell me things. And I had to go out and find her." In one motion she swung out from the wall and jumped down from it. "I'm tired of everybody blaming me."

"I'm not blaming you." But he was.

Ann hugged her notebook to her chest. She knew she was going to cry. It seemed like she cried all the time these days and she didn't know why she did that, either. She stomped up the sidewalk toward home.

"Ann. Stop! Ann . . . !" He came racing after her, finally trying to make amends.

She bolted ahead, not even caring that she had dropped her notebook. All she could think of was running as fast as she could to get away from Danny. She didn't want Danny's apology. She didn't want him to be sorry. The deed was done. And they had done it together.

Questions came to her mind, sharp and clear as she ran, like slides shining on a screen and then flicking off again. Maybe her father was right. Everything was going to be horrible. She wondered what it felt like to have a baby. She wondered if it hurt so badly she would scream. She wondered if the baby could feel her moving.

She stopped, bent over, gasping to catch her breath. When she did, she realized she wasn't bending in the same place anymore. She had counted just last night. She was only fourteen weeks along and already her body was changing. So many things were changing. A baby, a life, was growing inside her. She was on a track, like a train, speeding forward on one certain course.

This is going to change me, she thought. *There isn't anything I can do to fight it off.*

Richard opened the front door with a bang. At first he thought Ann was sleeping. But the house was cold. Obviously she hadn't been home to turn up the heat. He stood in the middle of the room, wondering where she might be. He had no idea at all.

He heard laughter outside and the dull thwacking of car doors. He heard Ann and Monica's voices, interwoven as they came up the front steps, their boots crunching on the brittle ice. "If I had known there was so much potassium in a *banana* . . ." He heard Monica giggling.

"You would have been eating banana splits all your life!" Ann finished.

"You guessed it."

Ann sounds like she used to sound before we lost Carolyn, Richard observed to himself. *She doesn't sound happy like that anymore when she talks to me.*

"The lights are on," Ann said. "He must be home."

He hated himself for the anger he felt, anger and jealousy kindled by the merriment in their voices. He opened the door and glared at Monica.

"Hi, Dad."

"Where have you been?" he asked, his tone full of accusation. Monica stopped when she saw the expression on his face. Why was he glowering at her?

"We went to a nutrition class," Ann began telling him. "So I can eat the right things." She marched past her father.

Richard stepped forward, his eyes still on Monica as he stood between them. For a moment it seemed as if he was trying to physically block them from one another.

He eyed Monica. "Why didn't you have her home earlier? She has homework on school nights."

"Excuse me?" Monica asked, astonished. She couldn't believe he was questioning her. She had driven here six times in six weeks and she hadn't seen the man once. Ann was always alone.

"I can't always count on her being with you," he told her. "Ann had a life before you came along, Miss Albright. She had a boyfriend who got her pregnant."

And a father who practically deserted her, Monica added to his statement in her mind.

"I'm sorry," Ann said from behind them. "I was going to tell you I had a class, Dad. I guess I never saw you. Or I forgot."

"Ann," Monica told her softly, "your father and I need to talk alone."

His eyes riveted on hers. He was silent while Ann left the room. Then he said accusingly, "You even give her orders now? Looks like you're in charge of everything."

Monica struggled with her words. "I'm not trying to take over. I asked you when I could have her and you told me I could take her anytime." It *had* been late tonight. And if Ann hadn't told him . . . But she wasn't going to back down now.

"I came home early," he said. "I thought it would be nice to see my daughter. I didn't know where she was. I was worried." He wouldn't admit it to Monica, but he had been really looking forward to spending the evening with Ann. And he was paying one of the station masters time and a half to cover for him.

Monica couldn't help herself; she had to say it. "It's a little late for you to start caring, don't you think?" But the minute the words left her mouth, she was sorry.

"Who are you?" He lashed out at her with words the way he wanted to flail away at the pain. "Who are you to tell me about my timing? You don't know me, Miss Albright. You don't know why I'm here. You don't know how Ann and I communicate. . . ."

"She's told me how you communicate. You don't."

He closed his mouth. Whatever point he was going to make next disappeared from his mind. "She said that? That we don't talk to each other?" His eyes were a void, endless and dark. Again she thought how handsome he would be if only he didn't look so exhausted and so angry.

"Yes," she almost whispered. "She's told me that. She's told me a great many things."

He hid his pain under a torrent of angry words. "Did you stop to think, Miss Albright, that Ann doesn't talk to *me?* It goes back and forth, you know. . . ."

"And when she tries to—" Monica's voice was soft, so soft he could barely hear it, and suddenly she hated herself for having to tell him exactly what she knew "—you end it by becoming angry. Like you did tonight."

Richard summoned the courage to tell her what he had been telling Ty at the station. "You don't have the right to come in here and try to fix things up between her and me. I know what you and that Joy Martin were

59

thinking while you were here. You were thinking I've had fourteen years to mess things up with her. You were thinking you'd step in with books and talk and take Ann's life and turn it around without me." Now he was trying to protect himself in the only way he knew. "You can't point fingers at me and say it's too late. Because it's too late for you, too, lady. Ann made a wreck of her life all by herself. Neither of us is going to be able to fix that."

"No wonder she feels lost . . . no wonder! You talk as if her whole life is over."

"Well, isn't it?"

She was furious with him. "I don't think so! You can stick by her. Someday you'll have a lovely grandchild to show for all this."

He practically roared at her. "I wanted to raise my daughter. I wanted to be with her. But I had to make a living for her instead. I don't *want* to raise a baby."

"You've given up all hope, haven't you?" she asked him.

He took one step toward her. "Go home. You don't want to be a part of this. You make it clear you don't agree with my view of the world. Just go home."

"I'm right. You have given up."

"I'm calling Joy Martin," he told her. "I'm telling her I don't want Ann to have a Big Sister. I don't want any more do-good ladies breathing down my neck."

"If you do that to Ann, you are despicable."

"Maybe so. But it's my life. Mine and Ann's."

Monica stared at him in silence. Then she turned, opened the front door and marched toward the

Cherokee without looking back. She climbed into the driver's seat and threw the electric door locks into position.

Richard followed her onto the front porch and stood watching. In his heart he knew she was right. He was aching with a combination of anger, pride and hopelessness—all the qualities for which she was condemning him.

Chapter Four

Monica stuffed the grant proposal she was working on back into the folder and stared at the storybook scene outside her office window. Children in bright snowsuits squealed as their sleds plowed through the slush in Heritage Grove.

That's how Sarah and I used to be, she reflected. That's how Ann must have been, too.

The sun made sparkling, multicolored gems out of the fallen snow. The boughs of the huge lodgepole pines dipped and danced in the light breeze. The day, like so many days in Evergreen, was dazzling.

Monica closed her eyes to it all. The brilliance outside contrasted with her somber mood, making it seem even darker. She couldn't stop thinking of Richard Small.

I was just being honest with him, she reminded herself. Yet his reaction to her words had been so strong. What if she'd been wrong? She had lain awake long hours last night thinking about it. Maybe the man cared more than Ann gave him credit for. *It's the only reason*

I can think of for his anger. And now I've ruined it for her.

"Monica?" Louise Kockler stuck her head in the door. "Good after*noon*," she said in the Georgia drawl that was by no means native to the little Colorado town where they lived. "You want me to take the grant proposals with me? I'm on my way to Longmont to pick up my grandbaby. I don't mind mailing them on my way down."

"Thanks. I just finished the last one." Monica tamped the papers together against her desk. "It would save me a trip."

The sleek, gray-haired woman flipped through the pages. "Looks good. I hope the Colorado Council of History will give us the money to purchase the hobby-horse collection in Aspen."

"Yes," Monica told her. "I have another lead on a horse brought over from Britain in 1903. Hopefully we can pick that one up, too."

"Delightful," the president of the historical society told her. "Something else for interested people in Denver to drive thirty miles into the mountains to see."

Monica nodded. "The Evergreen Chamber of Commerce should applaud us."

"I played bridge with the executive director's mother the other day. The chamber's getting calls about the museum almost daily. We're wondering if we should do a brochure. You know, something we can send to people who inquire."

"That's something I'd like to work on," Monica said. "We'll need to commission someone to take photographs. I could write the copy and play around with layouts. We'd have to pay to get it typeset and printed, but I think we could put something together that looks nice without being too expensive."

"Grand!" Mrs. Kockler said, making a two-syllable word out of it. "I'll propose it at the next historical society meeting."

The intercom buzzed at Monica's elbow. "Phone call on line one for you," Sylvia told her. "It's Joy Martin."

"I'll take it." *Ann and I are going to lose each other. And it's all my fault.*

The call rang through immediately. When Monica took it, she forced herself to sound confident. "Hello, Joy."

"Monica. What did you say to him last night?"

"You've talked to him?"

"I should say so," the caseworker informed her. "First thing this morning. He called from the station."

"What did he say?"

"What did *you* say?"

Monica stared at the wintry scene beyond her window. "I had to be honest with him. I had to tell him what Ann told me. And somehow it got all turned around. . . ." *Just like Ann says her conversations with him get turned around.* Monica felt like weeping but then resentment rose up in her and swept every other emotion away. He had done it. Not only had he threatened her, he had followed through and now Ann was the one who was paying. Monica steeled herself against Richard and Joy, too. "He needed to hear those things. He's got to face what he's done to her."

"Monica," Joy said diplomatically, and right away Monica knew the caseworker was going to tell her she had been wrong. "You are a loyal, lovely woman. You get right into a project and take it over and turn it into something monumental. But you can't do that now. I have to tell you—" Joy chose her words carefully "—that perhaps you were right. Perhaps Richard Small did need to hear the things you told him. But not from you. He needed to hear them from Ann. Things aren't going to get better for them if you move in and tell Richard everything she feels. You are overstepping your role."

"I'm sorry," Monica sighed. "I guess I'm getting too involved."

"You are Ann's Big Sister. You're in her life to be a positive role model to her. Nothing more."

"Not—" Monica spoke apologetically "—to cram my values down her father's throat."

"Exactly."

"Oh, Joy. I just . . . couldn't . . . He made me so angry. . . ."

"You were there for Ann, Monica," Joy said.

It was over then. Ann would get a new Big Sister. Or perhaps no Big Sister at all. "Have you talked to her?"

"Not yet. I asked Richard if she had seen or heard any of the . . . the animosity between the two of you. Ann apologized to him because she didn't tell him about the meeting. But she apparently didn't hear you and Richard arguing. You kept your voices down, didn't you?"

"We did," Monica said. "But if she doesn't know we

were arguing, she won't understand it when you match her with someone else," Monica said.

"I'm not matching her with someone else."

"You're letting him take her out completely? She won't have a Big Sister at all?"

"She will still have a Big Sister—you!"

"But Richard said—"

"I know what he said," Joy told her. "He said it to me, too. But I talked him out of it. I explained the reasons I couldn't change this match and he relented."

Monica let out her breath in a rush. "Oh, Joy. Thank you. How did you convince him?"

"I told him that, in Ann's case, stability is crucial. With everything she's been through and with all the decisions she will have to make, maintaining a balance for her should be his top priority. I won't create more upheaval in her life by giving her another match just when she's learning to love and depend on you."

"He agreed to that?"

"In the end—" Joy said quietly "—he agreed that a change would be detrimental to his child."

So he hadn't given in without a fight.

"I'm surprised by his initial reaction," Joy continued. "I had gathered from Ann that he didn't care about her life much. This anger apparently is new and . . . and different."

Monica was silent for a long moment before she decided to voice the thoughts plaguing her. "I think he wants to reach out to her and to have her turn to him almost as much as she wants it, Joy."

"You think he is honestly as unhappy with the relationship as she is?" Joy asked, seeking Monica's insight.

"I do." As she said the words, Monica pictured Richard's face, his eyes, the endless sorrow she had glimpsed there. And, true to her personality, her heart was totally absorbed again, not by anger this time but by something more. "Father God. Bless him for letting You soften his spirit. Oh, Father, draw this hurting man to your side." Richard Small was giving her another chance and she was going to use it. She couldn't help wondering about him—why he'd relented, and why he wouldn't talk to Ann when it seemed he cared so desperately. "Oh, Joy. I know he's really unhappy with things the way they are."

March 24
Dear Diary,
I hope when I grow up I'll remember how helpless it feels to be a teenager sometimes.

Where to start? First, I guess, with Dad and Monica, my Big Sister. I wish they liked each other but I don't think they do. Dad tried so hard when Joy Martin brought her over the first time. He even went to the store to get doughnuts. Sometimes I think he was even trying too hard . . . like he didn't want her to have me but he didn't want me to know. I don't know why.

What made me realize all that was because Monica took me to a nutrition class the other evening and I forgot to tell Dad about it and when we got home it was like he was madder at Monica than he was at me. I went to my room but I heard them arguing before she left. That makes me so mad at Dad. It isn't fair. It wasn't her fault, it was mine, you know.

I want to change things. I want to make things turn out right all the time only I don't know how. That's how come I feel helpless. Really, I think it would all be okay if Dad and Monica just tried to like each other. (Although I think maybe Monica is trying.)

I guess the other reason I feel real useless is Danny. I wish I could change stuff for him, too. It's like we started these things happening and now we can't stop them . . . like in that game called Mousetrap where you drop a marble down a chute. The marble knocks something into a basket and a boot kicks over a bucket and the trap falls, and you see it all coming but you can't do anything because you started it and you are just there.

Sometimes you don't realize that one little thing can make all this other stuff happen. I'm sorry I didn't know that before.

I'd better close

SOS. (Sorry So Sloppy)

Ann Leidy Small
(Age 14)

Danny's mother was stacking soup cans in the pantry. "What are you doing tonight?"

"Oh," Danny answered. "Nothing much. I'll probably just hang around and watch TV."

"Ann hasn't been around lately," she commented casually. "What's going on between you two?"

Danny wondered if she could look at him and see that his heart had stopped. "Ann's okay."

"You two broken up? I'm used to hearing you talk about her. You haven't said anything in a while."

"She's fine," he said absently. "We're still together. We haven't broken up or anything." *Our whole lives have changed, that's all. And I don't know what to do about it.*

As his mom moved to the kitchen counter and began sorting meats, there was a loud banging on the back door. "Anybody in there?"

"All right, Kev!" Danny swung the door open and greeted his classmate with feigned exuberance. "Come on in. At last I've found somebody to rescue me from grocery bags." *And from all these questions about Ann.*

Kevin punched Danny in the shoulder. "The ice is melting in our driveway. Thought you might wanna come over and shoot some hoops."

"Sure. Sounds great." He turned to his mother. "That okay?"

"That's much better than MTV," she said, smiling. "Supper's at six-fifteen."

Together they walked the three blocks to Kevin's house. Kevin dribbled the ball as they went, talking about school, the ice hockey team, the new swim coach. It wasn't until they were guarding each other one-on-one, dancing in jumps around the blacktop and shooting baskets, that Kevin asked him about Ann, too.

"So where has the little kid been?" All Danny's friends called her that to give him a hard time, since she was still in middle school and he was a junior at Sheridan. But even though they teased him, they all liked her.

"She's been around," he said offhandedly.

"I haven't seen her."

Danny lined up his shot, one eye squinted halfway shut, the ball delicately balanced between the tips of his fingers and his palm.

"And?"

The ball rolled twice around the hoop and dropped off to one side. "And what?"

Kevin was staring at him, waiting for an answer.

Danny sighed in frustration and bounced the ball at his side. He was distracted and didn't want to shoot again. "Why does everybody care so much about Ann Small all of a sudden?"

Kevin reached out in the middle of Danny's dribble and stole the ball away, catching it in two hands and stilling it. "I heard something about her today."

It was the second time that hour Danny had felt sheer panic. "What did you hear?"

"You don't know?"

"No."

"It's all around the high school that Ann Small is pregnant."

"Is she saying that?" he asked, doing his best not to show emotion.

"No. Of course not."

"Well, who is, then?"

"One of the girls in third period said she saw Ann at the doctor's office and the nurse was giving her all sorts of pamphlets about babies."

Danny bluffed his way through it. "I don't know anything about it."

"Well, we all thought since you're her boyfriend . . ."

"You *all* thought?" Danny interrupted Kevin. "You mean all the guys have been talking about it, too?"

"Yeah," Kevin pretended to examine the pavement, embarrassed. "I guess so."

"And you're going back tomorrow to tell them what you found out about Ann and me?"

"Yeah. Sort of."

The reality of what he was facing hit Danny full force. Even after talking with Ann, he'd been able to pretend it wasn't happening. But hearing the words coming from Kevin, information his friend had picked up as school gossip, made Danny absolutely frantic. "I'm going home now," he said, hedging.

"Hey, why?" Kevin tossed him the basketball. "It's not even five-thirty yet."

"I have to go." He had to talk to Ann. He had to do something, he just didn't know what. He was all the way down the driveway when he remembered to call back over his shoulder, "You tell them all tomorrow that she's not having a baby."

She'll have to get rid of it some way or another. I'll just have to tell her and she'll just have to do it. After all, I'm involved in this, too.

He ran back to his house, jumped on the ten-speed he kept in the garage and pedaled up the alley and onto

70

Hampden Avenue. When he got to the little town house, he saw her through the window, sitting with a book. He dropped his bike in the yard and pounded on the door.

She opened the door a crack. But when she saw it was him, she unfastened the chain lock. "Danny. Hi."

"We have to talk about this."

"Come on in."

He followed her to the sofa, and as he looked at her, the words he had rehearsed on the way over left him. She was so pretty and so young and she had depended on him. "You ran away from me the other day."

"Yeah. I did."

"I was just trying to tell you I was sorry. Why didn't you stop?"

"I guess I didn't want you to be sorry."

"I have to tell you what happened today," he said.

"What?"

"You're ruining everything, Ann. It's getting all over school. Kevin Black asked me if you were pregnant and I told him you weren't."

"You lied?"

"Not exactly," he said. He touched her hand as it lay beside him on the sofa. "I just told him you weren't going to have a baby."

"You lied."

"You don't have to have it, you know."

"Danny. Don't say that." He looked at her and he hated himself for the tears he saw in her eyes.

"How do you think *I* feel?" Ann went on. "Everybody at the middle school knows, too. All the people I thought were my friends are whispering about it behind my back."

"But I figured it out," he said. "Just get an abortion. Your dad already knows, so he'll sign the papers. You can take care of all the talking that way—just don't have the baby. Everybody'll think they were crazy for talking about it."

She jumped up from the sofa. She didn't want him to see her crying. "This is *my* baby. You have no idea how it feels, Danny, to have something alive inside your body. I'm keeping it because I want it. I want something that will always be mine. I want something I can always take care of."

"If you want something that's all yours to take care of, I'll win you a big teddy bear at Lakeside. You don't have to do something stupid like this."

"No. It's different," she said. "A teddy bear doesn't feel things." She saw it all on his face then, his fear, his absolute powerlessness. "What do you care anyway, Danny? You can just walk away from this, you know."

"You're right," he said, thinking about it and regaining his balance. "I can. And maybe I will."

"I'm keeping the baby." She pronounced each word carefully, disjointedly, as if he had to read her lips to understand what she was saying.

"So maybe I'd better just get my ID bracelet back and forget I ever knew you."

"Maybe so," she said. She was fighting for what she believed was right, daring him to do it, never thinking he would after everything they had been through. They needed each other so much. Especially now.

He touched the huge silver bracelet, too big for her wrist, and then he touched her face. He hardened against her. "Okay," he breathed. "Give it back then."

"You're kidding!" She wanted to scream at him. He couldn't want this. But he was being so unfair about the baby. Just now she wanted the baby more than she wanted anything. Keeping it was worth losing him. Maybe. She stared at him, noting that the fear was gone from his eyes. He was in command again. She yanked the bracelet off her arm. "Here. Take it then." She practically threw it at him.

"Fine." He stuffed the heavy chain into his pocket.

"I guess we've just wasted all this time."

"I have to go," he said.

"Go ahead."

"Good-bye, Ann." Once again he wanted to tell her he was sorry. But he didn't. He remembered her words from before: *I didn't want you to be sorry.* He sat on the sofa, looking at her.

"So go," she said. "Why don't you just go?"

He stood and the chain bracelet in his pocket seemed to weigh him down like lead, as if it was holding him there.

"You heard me," she whispered again. "Just go." This time, he heeded her.

It was over between them.

He went outside without looking back, grabbed his bike and jumped on it. When he made it out to Hampden again, he pedaled as hard as he could—left, right, left, right. The traffic rushed by him and his muscles burned.

• • •

Richard turned the doorknob and pushed the door open. "Ann? You in here?"

The room was dark. His daughter's tiny form, folded up against the bed, was shaking with sobs, and for one terrifying moment, he thought she was dying. He rushed in. "Annie?"

In a daze she turned her face toward him. Her eyes were swollen, her cheeks flushed, and her wet mascara was smeared in feathery tracks down to her chin. She looked as if she had been crying forever.

"What . . . do you want?" She could hardly ask the question, her voice was so broken. She was clutching a sweater Richard had seen hundreds of times before, a sweater he thought Danny Lovell had given her for Christmas.

"I wanted to make sure you were home. You didn't answer me."

"I . . . didn't want . . . to answer. . . . Just . . . go away. . . ." She buried her face in her arms again and he didn't know what to do for her. He stood behind her, silently protesting against whatever had hurt her. Beside him, his fists were an entity of their own, clenching, unclenching, clenching again. For an instant, he almost bent forward to touch her. He almost offered solace. But after so many years of holding back from her, the action was so foreign to him it just wouldn't come. "I . . . just want . . . to give up. . . . This is too . . . hard," Ann sobbed.

"No," he murmured gently, trying to touch her with his words the way he couldn't with his hands.

"You mustn't give up."

She was totally helpless, bending across the bed the way he had seen her bend across it so many years before, stooping there beside Carolyn to say her prayers. As he stood above her now a fortress inside his heart tumbled; she was his child again, his little Annie, not someone to be frightened of or angry with any longer.

She became familiar to him. Or at least a part of her did. She might have been six again, with her face buried in the bedcovers and her delicate spine visible right up to the nape of her neck.

"Ann," he whispered to her. "Ann Leidy Small . . ."

A long time ago he had pushed on the little bones in the back of her neck until she giggled like crazy, her wild hair flying as he circled her nape with his huge hand, teasing her and telling her he was pushing her "silly button." When she didn't answer him now, he felt one hand rise as if by its own bidding, reach toward her across a chasm and rest on her shoulder.

He thought he felt her flinch. Then she seemed to crumple beneath his fingers, crying again, as he reached for her with his other hand.

At last he spoke. "I—I'm your . . . dad, Ann," he said haltingly. "I'd . . . like to help. . . ."

He waited while her crying subsided and then, slowly, she turned her head sideways so she could see him. Her heart was beating in painful lurches against her chest. She had no idea what to say to him. "Dad? Would you . . ."

"I'd like to help."

"Would you . . . call my Big Sister Monica? I . . . need somebody . . . I can talk to."

Richard felt his guts wrench inside him. He had made such a grand effort, and for the first time in a long time, he had felt capable again. Here he was, trying so desperately, his hands still planted against the jutting bones of her shoulders.

Talk to me, Annie. I'm right here.

"Would you call her, Dad? Please?"

He felt as if he was drowning in his own inadequacy. Yet he was only a human being, after all. In a flash his resentment came back, assaulting him, consuming him. After everything he had said to Monica Albright last night and everything he had said to Joy Martin this morning, he was stuck here, eating his words, caught between his daughter's needs and his own pride.

He removed his hands from her shoulders.

He wanted—Please God, he wanted to do this himself. It was his first chance to step back to her. But she was looking at him as if he wasn't there, was looking through him, and in the desperation in her eyes he saw his own shortcomings. He had been too busy or too preoccupied for her too many times. Why should things be any different now?

Forget what you can't do, Small, he lectured himself. *All this dignity you hang on to hasn't done Ann one whit of good.*

"What's her number?" he asked.

"I don't know. I wrote it down on a piece of paper and stuck it by the phone. It says Monica on it."

"I'll find it."

She was watching him, really seeing him for the first time tonight. "Dad." Her nose was stuffed up and she sounded funny now that she wasn't crying. "Thank you."

"Here's a hanky." He pulled an old tattered handkerchief out of his back pocket. "Not to be ugly but you sound like a Canada goose honking."

She gave him a wry little grin. "Thanks a lot."

Richard went to the kitchen, flipped on the light and searched through the papers by the phone. But it wasn't until he dialed the Evergreen prefix that he realized how hard it was going to be to talk to Monica. Last night he had told the woman he was going to kick her out of their lives. Tonight he was calling her—probably getting her out of bed—to tell her Ann needed her after all.

Pride. Stupid pride, that's all it was?

Richard jabbed in the rest of her number. It seemed an eternity while he listened to the faint clicks of the interchange going through, and then at last it started ringing.

It rang five times.

She was asleep. She didn't want anybody bothering her. She wasn't going to answer, he knew it. Suddenly he was desperate to talk to her. It was the only way he could help Ann. He was just about to hang up when he heard Monica's soft, melodic voice. "Hello?"

He had to jostle the receiver around to get it back up to his mouth. "This is Richard Small." His voice sounded too gruff even in his own ears.

Oh, man. I sound scared to death. I am scared to death.

"Yes." At the sound of his voice, her breath hit a snag somewhere between her lungs and her throat. She was afraid of him, afraid to say anything more.

She waited for him to speak.

For a while Richard waited, too. He half expected her to hang up on him. "You still there?" he asked her at last. And for some unexplained reason, he pictured her sitting on his sofa, eating her doughnut.

"I'm here."

"I know it's awfully late."

The apologetic tone in his voice made her almost hopeful. "It's okay. We do need to talk about this. Joy told me . . . what you discussed. . . ."

"I'm sorry," he said, interrupting her. "I don't want to talk about that now."

She stopped herself right then from forgiving him. "Oh. What else is it, then?"

"It's Annie," he told her and his voice became much softer. She guessed he was whispering so his daughter wouldn't hear him. But there was something new tempering his voice as well, a warmth she hadn't heard before.

At the concern in his voice, she was worried, too. Her heart relented toward him just a bit because again, in that hidden way of his, he was proving he could care about his daughter. "What is it?"

"She's crying like it's the end of the world. She says she wants to give up, that everything's too hard. And I sure don't know what brought it on. She won't tell me about it even though I was trying . . ." He was talking faster and faster as he explained the situation, and he realized as he talked that he was feeling better about everything. Just having her listen made him feel he wasn't quite so alone anymore. "I got home and found her crying in the dark. I waited for her to tell me what was wrong but she wouldn't. She won't talk to me."

For the first time Monica wondered whether maybe Ann was to blame, too. He was trying, reaching out to her, wanting to be her father. And she wasn't letting him.

"She says she wants to talk to you and asked if I'd call. I didn't want to after everything I said last night. But I thought maybe it was best. . . . If we can help her . . ."

When Richard started the story, Monica had been prepared to speak with Ann over the telephone. But now, as she heard the concern in his voice and realized what courage it had taken for him to phone her, she wanted to do more. To comfort Ann over the telephone would be to exclude Richard. Despite their differences, she didn't want to cut him off from his daughter. She grabbed her keys off the banister by the telephone. "It'll take me a good while to get there. But I want to come. Is it okay with you if I do?"

"Yes," he told her. "Miss Albright, thank you."

"You'd better quit calling me Miss Albright and call me by my name, Monica." After all their talking, she couldn't keep from laughing at his formality. In a way, because of this one phone call, things were changing between them. "Thank you, too," she told him. "Sometimes I just need to be needed."

Chapter Five

Monica arrived just after eleven.

"It didn't take you long," he said.

"I didn't keep to the speed limit," she answered.

"Ann's in her room."

"Has she told you anything more?"

"No."

Her fingers fluttered briefly across his arm. The motion was so fast, Richard didn't know whether her hand had actually brushed the fabric of his sleeve or if he had just felt the rush of air as it swept by. In either case, his reaction was puzzling. His pulse quickened. After all this time of being angry, even jealous, he was suddenly, inexplicably, happy that she had come. It was the second time in an hour Richard had touched or been touched by another human being. It felt good. Better than good.

"Come in with me," she said. "Let's do this together."

He stared at her. "You want me in there? She probably won't talk."

"You sound like we're interrogating a prisoner."

"Sometimes I think she feels that way," he said, half joking, half serious.

They went in together. Richard stood in the corner while Monica knelt beside Ann and began to stroke her curls absently, the way a child would stroke a kitten. "Your father called me. I'm here, Little Sister." She muttered the endearment in an undertone, the same way she used to whisper it to Sarah. "Tell me what it is."

"I can't believe . . . he . . . did it," Ann cried to her. "I just can't believe . . . he did it. . . ."

"Who, Ann? What did he do?" she asked. Standing in the corner alone, Richard was aching again, wishing it could be him who comforted her.

"Danny!" Ann wailed.

"What did he do?"

"He took his bracelet back and broke up with me because of the baby!" she bawled.

Richard slammed his fist against Ann's desk. "Confounded boy," he shouted. "Just wait until I—"

"He wanted me to get rid of it and I told him I wouldn't because I wanted it. He says everybody at high school knows, that they're talking about it and he hates that. And everybody at my school knows, too— I know they do because they look at me when I walk by. I thought they were my friends," she blubbered, "and now they all hate me . . . and I thought Danny loved me, but he doesn't, and he was the only one who did. . . ."

Richard's anger subsided. *No, Ann,* he wanted to shout, *I love you.* But he couldn't say it aloud, not now after Ann had asked for Monica, after she hadn't wanted him.

Monica turned the girl's face with her hand until Ann was looking at her. "Listen to me, kiddo. I want to tell you something."

"What?"

"Losing Danny was bad. It's got to hurt a lot. But being untrue to what you believe would hurt you a lot, lot more." She glanced in Richard's direction, included

81

him, and he was grateful. "Your dad and I are both proud of you for that."

"But why couldn't Danny see it was important to me? Why couldn't he just want what I wanted?"

"It's never as easy as all that. Different people feel different ways about different things. It's a big part of growing up, having to learn that. Lots of people would want to get rid of a baby or give it away. Lots of people aren't as strong as you are." She knew from what Joy had told her that their lives hadn't been easy. Both Ann and Richard were stubborn and strong. It struck Monica how very much alike they were. "Some people change what they think so other people will still like them. You stood up for keeping the baby. Maybe you lost Danny. But you didn't bend. That's what's going to matter most when you look back on this."

Tears were streaming down Ann's face again and she was shaking her head. "But . . . I just can't do this . . . not without Danny. . . ."

Monica felt rather than saw Richard step toward his daughter.

"I just . . . can't do it. . . ."

"Don't be thinking of the things you can't do," Monica said to her. "Always think of the things you *can* do."

That's right, Richard wanted to say aloud. *That's right, Ann.* For one insane moment he wanted to reach out to Monica, to brush his hand across her arm, to tell her that her gentle words had found an audience with him, too.

She had echoed his own thoughts.

Think of the things I can do. I can find my way back to my daughter.

Somewhere, somehow, he was going to find a way to begin.

"Thank you," he told Monica quietly as they stood together beside the doorway.

"We seem to be thanking each other a lot," she said with a smile.

"Yeah." He smiled back, content for the first time in a long while. Something subtle had changed for him tonight and it was a relief just to share it with someone. He was quiet for a moment. "Ann and I have raised so many fences between us. I watch you with her and I look for ways to bring them down."

"That's quite a compliment," she said. "Thank you."

"There we go again, thanking each other." They looked at each other and both started chuckling.

"Yeah."

"I guess this is going to be hard on her for a while, isn't it?" he asked.

"It'll take her some time just to get over him."

"Seems like he could have stuck by her, Monica. After everything he's put her through, it makes me want to get my 12-gauge and find out what that boy's thinking."

She couldn't help teasing him. "You could always do what the hillbillies do—force him to marry her."

He gazed down at her. He was surprised at how small she suddenly seemed standing before him. He had already seen how capable she was. "No . . . no," he said with certainty. "She isn't ready to have a baby, nor is she ready to get married yet. Both moves are dumb. But just because one's coming doesn't mean she has to do the other."

Monica chuckled warmly. "You're saying that two dumbs don't make a smart."

"Something like that." Something about her kindness, the gentleness he had seen her use with his daughter, made him willing to open up to her now. "I want her to fall in love someday. And then I want her to know what it means to love someone the way I loved . . ." He stopped, realizing the conversation was becoming much too personal.

"Her mother?" Monica prodded.

He nodded. "Carolyn." He couldn't put the rest of it into words just then. But it came to him suddenly how hard it had been to love Carolyn . . . not at first, when he was falling for her, but later, when he wouldn't admit he was angry at her for being sick, for leaving them.

"I think," Monica said gingerly, "if you two get through the next six months together, she'll have learned about that kind of love."

"Maybe. Maybe not. Today while she was crying, I wanted to sit down beside her and say 'Ann, I'm your dad. I can make everything okay.' But I can't, you know?"

"You've got to be honest with her." Monica was listening to his words, watching his face, understanding his fears. It was as if she was seeing him for the first time. The bitterness, the anger that always seemed to consume him, was gone.

"Sometimes—" She was speaking to him but the words struck a simple chord in her, too, as she thought of Sarah. "Sometimes it's the trying that's enough."

His eyes were dark, obsidian, but at the same time gentle. "You really think so?"

"I do."

"Tell me," he said to her in a voice that sounded so lonely she wanted to weep for him, "about my daughter. What's it like just to talk to her? You seem to know which buttons to push."

"I was a teenage girl once, you know."

"And? Did you get your heart broken?" He asked it tenderly but he was teasing her, too. And when Monica turned her eyes up to his, her heart seemed to volley inside her, it's back and forth rhythm unsteady as she surveyed his face. She remembered thinking once he might be handsome if his eyes weren't so brutally angry. But now she was seeing a different man, a man who was boyish and proud, with a cock-eyed grin and sparkling eyes.

"Yeah. I got my heart broken a time or two. But I survived." She spun around. "See? I'm all here."

"Yeah," he said, grinning mischievously. "I see."

"It really was tough sometimes," she told him, looking away, wondering if she should interpret his appreciative expression.

He found that hard to believe. He was sure everything in her life had been easy. "I wish Ann would have told me about Danny tonight," he said. "I would have listened to her if she had given me the chance. But I

85

wouldn't have been capable of giving her the pep talk you gave her."

"When you two have time together, you ought to sit down with her and tell her how you were feeling. She can't read your mind, you know. . . ."

"Sometimes I think she doesn't hear what I say," he said, treading carefully again. "Everything gets turned around. If I tell her that, she'll decide I'm mad or hurt because she talked to you and not to me."

"Which you are," she stated. She could see by the rigid set of his jaw he was struggling with it, too.

"That isn't the point anymore. The point is that I *want* us to be able to talk. Neither of us ever gets past the judging part. There has to be a good common ground somewhere for us, doesn't there?"

Monica began to appreciate how difficult it must have been for him. Questions reared up in her mind, questions about Richard, about the choices he must have made. "She reminds me of myself," Monica said wryly. "She's very willing to tell her side of the story."

Richard was nodding, glad once more to have someone to confide in. "But Joy Martin says that's typical of every teenager."

"Only—" Monica said, "I'm not a teenager anymore."

He looked down at her again, openly assessing her. He wasn't thinking of Ann anymore, only of the woman who stood beside him now. Something akin to need was spiraling up inside of him as he watched Monica and thought of how grateful he was to her and how pretty she was. It had been ages—no, forever—

since he had taken the time to stop and look at a woman and feel anything. "No," he said at last, "you aren't."

She blushed, turned red just like a teenager, contradicting the words she had just spoken. He couldn't help grinning at her again.

"You're crazy." Monica grinned, too. Then she sobered. "Can I ask you something?"

"What?" He stood there, grinning down, his dark hair disheveled.

"Why did you call me? If you wanted her to talk to you?"

He closed his eyes, the little boy gone, in his place the man again. He sighed, and at last he told her the truth. "She wanted me to. It wasn't my choice to make."

She gazed up at him as another new idea jumped into her head. *I don't know if I'm as strong as all that. I don't know if I could ever admit I was failing someone who needed me.*

For one insane moment she wanted to reach out to him, to bind herself to him in much the same way he wanted to bind himself to his daughter.

I'm not here for that, she reminded herself. *I'm here for Ann.*

"I've got to get home," she told him softly. It was well past midnight. "Good night, Richard."

March 30
Dear Diary,
It's really early. I couldn't sleep. So many things happened yesterday and last night. First, Danny

broke up with me. I'm feeling so lonely today. But there's more to it than that. My Big Sister came over. She said it was good because I was like a tree that wouldn't bend. And last night, while I was lying in bed trying to go to sleep, I thought of something else. I was crying before Monica came, and Dad came in. He was standing behind me and he put his hand on my shoulder. I don't know if he even knows he did it or not. But just between you and me, that's a pretty spectacular thing. Maybe he wanted to hug me. Maybe he really wanted to hug me. This is so chicken of me—it's like I want to know, I think I wanted to know right when he did it, but I was scared I was making it all up and that I would turn to him and he wouldn't do it. But I just keep thinking maybe . . . maybe . . .

Today I feel funny inside because I'm finding out that people I thought liked me don't like me at all. I'm finding out that people I thought didn't care about me, like Dad, maybe do. Funny huh?

More later, I promise.
Ann Leidy Small

Eleanor Albright lifted one beef frank and held it with the tongs while the water dripped back into the Crockpot. "Okay," she sang out. "Who's ready for the next hot dog?"

"Me! Me!" It seemed as if a hundred tiny heads were bobbing up and down with arms waving above them, trying to call attention to themselves.

"Sarah?" Eleanor asked her daughter. "How many?"

"I don't know." Sarah draped one arm across her mother's shoulders. "It's hard counting all these moving targets."

Eleanor sighed wistfully. "I should never have given the housekeeper the day off."

"But, Mom," Sarah teased her. "I thought you said you could handle Kaylen's birthday party yourself, otherwise we could have done it at my house. You insisted on having it here."

"I did," the svelte, gray-haired woman nodded, "and here I am. Super Grandma of the magnificent Albright family—"

"And for about three hundred extra shouting four-year-olds," Monica interjected from behind them.

"Here's Monica," Sarah said, the smile dissipating from her lips somewhat. "Monica handles things so well. Let's put her in charge."

"No—" Monica held up a hand in mock desperation. "Please. Anything but that." She plopped down at the breakfast counter in the middle of Eleanor's modern kitchen. Even though the room had been redecorated several times, the little island with the bar stools was just as she remembered it. She and Sarah had always done their homework together right here, sharing books, pens and answers. "Hey! Kaylen's Grandma!" One of the preschoolers bounced up to Eleanor and tugged at her hand-painted sweatshirt. "When do we get cake?"

"Right now," Eleanor answered fervently. "I promise."

One-year-old Patrick waddled by, a shredded hot-dog

bun squeezed like dough between his tiny fingers. Kaylen came dancing up right behind her little brother. She climbed into Sarah's lap. "Hi, Mom. Grandma? When do I get to open my presents?"

"Right now," Eleanor echoed herself.

"As soon as we get the cake cut and the ice cream out and everybody settled," Sarah amended.

"That should only take about two more hours," Monica teased her niece. "This party adds new meaning to the word chaos." She turned and waved across the room at her father. "Hi, Dad."

Cohen Albright saluted Monica with his pipe. Despite all the bedlam, he was stretched out in his favorite chair, smoking his favorite flavor of English tobacco. "You can say that again."

"Now! Now! Now!" Kaylen shouted. "I want to open them now!"

"Monica," Sarah said. "Don't make fun of the party. Mother and I have worked very hard for this."

"I wasn't making fun," Monica said. "It's just a funny party, that's all."

Eleanor glanced back and forth from one daughter to the other.

"I'm sorry, Sarah." Monica was suddenly aching inside. She had done it again. Every time she and Sarah were together, she opened her mouth and said something wrong. "I'll get the ice cream."

When Monica came back, Kaylen was pushing for presents again. There seemed to be dozens of them. If she didn't start opening them soon, the party was going to last hours and hours. Monica didn't dare say anything, though, even though Sarah had left the room. "You're a good grandma," she said as she hugged her mother. "Someday Kaylen will remember this party with great fondness."

"If," Eleanor said, grinning, "she lives through today."

"Where did Sarah go?"

Eleanor glanced at her lovely blond daughter before she answered. "She and David are in the bathroom trying to get the white balance set on the video camera. They're going to tape the cake and presents."

"David's a good sport," Monica said. "I'm glad he married into the family." She had been maid of honor in their wedding and loved David as much as if he were her own brother. "Momma?" she asked abruptly. "Is everything okay? Is Sarah mad at me or something?"

Eleanor shook her head. "I don't know." The din of the party was rising to a roar around them. "I don't think it's you, Moni. David's working lots of overtime. And with the kids, Sarah doesn't get much time to herself anymore."

"It isn't me? You're sure?" Monica wanted to believe her mother. For some reason, Richard Small came to mind. In many ways her relationship with Sarah was similar to his with Ann. *But Richard admits he is failing his daughter. Do I have the strength to admit I am also failing someone who loves me?*

"Okay, everybody!" David stepped out of the guest bathroom with the camera raised to his left eye.

Sarah, her dark hair shining, came right behind him. "We're ready. Cake, please!"

Monica lit the four candles with one of Cohen's matches and carried the cherry-pink layer cake to the table.

"Happy birthday, darling." Sarah kissed her daughter on the forehead. All the children, with Monica leading, began to sing. Patrick stuck both hands in the icing. Everyone leaned toward the cake, helping Kaylen to blow out the candles. Even so, it took forever to get all four of them out.

Cohen began to pile mountains of presents around the little girl. He winked at Monica. "Little girls are such joys, you know. You need to have a little girl, too, Moni."

Monica felt Sarah's eyes on her. All the while Cohen spoke, she was hurting, wondering what had destroyed the love between Sarah and herself. The bond that used to give them strength was gone.

Monica turned to Sarah, but her sister wasn't beside her anymore. She had moved away to stand beside Kaylen, and she held Patrick, propped high on one hip. David was making funny gestures to them and running the video camera.

She's the rich one, Monica decided. *Look at everything she has.*

"I'm opening yours, Aunt Moni," Kaylen said, waving a silver-wrapped package. She was wearing a pair of neon green sunglasses a friend from preschool had brought her.

"I hope you like it," Monica called back. She was excited about the gift. It was a tiny wooden treasure box Ann had helped her pick out while they shopped. It came with tiny porcelain tiles and a tube of cement, so someday Kaylen could decorate the lid the way she liked it.

"Oh," said Kaylen, disappointed. "What's in here?"

"Nothing. It's a box for you to keep your treasures in."

"I don't have any treasures," Kaylen said.

"That's okay." Monica nodded at her, disappointed, too. "We'll find some, okay?"

Her words were lost in Kaylen's frenzy to open the next package, a Glitter Prom Barbie from Sarah and David, and the next and the next. The little box was lost under the pile and when Monica thought of how much Ann had liked it, she felt like crying.

I'm not that much different from Ann, she thought. *I just want to know I belong to them. I want to know they look at me and see me as a part of their lives. It isn't that I'm adopted. It's just that I'm different than I used to be, different from them.*

"Kaylen got so many nice things," Eleanor commented as the three of them gathered cake plates later.

"She did, didn't she?" Sarah was genuinely pleased. "And after all the trouble, David did a fine job with the video camera."

"That little box I gave her comes with hundreds of little tiles," Monica said. "You'll probably need to help her with those."

"I'll help her when she gets interested in it," Sarah said. "I'm sorry she didn't like it. You know how kids are. They get so much junk at once they're totally overwhelmed."

"She *could* say thank you, you know."

Sarah flung the tea towel across a chair as tears sprung up in her eyes. "You may think you know everything but you don't, Monica."

"I don't *pretend* to know everything," Monica answered. She wanted to cry, too. "Please, Sarah. You were my best friend once. Just be honest with me and tell me what I've done." Silently she was praying there would be something—some tangible *thing* she had unwittingly done to her sister—that she could make up for. That the problem wouldn't stem from the fact that Sarah didn't need her anymore, or that they had grown away from each other.

Is this how Richard feels, wondering if he can get through to Ann, wondering if she will let him?

"You haven't done anything." There was a hint of weariness in Sarah's voice.

"I wish you would tell me," Monica prodded her, gentler now. "Say anything, even if it's simple or stupid—like I insulted the birthday party or I was unkind to the guests."

"That isn't it." Sarah shook her head. "I don't know what's wrong."

"I could try to understand, you know," Monica pushed her.

"No."

Thoughts poured back to Monica, things she had said to Richard just the night before. "Tell me," he had asked, "about my daughter. What's it like just to talk to her? *You seem to know just which buttons to push.*"

"I was a teenage girl once, too, you know," she had answered him.

Oh Sarah, Monica thought. *Maybe that's it. I was a teenager once. But I've never been a wife and mother.*

Richard threw down his pen. He was getting nowhere. "Ty," he hollered to his colleague behind the cracked door. "I'm going to work on these schedules at home."

"Fine," Ty called back. "You coming back later?"

"Yeah. I have to."

"See you then."

He arrived home, glad to see Ann there. School was just out, so he figured she must have got home moments before him. "Hey," he called in to her. "What's going on?"

"Nothing much." She came into the family room. "I was just thinking about taking a nap."

"You tired?"

"Yeah," she told him. "I didn't sleep much last night."

"Me, neither," he confessed. "Bad dreams."

She nodded. "Me, too." Her dreams had all been about Danny. She gazed up at her father. For some reason, she thought he looked different. Even though he had puffy half-moons beneath his eyes, he looked happier. "You really had bad dreams?"

"Not real bad," he told her. "I just kept seeing your mother."

And Monica. I kept seeing Monica.

"I got up at four this morning. I couldn't sleep. I wrote in my diary a little bit. Then I just sat there, thinking how much I miss Mom. Sometimes it's like I almost forget her. And then I think of things, like how she used to take me to the swimming pool and how she used to scream and jump around on the Fourth of July when you shot off those bottle rockets she hated."

"You remember that?"

"Yeah."

"Well," he said, uncertain what else to say, but infinitely glad she remembered. "I never thought you'd think of that."

"Why are you home?"

"Couldn't think at the train station. I figured things would be easier here. I've got to work on some papers and take them back in."

"Oh."

He was gathering his things together when Ann stopped him.

"Dad, after I've slept a while, maybe I could go into Denver with you and we could stop at Joy Martin's office. I think I want to tell her about Danny."

He thought about it and decided it would be a good thing for them to do together. "Okay, we will." Then he teased, "Do you suppose Joy Martin gives good advice to the lovelorn?"

Ann paused. "She gives good advice, I think," she admitted at last. "But just about things in general. I wanted her to know about Danny because of the baby."

"Okay." He glanced in at the kitchen table and then back at his daughter, wondering if he should say anything more. He wondered if he should mention Monica. Maybe not. But then Ann did it for him.

"What time did Monica leave last night, Dad?"

"Pretty late. We talked a while after you went to sleep."

"She's nice, isn't she?"

For a minute Richard thought she was teasing him or matchmaking. But he measured the sincerity in his daughter's eyes and knew they were discussing the value of a genuine friend. "She's nice."

"I guess I shouldn't have asked her to come down here last night," Ann said. "It was so late and she had a long way to drive."

Richard smiled, reassuringly. "I think it was okay, Ann. I think she was happy to do it."

"Thanks, Dad. I needed to hear that. I don't ever want to make her feel like she has to do too much with me or anything."

"I don't think she does." He was surprised as he said it to realize he wasn't jealous of Monica anymore, not after they had been together, comforting Ann.

All this time I've been waiting for Ann to open up to me. The enormity of what he had just discovered astounded him. *All this time. And all I needed to do was to quit worrying about her telling me what she was thinking. All I needed to do was tell her what I was thinking.*

When he spoke again, he echoed the exact words Joy Martin had spoken to him just two days before at the time he had been desperate to keep Monica from taking his daughter. "I think she has the makings of a good friend for you, Ann."

"She already is," Ann told him. "She already is."

Chapter Six

Danny Lovell frowned at the rows and rows of metal cages. There was no way. When he had come here looking for a present for Ann, he'd had no idea the Jefferson County Humane Society would have so many puppies.

They all looked so cute and so lonely. Their tails were wagging so hard their bodies were shaking.

He wasn't even sure why he was here. All he knew was that a puppy stayed your friend even if you did something stupid.

Today had been a horrible, decisive day for Danny. Everything had been fine during the first two periods. But in third-period algebra Alyssa Edwards, one of the sophomore cheerleaders, had stomped up to him and just started yelling. She was so mad at him she was almost crying. She said all her friends knew Ann Small was pregnant and that he had broken up with her because she was having the baby. And that he was a stupid jerk, not the way they had all thought he was, and she hoped Ann told everybody in middle school and high school and the world what he had done.

Danny's first reaction was to get angry at Ann again. But as Alyssa kept yelling at him, he reasoned it out. Ann had probably been feeling sad, and in first period she must have told one or two of the girls she went around with what had happened between them. And now everybody knew. Alyssa was right. Maybe he was a stupid jerk.

But he had a life to live, too. Ann wouldn't listen to him. She couldn't just decide to have a kid all by herself when the baby was a part of him, too.

I mean, it is not her decision to make alone. Surely I have some say as well.

Maybe that's what he was trying to prove to Ann. Maybe that's what he should have said.

He had turned to Alyssa. "You wanna go out with me, don't you? I mean, now that I've broken up with Ann Small." He was being as obnoxious as he knew how to be, trying to embarrass her as much as she had embarrassed him, just so she would leave him alone.

It worked. After she tromped off, things were better for a while—until he went to the lunchroom and a whole table of his friends grinned knowingly at him.

"Good thinking, Lovell," one of them leaned over the table and shouted.

Danny wanted to run away but he didn't. He held his head high and carried his tray over to sit with them. Then they started in on him full force, almost before his bottom hit the chair.

"Little kid handles life all on her own. Ann Small's gonna have a *kid*."

"You're a real cool guy, Lovell."

"I'll bet Ann Small thinks so."

Danny threw both his fists against the table. "Shut up about her. Just shut up."

"Why don't you marry her?" Tony Hubbard got in one last jab in his singsong voice. "Then you can get some every night. And Ann Small can have lots and lots of babies."

"Then Ann Small—" somebody else added with a hoot "—won't be so *small* anymore."

Danny didn't remember whom he had hit first. His whole body flew up and the metal cafeteria chair clanged to the floor and he just started decking people. He knew his nose was bleeding as he pounded against whatever body parts were the clearest shots. He was hurting so badly inside he didn't even feel the physical blows.

It took three teachers, the assistant principal and the school custodian to break up the fight. And he had been in Mr. Evans's office for what seemed like hours, waiting while they called his mother at work and told her what he had done. Then they assigned him enough detentions to last him for the rest of the year. Danny had had all that time sitting in the principal's office to think about Ann and the baby.

He hadn't wanted to be physical with her at first. He had been scared about it. But everybody at the same stupid lunch table had told him how good it would be. One day when he and Ann were walking back from the bowling alley, holding hands, it had just seemed right to kiss her, and when he did, he felt this fever pitch curling up and shooting straight out of him. When he hugged her, she clung to him like she had never been hugged by anybody before.

It went from there and he knew he had to do it, had to prove something to himself, to her. Had to prove how much taking care of her had made him love her.

Ann had befriended him, worshipped him, needed him. She'd looked at him and everything he saw in her eyes made him feel like a hero.

Well, I don't feel like a hero anymore.

Danny had known even less about sex than Ann had. He had developed all his prowess from the short film he'd seen in sixth grade physical education class and from the stupid things the stupid guys had told him at lunch.

He had visited a church youth group once, and he remembered the leader talking about it. He remembered thinking those church people had no idea what life was like. But now, he knew they did.

Once something like this happened, you could never go back.

He should never have accused Ann of anything. But he couldn't take any of it back now. He didn't know what he should say, what he could say, to make it right again.

The animal control officer sauntered up beside him. "Are you looking for a dog, young man?"

"Yes," he said. "I just don't know which one."

"What kind of dog do you like?"

"It isn't for me. It's a present for a friend." If he had been older or even more mature, he might have been able to put a name on his feelings. He was trying his best to absolve himself of an unabsolvable guilt. He was trying to make it up to her. He was trying to give Ann something alive, like a baby only different, for her to care for.

"Does your friend know you are bringing a pet?"

He started to say no but thought better of it. "She knows," he lied, "and it's okay." Maybe they wouldn't

101

let him adopt a puppy. He couldn't afford to buy one. Ann's dad was never home. He probably wouldn't even know there was a puppy around.

"Perhaps she would like to start with a kitten or a cat," the officer suggested. "They're much easier."

"No." Danny was certain. It had to be a puppy. A cat wouldn't like her enough. "A pup, please. But maybe something little."

They walked through the rows of cages, just looking, as the woman pointed out the assets of each dog and reminded him over and over again how much trouble an animal could be. They ended up standing beside a cage talking, and as Danny stood there, he felt something yanking on his shoestrings. He looked down and saw a puppy he hadn't noticed before, whimpering from a cage close to the floor. It had floppy ears, a brown patch around one eye and a tail that was flashing back and forth so fast he could hardly see it.

"That's him!" He bent down to peer inside the cage and to retrieve what was left of his shoelace, and as the little dog nuzzled against his fingers through the metal bars, he knew he had found Ann's newest friend. "Right here."

"Okay," the warden told him. "Come with me and we'll fill out the papers."

Danny sat beside the desk covered with cartoon clippings of Marmaduke and Snoopy and Heathcliff. The woman asked him so many questions he felt as if he was adopting a child instead of a puppy. Would the pup have a fenced yard? Would the new owner be willing to have the dog neutered? Would they feed him Puppy Chow twice a day?

Danny couldn't help it, he started giggling like a little kid. It just seemed so weird. Here they were asking him all these questions about a *dog* and Ann was going to have a baby. He was going to be a *father*. Nobody had interviewed him about that.

Are you sure you want him? Do you have a crib for him? Will you feed him seven or eight meals each day?

Danny signed the papers and carried the little puppy to the cardboard box he had attached to the back of his bike with bungee cords. As he pedaled down Sheridan toward Ann's house, he kept sticking his hand behind him into the box, scratching the pup behind his ears and talking to him.

When he arrived, Danny carried the box with both hands to the front porch. He'd planned just to leave it and go. But in the end, after the interrogation he had just been through, he decided he'd better make sure the dog would be okay there.

When he knocked, Ann opened the door a crack, then all the way. "Danny?"

He held the box out to her without saying anything more.

"What's this?"

"A friend." A precious, wet nose poked out at her. "I wasn't sure you'd be home."

"Yeah. I'm here." Her father had just brought her back from Joy Martin's office, then he had gone back to Denver Union Terminal again. "Is he yours?"

"No, dummy," he said, grinning at her. He took the

box from her so she could scoop the puppy up in her arms. "He's yours, Ann. I just thought you needed . . . a present. I named him on the way. His name's Abraham."

She wrinkled her nose. "What a weird name for a dog."

"I had a weird time getting him."

"He's cute." She didn't quite know what else to say.

"He's part beagle and part something else, and I know he'll get bigger but probably not by much. Somebody abandoned him and they weren't sure how old he is, but he's probably four or five months. . . ." He trailed off. Ann was staring at him as if she didn't know what to say and wasn't certain she should say anything. All of a sudden he wanted to hug her, to tell her he was very, very sorry for what they had done.

"What are you doing this for?" she asked. She wanted to cry again, just seeing Danny here. She knew her father would never let her keep a dog.

"I guess because I've been thinking about things. I kind of wanted to give you something that can take care of you and that you can take care of, too. I just thought maybe Abraham could be with you since your dad isn't and I'm not anymore, either."

"You don't want to get back together?" She had been hoping that was why he had come, that it was okay with him now for her to keep the baby. But just looking at him, she knew it wasn't.

"No. I don't."

"You wanna come in?"

He shook his head. "I'd better not. I had sort of a bad

day at school today. They called my mom. She's going to be really mad at me when she gets home from work."

"What did you get in trouble for?"

"Fighting in the lunchroom."

It was the first time she noticed the bruises on his jaw. "Danny? Are you okay?"

"No," he said. "I'm not." He eyed her. "Ann." He said her name softly and his eyes were sad, as if he was carrying a huge burden on his shoulders. Perhaps, after the interview about adopting the puppy and after thinking about the baby, in a way he was. "I'm sorry."

"You go to school," Joan Lovell admonished her son, "to learn. You do not go to school to fight with your friends."

Danny hung his head. "I know that."

"Do you know how I felt when Peter Evans called my office today? I thought they had called the wrong mom at first. 'Things like this do not happen to my son,' I told myself. 'Danny does not pick fights.' But Evans kept telling me it was you. They wanted me to come but I couldn't. I just can't take off work in the middle of the day to discuss why my son is in the principal's office. Danny? What is it? Why did you act this way? What makes you think you could get away with something like this? Why do you want to make me drive over there right at 1:30, the busiest part of my day, to talk to . . ."

"Mom. Mom . . ." He said it over and over again, the entire time she was talking. "Mom . . ."

"Why did you hit your friends? Why did you think you wouldn't be punished for behavior like that? Why did you think you could get away—"

"Mom!" He finally had to yell at her to make her stop raving. "If you'll stop talking, I'll tell you!"

"Why did you—"

He shouted at her. "I hit my friends because they aren't my friends anymore, okay?"

"Why? What could possibly have happened . . ."

"They were making fun of Ann and me." As he started the sentence, he knew he would have to tell her the rest of it. "She's pregnant, okay? I got her pregnant and I hit people for making fun of us."

"Oh, Danny." His mother's feet went out from under her. Luckily there was a sofa behind her or she would have hit the floor. She couldn't cry. She couldn't rave anymore. She could only stare at him. She knew the tears would come later. "What are you going to do about it?"

"I don't know."

"That's why she hasn't been around."

"She avoided me for a while before she told me."

"She's keeping the baby?"

"I think so."

"There's only one thing you can do," his mother told him. "Break up with her. You're too young for this. Nobody has to know it's your baby." She covered her face with her hands. "No . . . no . . . that's wrong, too. You can't . . ."

"I know I can't," he interrupted her. "I already tried it. I tried to reason all that out, too. But it didn't work."

• • •

Ann met Richard at the front door when he arrived home from the station. "You're gonna be mad when you see the rug in here. Get prepared."

"Why?"

She was holding a rag and a spray bottle of disinfectant. "Abraham isn't housebroken yet."

"Who is Abraham?"

She just looked at him and didn't say anything. He was going to kill her.

"Ann. Can I come in my own house, please?"

"I guess so."

"Now?"

She stepped back so he could walk inside.

The first thing Richard saw was the huge, dark wet spot in the corner of the carpet by the lamp. The second he saw was the tiny puppy tearing at the skirt on the sofa like a lion overcoming its prey. The house smelled like dog.

"What have you done?" he asked, forgetting everything he had discovered with her the day before, forgetting everything except the fact she was bringing a baby into the house and now she had brought a puppy, too. "Get that dog under control before it eats the whole sofa. Give me the rag. It's gonna stain. We're going to have a horrible spot there."

"Daddy, I'm sorry," she started to explain.

But he wouldn't let her. "Give me the rag *now*." He threw his things on the floor and started scrubbing. He was panicking. He didn't know why, it just seemed as if everything that was happening to them was overtaking him, drowning him. The biggest thing—Ann's pregnancy—he couldn't change. The only thing he could fight was the cute little dog.

He let Ann have it with everything he had. "While I clean this, I want you to get rid of the dog. I want you to take it back where you got it. It will not spend the night in this house. Do you hear me?" He looked up from the carpet and saw the devastation on her face. "That dog will not spend the night in this house. Get rid of it!"

"Dad," she said, "give me a chance. It's night and I didn't think you'd let me keep it, but I—"

"Then why did you take it in? Out the door with it . . ."

"Dad!"

"There will be no discussion. We cannot have a dog."

There were tears streaming down her face. "I can't get rid of it *tonight*. It doesn't have a *place*."

But he wasn't listening anymore. He was thinking of a baby, one more mouth to feed, after he had worked so hard all these years so she could get set up on her own some day. And now she thought they could feed a puppy, too. "I don't care. I'm your father. You do what I say."

"Fine," Ann hollered at him. "I don't care, either. This puppy doesn't have a place to spend the night and neither do I. But that's fine. That's just *fine*." The box Danny had brought him in was still in the kitchen, and she stuffed Abraham into it. She covered him with a towel so he wouldn't get cold and grabbed her jacket.

Her father was standing now, towel in hand, staring

at what was left of the fringed trim on the sofa.

"Don't you even want to know where he came from?" Ann asked, hoping he would soften enough for her to explain about Danny's gift.

"No," he told her. "I don't. I want him out of here. I don't want a dog in this family."

Inside her heart was breaking. She had thought things were better. But maybe they never would be. "*You* don't want a dog in this family. *You* don't want a baby. You don't want *me*." She slammed the door and she was gone.

He stared after her, not feeling a thing. She was asking him to accept too much. He couldn't do it.

As he put the cleaning supplies away and gathered his things, he decided he had overreacted about the spot on the carpet. Ann had already cleaned it well. It had just looked so *wet*. He adjusted the throw cover on the sofa so the rips wouldn't be quite so visible. He glanced at his watch.

It was 10:45 p.m.

I never would have let her go if I had realized it was this late.

The pup could have spent one night here, I suppose.

He sat on the sofa to wait for her. He must have dozed off, because when he looked at his watch again, it was after midnight and she still wasn't back.

He didn't know who to call. He didn't know where the puppy had come from. *I didn't even ask. She's right to think I didn't care.* But he had been so angry—not at Ann, but at her choices, at the circumstances that governed them now.

109

He put on his coat and walked outside, up and down the street, hoping he might see her. It was cold and clear, twenty degrees already and dropping. Above him a thousand stars shone like crystals in the sky. He had to find her. He walked farther, calling her name, but she never responded. Finally, at 2:00 a.m., cold and numb with desperation, he went inside and called the police.

"We had a terrible fight," he told them. "She wanted a puppy but I made her take it back. I had no idea how late it was. She's been gone for hours. It's so cold and all she had on was her jacket."

"Mister," the dispatcher drawled to him. "You shouldn't have sent her out there. You should have looked at your watch. Unless we have clear evidence she's a runaway or until she's missing for another . . . ah . . . twenty hours, we can't do anything."

"I'm not asking you to launch a full-scale investigation. You've got squad cars out there at this time of night, don't you. Well, use them. If anybody sees a teenage girl walking around with a puppy—" He knew how stubborn Ann was. She would still have the dog with her. For some reason that thought made him feel better. "Let them know where she belongs and have somebody bring her home."

"We'll do what we can, sir. We can do more tomorrow night." He heard the sarcasm in the man's voice. He knew what the guy was thinking. *If you were my father, I'd probably run away, too.*

At 5:00 a.m. he called Monica on his cell phone. He'd been driving around looking for Ann for hours.

Monica was his last resort. And when he reached her, she didn't ask for explanations, she just said she would look with him. Forty minutes later she was pulling into his driveway.

She cares, he thought as he stood in the window, alone and frightened, watching her come up the sidewalk. *I don't understand why she cares this much.*

When she walked in the door, he could tell she had been crying. She gave him a sad little smile and handed him a bakery bag. "They're chocolate-covered. I stopped to get them. I knew you liked them."

"Thanks." He took the bag out of her hand, and for some insane reason, he wanted to hug her for coming, but he didn't. "Oh, Monica. Thanks."

"Let's make some coffee," she suggested.

They sat down at the kitchen table together, drank the whole pot of coffee and ate the doughnuts while he told her what he had done.

"I know the dispatcher thought I was a kook. I know I come off as too stern with Ann sometimes. All I know is I walked into the house and there was that dog, and it reminded me of the baby and Ann's life and everything that's going to happen. At that moment I decided I couldn't handle it anymore. I took it all out on her and that mutt."

"Poor mutt," Monica commented sadly.

"Do you have any idea where she might have gotten that dog?"

"No." She shook her head. "I didn't talk to her yesterday at all. I was at my niece's birthday party all afternoon and then I worked on another grant proposal last night." She hadn't called on purpose, but she didn't tell him that. She had felt that he and Ann needed some time on their own.

"I hate myself when I blow up at her like that," he confided. "I have this horrible way of losing myself when I lose control of things. It's something about me. I sat and watched Carolyn's life slip away. And whenever things in my own life start going wrong, I feel as if they're slipping away, too. I lose control and just . . . panic."

Monica held her coffee cup in one hand, circling the rim of it with a finger from the other as she looked through the window at the rising sun. Its first burnished rays stretched across the eastern plains. "Maybe they'll find her soon," she said softly.

"Oh," he said, "please, God, I hope so."

Monica reached for his wrists and held them. "Richard," she whispered. "You're the one who mentioned God. Do you mind if we pray together?"

"What?"

Her ears were humming, and she was afraid. But fear didn't matter this moment because, suddenly, Monica could not turn back from what the Holy Spirit was urging her to do. "Do you mind if we commit Ann's safety into the Lord's hands?"

"A prayer?" he asked, bewildered.

"Yes."

"Well, I . . ." He reached across the gap and gripped her hands, too. Silence. Then, "I wouldn't say no to that. I wouldn't say no to any offer of help." He fixed his eyes on hers. "I would be *grateful,* in fact."

Monica smiled and lowered her eyes. Richard lowered his, too. And the fumbling words Monica prayed aloud didn't matter; what mattered was Richard's sharing them with her, and her insistent inner yearning that went beyond words, for Jesus Christ to bring healing to this torn family that she loved.

At 6:45 a.m. the telephone rang. They both jumped. Monica stood, frozen, while Richard moved to answer it. "Okay," he said. "Okay. Okay. Is she all right? Thank you. Yes. Okay." He hung up the phone and turned to her, looking like he was going to collapse. "They found her, Monica."

"Where?"

"Sleeping on the front porch of the Jefferson County Humane Society, all bundled up in her parka. Monica, she could have frozen out there. She kept going into the 24-hour convenience store to warm up but they wouldn't let her stay."

"Poor little Ann. Why was she at the Humane Society?"

"That must be where she got that dog. I don't know how she got there. Someone must have taken her. She was trying to take him back just like I said. Only she couldn't get in." He felt tears rising in his throat like a tide. He was horrified but he couldn't stop himself, he was so relieved and sorry. "She was just trying to do what I told her to do. . . ."

He was crying then—a grown man. Standing there, his fists balled up, crying like a baby. They had found Ann and she was okay. She had hidden in the shadows all night in the corner of the porch so the patrol officers

113

hadn't seen her. And now she was coming home.

Monica stood beside him, aching for him. His pain was almost tangible. In that moment she was certain; everything she had thought about him at first had been wrong. The things she had guessed about him since had been right. Maybe he didn't know how to tell Ann he loved her. But he did love her.

When Monica stretched out her arms to Richard, she wasn't reaching out to the man. She was reaching out to the friend who needed solace, understanding and strength. She gathered him into her arms and they stood against each other, their bodies rigid, while he wept on her shoulder. It was a profoundly moving moment for both of them, one that was entirely spontaneous.

Monica smelled sweet and fresh, like the morning smell of sunshine burning moisture off the evergreens. For a moment Richard imagined he could taste her skin, imagined the faint salty flavor of her against his tongue.

What am I thinking?

His mind was in turmoil. She was such a comfort to him, being there. He raised his head and looked at her. He wiped his eyes with a sleeve from the flannel shirt he had donned the morning before. He smiled for the first time in hours. He couldn't help it. He was only human, after all. She looked tiny and beautiful, like a little elf who had come to rescue Ann and him, too. "Thanks one more time."

He took three steps away from her.

"No problem," she smiled back, a half smile, and he could have sworn she was shaking.

Monica couldn't stop herself. She was overwhelmed by how solid his body had felt next to hers, how tight his muscles had been, how wrinkled and soft his shirt had felt next to her skin. And the scent of him. All smoky, musky and real, like the earth.

The squad car had pulled up beside the curb and they could hear Ann talking as she climbed out. Richard hurried to the front room and peered out the window. "She's still carrying the box," he said wryly. "I knew she'd keep that mongrel all night." He laughed. "It was kind of a comforting thought."

Monica stepped up beside him. "She couldn't have left him if she wanted to. I don't think the Humane Society opens until ten."

"She had three or four more hours to wait."

She walked in then, still holding the box. Richard froze. Reaching out to his daughter was still so foreign to him. He thought of Monica, of how easily she had reached her arms to him. He thought of the feeling she had offered him, the feeling of walking from desperation into solace, of walking into strength. "Put the box down," he told Ann. "Come here."

She set Abraham on the floor and the pup whimpered.

"Come here." He said it again and held out his arms. And Ann was whimpering, too, as she walked into his embrace. "It's okay," he told her, stroking her hair the same way he had seen Monica stroke it. "It's okay. Last night was my fault. I wasn't angry at you or at the puppy. I was angry at life and I took it out on you."

"I just had to stay with Abraham . . . through the night. . . ." she said into his chest.

"I know. I know."

"I couldn't leave him," she told him. "They weren't open yet."

"Want to know something funny? I knew you wouldn't leave him until you had someplace safe for him. I knew, this morning, you would show up together."

"I can take him back at ten. That's where Danny got him. I didn't mean to get a puppy without asking. But he was sort of a present. A funny present. Danny wanted to give me something that would take care of me a little bit."

He pulled back from her so she could see his face. "Maybe you won't have to take him back."

"Dad?" She couldn't believe it. He was smiling. He was serious.

"I mean it. Do you want to keep him?"

She surveyed her father's face, staring at him. She couldn't believe he had even asked. She nodded vigorously as hope began to mushroom in her heart. "Yes. Oh, yes."

"Where will we keep him while you're at school? It's too cold for the little mutt to stay outside."

"I can keep him in my room. He won't hurt anything."

Richard eyed her. "Except for the rug and the bedspread and everything else you leave lying on the floor."

She grinned at him and wiped her nose on the sleeve

of her coat. Monica's soul filled as she watched them. It was the very same gesture Richard had used, wiping his eyes with his sleeve. "I forgot about that part. I guess I'll clean up my room. I can roll the rug up when I leave. And I don't have to use the bedspread."

"It might work."

"Oh, *Dad!*" She threw her arms around Richard's neck. "Thank you!" She was staring at him in utter amazement. "Thank you, thank you, thank you!"

"You'll need to budget some of your allowance to pay for his dog food."

"Puppy Chow," Ann corrected him. "Right now he eats Puppy Chow."

"Whatever . . ." His face softened as he watched his daughter. "Now I'd like to know about Danny. Do you really think you love him?"

"I don't know," she said. "After what's happened, nothing's going to be easy anymore."

"I'm sorry," he said to her gently, "for not telling you more."

"I'm sorry, too." She was gazing up at him, her eyes huge and dark and filled with honesty. "But I think I understand. Monica told me it's hard for dads to talk about that sort of thing."

He was grateful to Monica again. He turned his face toward hers, remembering the gentle way she had comforted him. Suddenly he was aching to include her in their embrace, too.

"You know," he said carefully, heart pounding like a tom-tom against his rib cage, "You found yourself a pretty special Big Sister."

Abraham was whining from his box. "I'd better go take care of him," Ann said. "I think he needs out."

"You also know," he said, broaching the subject that had been alien to him only weeks before, "that caring for a baby takes a whole lot more planning than caring for a puppy does."

She nodded. "I know. I've been thinking about that a lot." She had thought about it for hours last night while she sat alone in the cold, trying to sleep.

"We've got to do some planning," he told her.

"Okay." She hugged him again. "We will. But right now, I'd just like to go to sleep."

He grinned. "Me, too." Gently he lifted the little dog from the damp box. "You said his name was Abraham?"

"Yeah."

"A big name for such a little dog."

"Yeah. Danny named him. It's funny, isn't it?"

"Yes," Richard conceded. "But in a way, it sort of fits him."

"I thought so, too."

"Here." Richard handed Abraham to his daughter. "Take him out. Then the two of you can crawl under the covers and get some shut-eye."

Chapter Seven

"You must be exhausted," Monica told Richard after Ann had gone to bed.

"Oh, stop feeling sorry for me," he kidded her, smiling at her, thinking for the umpteenth time how pretty she was and how kind. "Besides, you have to be tired, too."

"At least I slept until five this morning."

"I've got to call Ty and tell him why I'm late coming in. He's going to have to cover for me on the first two trains. He's probably about ready to fire me."

"Is he your boss?" Monica asked.

"No," Richard said, grinning tiredly. "I'm his."

"Great." She draped her coat over one arm, then reached for the doorknob. "I'd better get out of here. It's a pretty bad sign when employees start firing their bosses."

"He's also my friend. . . ."

"Or when friends start firing their friends. . . ."

Directly outside the window beside Monica, Richard could see the honeysuckle vine he had planted for Ann the year they moved here. This early in the season it was bare. But any time now the days would grow warmer and the vine would begin to bud with tiny ivory flowers. Ivory petals, soft and perfect, like Monica's face. "Thank you for being a friend, too," he told her quietly.

She stood silently for a moment as their eyes held. She was worried about him. He looked exhausted. He had been through so much with Ann. She was infinitely glad he had called her.

"She still scares me, Monica. She's turning into such a beautiful young woman. I feel out of place with her sometimes."

"I think that's normal, isn't it?"

"I haven't felt that tongue-tied since I knew I was

falling in love with Carolyn. She was so pretty. She'd walk into history class and I could talk to everybody else just fine. Then I'd turn to her and it was like somebody had erased my whole mind. Or, worst of all, I'd manage to spit something out and it was so jumbled it sounded like nonsense."

"I think that's normal," Monica said with a laugh. He was looking at her with eyes so dark, so penetrating, she almost couldn't bear it.

"I cared too much, I think." Richard had never told the story to anyone before. But with Monica he felt comfortable talking about himself. "It's like I'd turn into a different person. I'd turn into someone who was incapable of functioning. Now here I am after all those years, a grown man, and I'm feeling the same way with my own daughter."

"I did that, too." He had shared so much of himself with her. She wanted to give him something of herself as well. "There was this guy in the ninth grade. Johnny Brooks. He was on the football team, of course. We were in speech together. We went to a speech tournament and I had the teacher put me on the same debate team."

"So what happened?" He bit his lip in amusement.

"We lost the tournament. I did the same thing you did. I was so nervous I couldn't speak in front of Johnny. The other team didn't matter at all. I defeated us."

"And?" he asked.

"And the rest is history," she said, giggling because it all sounded so silly now. "Johnny married Jennie Patterson, our other team member. They went out for hamburgers that day and left me behind because they were so mad at me. I graduated with Jennie. They invited me to their wedding."

He let out a little snort. "And is that why you aren't married now? Are you still pining away for Johnny Brooks?"

She almost punched him. "Not by a long shot. I didn't tell you this story so you could tease me."

"Then why aren't you married?"

She thought about it for a minute. "I don't know. I never fell in love, for one thing. For another, I was always just too busy. I always had these plans. I always wanted to make something *happen*."

"Did your parents bring you up to make things happen?"

She thought about it again. "I don't think so. My sister and I are very different from each other. Sarah couldn't wait to grow up and get married. She and David got married while they were both still at the University of Colorado." She purposely asked the next question to get him talking about himself again. "What about you? If you were so self-conscious around Carolyn, what did you ever do to make her fall in love with you?"

"I quit trying so hard. She was unattainable so I gave up. I just went back to being me again. My dad came to class and talked about trains one day. I was walking home that day and she chased after me to find out what it was like having a dad gone all the time, riding the rails. . . ."

He trailed off, staring into space, just remembering that day. There was an expression on his face Monica had never seen before. He was relaxed, introspective, as if he was touching a portion of himself he had long since abandoned. "I guess it all happened when we were the same age as Danny Lovell." He hadn't thought of those days in so long. He could remember all the incredible emotions he had felt as he learned to love Carolyn, and how strongly he had embraced them.

"Oh, Monica," he said quietly. There was a hint of wonder in his voice. "Do you suppose Ann's feeling things as strongly as all that?"

She gazed at him, unable to harness her own feelings, unable to erase the memory of his lanky torso pressed up against her own. "Probably so." His innocent, self-examining question tugged at her almost as much as thinking of him as a young man did. "I'm betting she does."

"Oh, Monica." He was just staring at her. "I had forgotten what it felt like . . . to want somebody. . . ."

"You said the right things, I think. You know—" she smiled again "—you forgot to be nervous and you were just yourself. It was okay."

Monica thought of her own life then, of how easy everything had always been with Cohen and Eleanor and Sarah. Sometimes she felt as if they had handed her life on a silver platter.

Richard and Ann don't know they're lucky. She had spent years caring for her own family but she had never had to stand by them, love them, even while it hurt. *I want to care about someone that much. Like Richard cares for Ann. Like he once cared for Carolyn.*

"You were okay with me, too," she wanted to add aloud to him, but she didn't.

Monica and Ann had planned for weeks to go up into the mountains once the snow started melting. As Monica drove toward the little town house once more, her heart and her body were both betraying her.

I'd give anything to see him.

I'd give anything not to see him.

Her expectancy and caution seemed to constrict inside her like a fist. When she turned up the street and saw that his mustard-yellow Dodge was gone, her limbs went limp with disappointment and with relief.

Ann came bounding down the front steps with Abraham in her arms. She was wearing a floppy red flannel shirt that must have been Richard's. It smelled of him.

Monica reached out and hugged her Little Sister. She realized Ann's pregnancy was starting to show. Mentally she counted the weeks. It was early May, after all. It was time.

"Hi," Ann said, grinning. "Here's the picnic. Turkey sandwiches and graham crackers and peaches and celery with peanut butter." Since they had been going to class together, Ann was paying a lot of attention to her nutrition. "I cooked the turkey yesterday afternoon after school. Dad came home early again last night, Monica. Can you believe it? We even ate supper together. We had to wait until eight when the turkey was done. But it was wonderful."

"I'm glad," Monica told the girl, and she meant it. But she had to sit there for a moment to get her bearings, she had been so afraid and so hoping he would miraculously be there.

"This is Dad's shirt," Ann told her proudly. "None of mine even fit anymore."

"The baby's growing. I can tell."

Ann flipped up the shirt and showed Monica the rest. "I had to wear sweatpants, too. No more jeans. And last night, while I was sitting at the table, I felt this little flop inside me and I think it might be the baby moving."

"I'll bet it was."

They drove up Sixth Avenue to the interstate in silence, then on past Evergreen. When they got to Idaho Springs, Monica stopped to let Ann take pictures of the ice-bound waterfall. She'd brought a camera that she'd checked out from school. She was taking a photography class just this semester.

"You even know how to set the f-stops?" Monica asked her Little Sister. "You do better than me. I never can figure out what the right aperture should be."

"My teacher taught us to pick the setting we think is right for the sun and then take two or three shots on either side of it," Ann said, grinning. "That's how all the professionals do it. Then you always know you've come close."

"I'm impressed," Monica said. "You'll have to teach me."

They spent hours taking pictures, playing with the camera so Ann could get backlighting on the waterwheel and sunlight shining through the ice just the way she wanted it. After that it seemed like they found hundreds of things to take pictures of—a chipmunk at their picnic waiting to be fed; dilapidated gray mines and yellow tailings that clung to the sides of the mountains near Silverthorne; weathered, wooden grave markers protruding through the snow at the old cemetery in Central City. They even found crocuses and harebells just starting to brave their way up through the ice. It was a wonderful day for both of them.

"I've had so much fun today," Ann said as they drove back toward the city.

"Me, too."

"I love taking pictures. Maybe someday I can save up and get a really good camera."

"I don't mind if you borrow mine," Monica told her. "I don't use it much. I'll bring it the next time we get together."

"I might. I don't know if Dad will let me."

For a long while there was silence between them. Then Ann spoke again.

"Don't tell anybody, but I used to think I wanted to be a professional photographer some day. You know, like the people who take pictures of people's kids or their weddings and make them look really good."

"Ann," Monica grinned, happy to encourage her. "That would be wonderful for you."

"I used to think so, too."

"Well," Monica said, "just go for it."

Ann shook her head. "It's too late for that now."

Monica remained silent. She knew there were times

it was best to let Ann reason out the future for herself.

"You know what I really wanted to do? I wanted to be on the yearbook staff. I wanted to take pictures of everybody in school. It's real hard to make it. You submit pictures and then you take a test, and the people already on the staff get to choose what they like best. You don't put your name on your picture or anything. The teacher won't let them just pick their friends."

"It sounds like a great place to start, young lady."

But Ann was shaking her head again. "I can never do it now." She shouldn't even have been talking about it. But every so often she forgot about the future she was choosing and just remembered her dreams.

"It is an extracurricular activity," Monica said, urging her now. "But I'll bet when they see how hard you're working to do everything, they'll be willing to figure something out. Don't quit without even trying."

"You don't understand, Monica. It isn't that easy."

"And why not?"

"Because I'm dropping out of school."

Monica stared at her. "Ann. No. It's so important—"

"The baby is important, too. I want to be home with my kid. And I have to get a job anyway. Dad says I have to or we'll never be able to get by."

Monica wanted to cry out at the injustice of it all. "If you don't finish school, you'll have to work hard your whole life to make *anything*. It's just a few years out of your life, Ann."

"You're the kind of person who's lucky," Ann told her Big Sister. "Things just work out for you. Things have never worked out for me."

"You have to at least *try*."

"I want to have time for the kid now." Ann touched her stomach gingerly with one hand, the stomach that was just now beginning to grow.

Surely Richard wouldn't let her make this decision. "You've discussed this with your father?"

"Yes."

"What did he say?"

"He agrees with me."

"He can't."

"Dad says it's the only thing I can do," Ann said.

"There must be something." Monica was grasping for ideas. "Some way for you to compromise." There had to be a way for Ann to keep the baby and finish school, too. She only had three years left to go. Surely Richard had to see what an incredible difference it would make in her life.

Monica wanted to cry for both of them.

He's not even trying to help her. He's given up already. He isn't making it any easier for her or any better.

Monica's mind was roiling with emotions she had never imagined she could feel. Disbelief. Despair. She cared for Richard and had thought she was getting to know him. But this decision was that of a stranger.

Ann read the indignation on her Big Sister's face. "Sometimes I think it really is fair, you know. I did this to myself."

"No, you didn't. Danny Lovell was there, too, if you remember correctly. And there were things your father should have told you. . . ."

"Yet it wasn't all Danny's fault. Or Dad's, either. You want to know something funny? When I first found out about being pregnant, I used to pretend this baby would make Dad happy again. He's never happy anymore."

"I know he isn't happy," Monica told Ann. "I've known that for a while."

She steered the Cherokee around a turn onto Ann's street. The truck was in the driveway. Ann reached across the front seat and touched Monica's hand. "Come in, why don't you? Just for a minute? Please?"

"Ann. I'd better not."

"Please? I'll ask Dad if I can use your camera."

Richard opened the door to greet them. "Come on in," he called out to both of them. Strange that they had just been talking about him not being happy. Now it seemed he was.

In four days I had forgotten how pretty Monica is, he was thinking. *She's all country delicate and city fine rolled into one.*

"I took pictures with this camera and taught Monica how to change f-stops," Ann was telling him. "I got this great close-up of a chipmunk eating celery. I focused on his whiskers. I'll bet you'll even be able to see them."

"That's nice, Ann." He couldn't take his eyes off Monica.

Abraham tugged on the curtains in little fierce jerks. "Oops," Ann said as she scooped him up. "I'd better get him out of here."

Monica waited before the back door closed before she said anything. She was aching inside. She wanted

128

to touch him. She was furious with him. "Ann tells me you two have decided she isn't finishing school."

He looked surprised. "That's right."

"Richard . . ."

"She has to learn to take responsibility for her own actions."

"Yeah," Monica stepped toward him, her eyes narrowed, her fists clenched. "But asking her to give up her education is a bit tough, don't you think?"

"We're in a bad situation, Monica. We're in it together. We're trying to make it through the best we can."

"You're either punishing her or you're punishing yourself, and I haven't figured out which."

His eyes were blazing, too. "You don't need to figure it out. That isn't your job."

"But I thought you were trying . . ."

"She wants to be with the baby. She wants to do things differently than I've done them. Is that so hard to understand?"

"Is there any particular reason you're trying to make everything as hard as possible for her?"

He sighed. He didn't know how to explain this to her. "Your life has been a storybook life. Look at yourself now. You live in one of the prettiest little communities in the mountains and you run a toy museum. That ought to give you a clue. You deal with replicas and models while the rest of us deal with the real thing. You don't have the right to judge us."

A little twist of pain started in her heart and spiraled outward. She hated this part of him, the part that seemed to cover his gentle qualities with hardness. "My, but you are a cynic."

"Don't call me a cynic until you've lived my life."

"Don't tell me I don't know what I'm talking about." She was fighting now, for Richard, for his daughter. She felt incredible pain and she embraced it. "What you say isn't new or different. If you care about Ann, you'll search and find out there are compromises you can make."

He wanted to shake her. How dare she come into his home—so beautiful and so damned enticing—and say these things about his life? She had grown up with options he had never known. Nothing was real to her, nothing too difficult. Her life was a toy museum, neatly displayed, playthings all in order.

She saw it in his eyes. "We're viewing things from different angles."

"Why don't you go ahead and say it, Monica? You think it's all my fault, don't you? You think it's my fault she's pregnant. You think it's my fault she's dropping out of school."

Her eyes were bitter. She hated saying it, knew it would hurt him, but she had to. Had to make him see what he was doing to his daughter. "Yes. Sometimes I think it's your fault."

"Oh, man," he said clenching his fists and then staring at them, as if he had been trying to hold onto something that had just been ripped away. "Oh, man."

She saw the raw pain in his eyes then, saw how she had shattered him. But it was too late now, too late for anything except saving Ann. "I've got to go."

He took one step toward her. He was going to fight her now the only way he knew how. "No. You aren't going to leave this way."

"I don't want Ann to see us this way."

"What," he asked her. "Fighting?" He came toward her, his eyes smoldering with anger. "Don't use Ann as an excuse. Don't accuse me and then run away so I can't fight back. That isn't how it's done."

"I can't help it," she told him. And as she said it, she realized it was true. It was how she and Sarah had disagreed as children. She had been taught a long time ago that it was the ladylike thing to do.

"Tell me why you look at me one moment like you admire me and then the next like you want to hit me?"

"There are times," she said simply, "when I have to judge you by what Ann tells me."

"Like today?"

"Like today."

"Every so often I look at you and you seem surprised. As if I'm someone else, not someone you thought I was. . . ."

"It's true," she conceded. She was shaking, frightened. She would have backed away if his eyes hadn't held her. "You do . . . surprise me . . . sometimes. . . ."

"Why?" he demanded of her. "Why do I surprise you?" He reached out and gripped her shoulders. "Is it when we're fighting about Ann? Or is when we're attracted to each other?"

She met his eyes head-on. "It isn't that at all." *Please, God. Have I been that transparent?* "It's when she tells me you don't care about her. I believe her

131

sometimes because you're so hard on her—"

"Life will be hard on her."

"And then I see you caring about her even though you don't know how to show it."

"And when you look at me sometimes I see wistfulness in your gray eyes . . . like a storm coming in from the sea. Is that the same thing? Is it because you're glad you can forgive me? Because you—"

"Don't put me on the spot like this, Richard." She was furious with him for seeking those answers, furious and yet aching.

His hands tightened almost imperceptibly on her arms. "I may not always be as gentle or as sensitive as I need to be with my daughter. But at least I know how to be honest, Monica." His eyes were deep black pools, threatening to drown her. "I tell Ann what I'm capable of. She doesn't harbor any false hopes about what I can provide for her."

"My father taught me to have dreams," Monica told him. "Sometimes that was more precious than honesty."

"No," he said. "Not more precious. Just easier."

She wanted to scream at him. And she would have given anything to step into his arms just then, to cry as he had, to have him hold her. He wouldn't apologize, not for this. It was her fault. She was the one condemning him. "Maybe easier," she told him vehemently. "But maybe more fair, Richard." With that, she turned and fled.

Chapter Eight

"Joy is with a little sister right now," Gwen, the receptionist, told her. "Can anyone else help you?"

"No," Monica answered. "I know I don't have an appointment or anything. There just wasn't time. I have to see her. Please. I'm willing to wait as long as I have to."

"I'll let her know," Gwen reassured her. "I'll see what she says, okay?" A few minutes later she was off the intercom and smiling. "Joy says it's fine, Monica. She'll be finished with her interview in about ten minutes. She'll talk to you then."

"Thanks, Gwen."

Ten minutes later, Gwen led her up the hallway to Joy's office.

"Monica. Sit down." Joy rose to take her hands. She had known the minute Gwen buzzed her that something was terribly wrong. "Is Ann okay?"

"She's okay," Monica answered. But she looked beaten and Joy couldn't help thinking how different she seemed from the confident woman who had come to her office three months before for her initial interview.

"It isn't Ann. It's me, Joy. I'm trying too hard to do what's right. And I don't think I am."

"Ann tells me you're doing a lovely job, that you're best of friends. . . ."

"It isn't that. It's just . . . the relationship." She pushed on, uncertain of how to put it, uncertain, really, of what it was she was trying to say. "It's Richard

Small. I can't agree with him. And it's . . . hard . . ."

"You're questioning his competence as a father?"

"No. Not that," she was shaking her head again, close to tears, desperate. "It's more than that. Or less than that. He won't compromise about her finishing school, won't help her . . ." She stopped, uncertain of what else to say. She couldn't say Richard wouldn't reach out to Ann. He was trying to. And she admired him so much for his effort. "He's just so . . . so *steadfast*. . . ."

Now that Monica was releasing her emotions, she wanted to strike out at something. She was angrier at herself than she was at Richard. She had absolutely no idea what she was feeling. He had talked about attraction.

Attraction.

She was angry at him but she respected him, and truly, truly, she cared for him. The only thing she could accuse him of was being honest.

I told Ann she would look back at herself, be glad, because she had been strong. Now I am the one who is bending.

"I don't know how to help him." She glanced up at Joy like a little lost child. "He's trying so hard but he's trying in some of the wrong *ways*—"

It was Joy, another woman, who understood exactly where she was coming from. "Monica? What are you feeling for this man?"

Monica stared at the caseworker before she answered her. "Anger."

"Your anger is covering something else. You are here building walls. Why?"

Monica seemed to crumple as Joy watched her. "I don't know. I'm mad at him. I want to help him. I love Ann. Ann needs me. And I think *he* needs me. . . ."

Her answer made Joy take Monica in her arms and hold her for a long moment, rocking her. Joy knew she had to ask the next question—had to know Monica's answer. "Monica? Are you attracted to Richard Small?"

Monica was silent for a breath, just a breath. Then she answered in a whisper. "I'm trying not to be. But, yes. Yes, I am."

Joy hated herself for what she had to do next. She knew she had to harden herself, had to show Monica that she and Richard couldn't allow their feelings to surface. A young girl's happiness was at stake.

"Does he feel the same way, Monica?"

"I don't know. I mean, I didn't know . . . I thought it was just me. But today, while we were disagreeing, I told him he surprised me sometimes. He asked if it was when we were fighting about Ann or if it was when we were attracted to each other."

"He's feeling it, too, then."

Monica closed her eyes and remembered reaching out to him, remembered holding him, how stalwart he had felt against her even while he was so desperately afraid for his daughter. She nodded.

"Listen to me, Monica. Listen to me carefully." Joy held Monica by the shoulders. "You mustn't feel this way. For Ann's sake, you can't. And neither can her father."

"Joy. I'm so sorry."

"There isn't anything to be sorry for. We will handle it now," Joy said firmly. "Besides today, have you voiced any of these feelings to each other?"

"No." Monica shook her head. "If I hadn't been so unfair to him, if he hadn't been so angry, I don't think we ever would have."

"First of all, we'll have a meeting between you and Richard here in the office. I'll ring him, too, and schedule it. The two of you can iron out your differences. After that, you will not discuss them again. If there is any animosity or friction between the two of you, Ann will sense it. She's a smart one. I don't need to tell you she needs support from every direction."

"I'll be here," Monica said. "I can't speak for Richard."

"As for the attraction between you," Joy said matter-of-factly, as if she was discussing bad grades with a schoolgirl, "it will remain unexpressed at the meeting." Perhaps, if left alone, the matter would take care of itself in time. But it could be awful for Ann and Joy wanted Monica to realize that. "I don't think I have to tell you how detrimental it could be to Ann. If Ann weren't pregnant, I would advise a new match right now. I would get you and Richard away from each other as quickly as possible."

Would they take Ann and me away from each other? It sounded horrible to Monica. She had grown to love Ann so much. But she knew Joy was right and, for Ann's sake, she wanted to do what was right more than anything.

"What we want here is a certain kind of focused

concern and attention from both of you onto Ann Small."

"Do you think Ann would want a new Big Sister?"

"Maybe. But I'm not even going to ask her. A pregnant teen needs stability. Ann has many decisions to make about her own life and the life of her baby. Her attention has to be centered on those decisions, not on hurt or rejection because she's been matched with somebody new. You two have made great strides together. Right now she needs *you*. That's what you have to remember."

"I will. I do."

"She needs stability," the caseworker repeated. "A romantic involvement between you and her father would make things too volatile and uncertain. Ask yourself questions. How can you keep an evenness in your relationship with Ann when your own life suddenly becomes topsy-turvy? What if you or Richard initiates this and you eventually decide to break it off? What will that do to Ann? Also, she might feel jealous of you."

Joy kept on. "How can she make decisions about her pregnancy when she is worried about what will happen between her father and you? You are in her life as a role model and a friend, not as a parent or a provider. Will caring for him cause you to take a parental role in her life instead?"

"I won't let it happen, Joy," Monica said, and in her heart of hearts she meant it. Quietly, carefully, she acknowledged her attraction to Richard and then swept it away.

It will be easy, she decided, *because I love Ann so much.*

May 5
Dear Diary,
Hi. I'm tired tonight. This crazy dog is really trouble. Sometimes I think about walking over to the Lovell's house and giving Abraham back. But if I did, I know I'd miss him.

I had a good time with Monica the other day and I haven't had time to write since. Days when I don't have to go to school or see Danny are pretty good. It's hard to see him and have to be just his friend when I used to be his girlfriend and now there's this baby.

Monica's letting me borrow her camera while I'm in this class. It will be great. Something I've always dreamed about. But I'm fourteen years old and I don't really have a reason to dream about things anymore.

Here is a list of all the things I owe my dad for:
1) Puppy Chow for Abraham.
2) Anything he has to pay for when the baby comes.
3) New curtains for the front window. Abraham ate them tonight.

So, I really don't know what to do. I need a job, I think, but one that pays pretty good. And Monica thinks I should stay in school. Sometimes I get confused. I get worried. And scared. This really is a little baby inside of me. And maybe, when it starts growing it'll do things like Abraham did and pull down the curtains and eat them. Today I didn't want to love Abraham. I wanted to throw him out the window.

Love,
Ann Small

Sarah Albright Taylor stood out in the corrals, alone with the horse, her taupe leather boots up to their ankles in mud. The gray ooze sucked at her feet but she loved the feel of it. The horse, a huge buckskin, trotted around her in a circle, just the circumference of the lead she gave him.

She pushed up the sleeves on the funny turquoise sweatshirt David had given her. It said "I'm the Mommy. That's Why." Sarah cracked her little whip then and made the horse gallop. His mane and his tail streamed in little ripples in the wind. *Look at him go,* she said to herself as his hooves kicked up clods of mud and threw them. *A free animal.* But then she corrected herself. The horse was nothing special, he was just like her, inside a corral and on a tether, galloping in circles, going nowhere.

It had been, she thought, a long time since she'd been happy.

"Sarah!" Eleanor called to her, her voice echoing through the trees. "Do you want to eat lunch with us? Agnes is making fried tortilla soup. Kaylen says we should wait for you."

"Don't wait. I'll be in later." She loved being out with the horses, always had, ever since she and Monica were old enough to be allowed down here by themselves. The corrals and the stables had always been cool and damp, wonderful places to play make-believe. She and Monica had dreamed up handsome princes and castles, and the horses had been dragons. It had been their own pretend fairy tale.

I am thirty-two years old and I'm just now figuring out fairy tales aren't real.

She supposed she should be mad at Cohen for sheltering them all so. He had done everything he knew to make things easy for her and Monica. He had sent them to college and paid their way. He had bought them cars when they were sixteen and helped them open their own checking account. She had expected it always to be that easy.

But somehow it wasn't. She and David had everything except for each other. He was working incredible hours every day and she couldn't help him because of Kaylen and Patrick. When they first got married, they'd run the office together. But now it was crazy for her to try to work. Day-care facilities in the little mountain town were hard to come by. Sarah had put the kids on three waiting lists but space never became available. And, really, she preferred to care for her children herself.

Their grandma had a life of her own, too, Sarah knew she couldn't saddle her mother with kids every day. Eleanor played bridge on Thursdays, volunteered at the hospice and was president of the homeowner's association. She accompanied Cohen to all the Denver Bronco games and helped him organize elaborate tailgate parties at Mile High Stadium. She was living the life she deserved to live after bringing up two children of her own.

"Momma! Momma!" Kaylen slammed the screen door shut and came racing down the hillside. "I ate all my lunch and Agnes says I can have ice cream and I don't have to take a nap!"

The horse bolted, spooked by the rocks, dust and pinecones the running child's feet sent flying toward the fence.

"Stop, honey. Don't come closer. You're scaring him."

"Momma? Can I ride him? Please?"

"No."

"Oh, please. Just for a little while?"

"I said no. Don't ask again. He's frightened by you."

"You're mean."

Sarah shot Kaylen a look that said *I'll show you what mean is*. She should have spanked her for that comment. But she had the horse on the end of the rope and could do nothing. "Go back inside. Tell Grandma I'm coming in."

"Momma? Is Daddy coming home any earlier tonight? Will I get to see him before I go to bed?"

"I don't know, Kaylen. We'll see." She never knew the answer to that one lately.

As Kaylen climbed back up the hill again, Sarah watched her go, watched her chubby little legs and the long hair that was too often tangled. *I do love her so much.*

As she put the horse away, it occurred to her that she

had been a good mother until the baby came along. Even though she had grown up almost a twin, she was still a private person. She treasured her time alone. Before Patrick was born, she had always found time to relax and reflect on things during Kaylen's naps.

Before the second baby came, she and David had employed a housekeeper. But David's business declined after that and they couldn't afford her anymore. Now it seemed like the children played off one another. One slept while the other needed her attention, and vice versa. It was hard keeping the house up and sometimes she felt as if there was no time to think . . . much less to read or stitch or do something just for herself.

It isn't selfish. It's something I need. In order to give myself to other people.

"So? Did Kwan do all right for you?" Eleanor asked her when she came into the house. Cohen had named the mare after Michelle Kwan, one of his favorite figure skaters. Not long ago they had all driven to Colorado Springs to see her perform at the Broadmoor.

"She did fine. She's a beautiful horse. She certainly needed the exercise. Maybe one of these days I can take her out and ride her."

Eleanor glanced at her watch. She had to drive a hospice patient to the grocery store by two. "Monica's been wanting to come up and ride, too. Maybe the two of you could go out together."

"I would rather go by myself," Sarah said.

Eleanor sat the teapot down, cradled her chin in one palm and surveyed her daughter. "Sarah. Baby," she said. "Are you and David having troubles?"

Sarah laughed once. "I don't think we see each other enough to be having troubles."

"Is he working that hard?"

"He's trying to do the work of two people, Momma. It's everything he can manage just to do the day's transactions with the brokerage. When any new accounts come in, it's just impossible."

"Could he hire somebody to help him?"

"Yes. We've discussed it. We could afford it if we paid somebody a draw against commission. But it's not easy to find someone."

"Are you depressed?" Eleanor asked her.

"No." But that wasn't entirely true.

"Feeling alone?"

Sarah had to smile. Anything but that. She definitely didn't feel alone. "Sometimes I think I'd like to be alone—to cut myself off from people for a while . . ."

"From everybody?" Eleanor was prying now and she knew it. But she didn't think she'd get answers any other way. "Or just from Monica?"

Sarah shot her a look. "What do you mean?"

"Whatever's wrong, you've been taking it out on Monica."

"I don't mean to. I don't know what it is." But she did know—she just didn't want to voice it. *Monica's life is still easy. Monica is still living the fairy tales Cohen made for her.*

Sarah buried her face in her hands for a moment, her thick, dark hair hanging around her hands like a curtain. When she raised her face, her eyes were wet but she wasn't crying. "Okay. I'll tell you." She stopped, swallowed and plunged on. "I'll say it." She paused again, then finished. "I think I'm jealous of her."

"Jealous?" Eleanor was shocked. "Why?"

"I don't even know," she said. "Monica's just so free. But I have two precious kids and I do love David so much. We have our own business. We have the new house in Hiwan."

"You have everything she doesn't have."

"I know that. She's my sister and she used to be my best friend. Sometimes I think it's just *time* I begrudge her. She's who I *used* to be. And she does all these great things for society like taking Ann Small and changing her life. . . ."

Eleanor took her hands, holding them, aching for the daughter who had always been the popular one. "You have two little lives in your charge right now, precious gifts. You can change their lives. Ann is the way she is because she doesn't have a mother any longer."

"I know that. I *know* that."

"Don't be guilty for what you feel, Sarah. Think back to when you made cheerleader and Monica didn't. Remember? She didn't talk to you for two days. And then, after she told you she was sorry, she cried for another three. Do you remember how you felt?"

Sarah stared off into space for a minute and smiled for the first time in weeks, remembering how she and Monica had cared for each other then. "I haven't thought about that in ages. Monica moped around until I wanted to scream at her. And after I found out what was wrong, I would have traded places with her, given her my pompoms, if I could have."

"She might trade places with you now, Sarah."

Sarah propped her chin on her hands. "It's crazy, isn't it?"

"You two are sisters," Eleanor said wisely. "That's what matters. And I'm guessing that's what will win out for you in the end."

Ann couldn't find her math book. It was always on the bottom of her locker. She hardly ever took it to class because the teacher always wrote the formulas on the board and handed out copies of the problems. Today they were doing word problems and Mr. Samuels had said to dig out their books.

She pulled out one dirty white gym shoe that had been there since last semester P.E. and a magazine she had saved from four months back because it had an article about Clay Aiken in it.

She was still rummaging when she felt two arms go around her expanding waist. Then somebody started tickling her.

"Hey." She rocked back on her heels but she didn't have to look. She already knew it was Danny. He used to come across the street from the high school and do that during break all the time. "What are you doing?"

"Bugging you."

"I can feel that." She was glad to see him. It had been hard at first but now she had stopped expecting him to want to get back together. Her heart had stopped jumping every time she saw him. And now they were becoming friends.

"I didn't want to abandon you," he said. "I guess . . . I really just wanted to see how you're doing."

"I'm doing okay."

"Everybody at the high school knows now. Every single person."

"Yeah," she said softly, wanting to cry suddenly for no reason and knowing she couldn't. "It got around really fast."

"I talked to my mom. She knows, too."

"What did she say?"

He hesitated. He didn't want to tell her. "She was upset. So—" He was searching for another subject. He wanted to quit talking about the baby. "Has the— Humane Society called to check on Abraham? They always do that. They want to make sure their animals are okay."

"Ha!" Ann snickered. "They're like an adoption agency or something."

"I know. I was thinking about that the day I got him. God's going to give you and me a kid without any questions, but when I went to get that dog I had to answer all sort of questions and stuff and prove you could really take care of Abraham. It was pretty funny."

Her voice was low. She had written in her diary just days before and, as she was writing, she had begun to see the baby for what it would be, an awesome responsibility. "It *is* strange, you know?"

"So tell me about Abraham."

She grinned at him. "You really want to know? I think you gave me that wild animal to totally sabotage

146

my life." She furrowed her brows, trying to tease him. She was trying to look disgusted and angry but she couldn't help laughing just the same. "As if you haven't sabotaged it enough already, Danny Lovell."

"What has he done?"

"You know the curtains in the front window? He yanked them down off the rod and ate them. The rod hit my dad on the head. Remember the sweater you gave me? He ate that, too. Chewed one whole arm off and unraveled the other one. And my new CD?" It was by Hilary Duff and he had given it to her for Valentine's before she found out she was pregnant. "He unraveled that, too. He ate my mascara and two kitchen sponges, the skirt off the sofa and Dad's gasket sealer for his truck."

"Oh, *no.*" Danny was doing his best to look mournful but it was hilarious and he was laughing, too. "He must be teething. They say puppies eat everything when they're teething."

"He's teething, all right. I've got to pay Dad back for the curtains. And I really need to get things for the baby."

He looked at her. They had done it again—gotten away from it, talked about everything else and then come back full circle. "You're getting sort of fat."

"I know." Ann gazed down at the paunch that was developing and smoothed one hand over her stomach. "The nurse says the baby's about as big as a telephone receiver."

Finally she spied her math book. She couldn't bend to get it so she knelt down for it and then stood again.

She tried to close her locker but Danny was leaning up against the door.

"Break's almost over. We can't be late for class."

"Detentions are fun," he said wryly. "I've had lots of them."

"Yeah," she said. "I heard about that, too."

"I miss you a lot sometimes, Ann."

"I miss you, too."

He was just standing there, looking at her, and all of a sudden he thought of something he could do to help her. He started fumbling around in his jeans pocket. He pulled out a wad of one-dollar bills. "Here."

"Danny . . . don't . . ."

But he insisted, shoving them at her, and suddenly, it felt good. Like when he gave her the puppy. "For the curtains," he said. "I gave you that dumb dog. Let this help pay for the curtains."

She wouldn't take it.

"Come on." He jabbed the money into her T-shirt pocket and backed away so she couldn't return it. "It's just my allowance. I was going to blow it all on video games at Celebrity Sports Center anyway."

"Danny."

"I've been thinking a lot about what you and I did."

"Have you?"

"Yeah. And I keep thinking about you having a baby. I've been thinking a lot about what you having a baby means. What we did . . . I wanted it, too, you know. I just saw how bad you wanted somebody. I care about you lots, Ann. I never would have hurt you . . . or used you . . . or made this happen."

"It's okay, Danny. We're a long way past that point. Don't apologize now."

"I'm not apologizing," he said to her slowly and, as he did, he admitted it to himself for the first time, too. "I'm just telling you that . . . I think all this is . . . important. That . . . doing what we did . . . means something to me. I've had to think about us, you and me, making something that is going to be a real person."

"It's pretty neat, huh?"

"Yeah."

The bell rang then, from the hall clock just behind them. "Danny. You're going to be really late."

"That's okay. I can't do any more detentions. They've got me set up to attend every one until the end of school."

"Well," she said. "*I* have to go."

"Okay. Okay. I'll go, too, then."

But before he turned to leave, she reached out to him once, barely grazed his forearm, and then pulled her hand away. "Thanks."

Chapter Nine

Richard sat on one side of the gray sofa in the Colorado Big Brothers/Big Sisters agency, watching Gwen answer the phones. He folded his long arms across his chest. He crossed his lanky legs. His left foot, clad in one slightly chewed work boot, kept a rough cadence with the traffic that was rushing by outside.

Monica sat at the opposite end of the couch. It was

the only place to sit in the entire office except for the receptionist's chair. She sat motionless, her tiny knees and feet aligned perfectly side by side, her gray wool skirt straight around her hips.

Richard turned his head slightly to one side so he could see her. She didn't seem to notice.

She looks so good sitting there. But she's as much out of her element as I am.

He looked away, then looked at her again. She was staring at a tile picture hanging on the wall. It was huge, maybe nine feet square, and mostly of Easter colors—blues and purples and yellows and pinks. The scene—of two birds, one big and one small, riding atop a wave—was made entirely from little tiles and set in cement.

"It's pretty, isn't it?" she said.

So she knew he was looking at it. She probably knew he was looking at her, too.

"It must weigh a ton," he said.

The receptionist nodded. "It really does. It's set in solid cement. We'll never move it, thank heavens. One of our matches made it for us."

"A match?" Richard asked, still tapping his foot. "You mean a Big Sister?"

"No," she answered. "A Big Sister and a Little Sister together. That's what we're all about here."

She was right, Richard realized. It wasn't the drabness of the carpet or the walls, it was how the place felt around him, the warmth of it and the hope.

That's what we're doing, being here, he decided. *We're making part of that hope. I should have come*

150

here a long time ago. Back when I thought they were trying to take my daughter away. Being here might have changed my mind.

He glanced at Monica one more time. A sudden, overwhelming emotion washed over him. She was so beautiful and busy and strong. And, of course, she had started it all here, finding Ann and coming to them—to him—to help.

The next thought crashed down upon him like a devastating blow. *A Big Sister and a Little Sister together. That's what we're all about here.* The receptionist's words echoed again in his mind. He added the rest himself.

It isn't about a Big Sister and a Little Sister's father.

It was this place, this feeling, and everything they were doing for him, Ann and so many others, that forced him to face an indisputable fact.

I cannot want more from Monica.

Joy Martin appeared and beckoned for them to follow her up the long narrow hallway.

"Have a seat." Joy motioned to two very utilitarian chairs placed side by side. Monica sat in one and smoothed her skirt. Richard sat down in the other. He didn't cross his arms this time.

"Thank you both for coming," the caseworker was saying. "I know this meeting may be a hard one. We owe it to Ann to talk frankly about things."

Richard was brutally aware of Monica beside him. Now that he had decided the doors were shut between them, something about her had been magnified, consuming him; he was a child again, wanting to turn to

151

her so badly he was aching with it. *Talk about losing control of things.* All of a sudden, he was mad. Mad once more.

"We have to keep Ann's life as stable as possible. We've got to discuss this—" she didn't know exactly how to put it "—this *tension* between you."

When Joy looked at him first, he stumbled through his anger to find something to say. "I know a lot is my fault. I haven't been able to see much good in the world lately. Ann's sensed that from me." He turned slightly in his chair, talking about Monica now but looking at the wall. "Ann told Monica the other day that she had hoped this baby would make me happy. In a way, it *has* done good things."

Immediately, Monica leapt into the conversation. "It's more than just happiness she wants for him, Joy. She's searching for some way, any way, to bring back the father/daughter relationship they used to have." Her silken-clad knees tipped toward his. "Until lately, you haven't given her anything to go by. Sure she's still grasping at straws. You haven't given her any other choice for so long."

"I know that," he stormed back at her. "Because I don't think she has any other choices."

"You just . . . won't . . . make anything easy for her. She has options you won't even consider."

Richard let her speak. In a way, it was good to hear her. Because Ann was usually no more than a closed door away whenever they disagreed, everything they had to say to one another was in whispers, fraught with emotion. Bringing everything out into the open with

152

the objectivity Joy Martin was forcing on them was probably good.

Joy turned to Richard. "You want a chance to tell your side?"

He nodded, thought a moment, then began. "Life has been unfair to Ann. It's thrown some hardships my way, too. I want her to be able to face things better than I did. I'm teaching my daughter the only way I know how to teach her."

When Monica heard the conviction in his voice, she wanted to root for him, too. This was the first time she had heard him voice it. She looked away, dangerously close to tears. She had thought about the things she'd accused him of for a week now. In trying so hard not to hurt Ann, she was hurting him instead, and suddenly, uncannily, that seemed to be equally tragic.

"I'm glad to see the two of you caring so much for Ann," Joy said, "albeit in different ways."

"I want to give Ann everything I know to give her," Richard said slowly.

"I know that," Monica said. "I'm not trying to undermine anything you want to do for your daughter." She felt as if her loyalties were being torn into portions, a portion that wanted to reach for Richard, a portion that wanted to remain true to Ann. "I love her, too. Maybe I keep trying too hard to do things right for her. But I don't think so."

As Richard listened to her speak, he realized how different his life would have been now if she hadn't wanted to help them. It was a time of taking stock for him, of counting his blessings—blessings that would increase if he could stick by his daughter.

Because of Monica, I'm learning to be a father to Ann again. And maybe, the thought came from some unexpected place, *I'm learning because of God, too.*

"I don't think so, either, Monica." When he said it, he was reassuring himself. "I can't give my daughter too much. But I am giving her everything I know to give her."

The caring and the commitment in his voice brought back emotions Monica had forced herself to forget. She found herself longing for someone to care for her, too, maybe even for it to be him.

"I never meant to say you weren't capable of giving, Richard," she said softly, her heart tottering on an edge, ready to plunge. "I know that you . . . are. . . ."

As he watched her, she looked so much like a little girl—so forlorn and alone—that some of the joy was gone from Richard's victory. At long last he met her eyes. "I have an awful way of hurting people when they get in the way of my pride."

Joy Martin stood and looked at both of them from across her desk. "Richard. Monica. I think you both have valid points. But from now on, you mustn't make them. You cannot allow anything volatile to enter the relationship between the two of you. Ann's future depends on it."

The caseworker glanced down at her blotter and shuffled papers there, while Richard sat upright again and Monica leaned back in her chair. They both knew what Joy meant. Only, in a way, it was worse now, because they had aired their differences and found a common place between them. Now it was only Ann standing in their way.

Only Ann.

It might as well have been an ocean or a bottomless chasm or a lifetime. Hurting Ann was unthinkable to both of them.

"Your daughter places her value in your hands," Joy said, her eyes on Richard. "She needs your caring and your stability. She needs you. Be certain to nurture her self-esteem wisely."

Ann hiked herself up on the pine corral fence at the Albright's. "I told you the doctor wouldn't mind if I still rode horses. He said just to remember my center of gravity is off a little bit and I should do fine."

Monica patted Ann's stomach. The baby was in there turning something akin to somersaults. "If you are both sure . . ."

"Sure," Ann said. "Besides, I can't get into much trouble riding on a horse named Molasses."

Monica laughed. "Sarah named that little horse Molasses because he walks slowly, not because of the way he runs."

"You don't fool me," Ann teased her. "I wish I was riding Thunder." She pointed to the gray Appaloosa Monica had saddled for herself.

"Sorry," Monica said, laughing. "I promise you if we had a horse named Lightning or Diablo or Freeway, I'd let you ride him. But we don't. So Molasses it is, take it or leave it."

"I'd better take it."

There came a rustle of pine needles from behind them. Sarah stepped out, balancing Patrick on her left hip. "Hi," she said as Patrick grabbed a strand of her dark hair and yanked at it, trying to get it to his mouth. "Hope it was okay for me to stop over. Mom said the two of you were coming up today." She had come because Eleanor had urged her to. "I wanted to meet Ann, the *other* little sister—" she grinned at the teenager "—besides me."

"You're Sarah," Ann said, her voice filled with enthusiasm. Monica could have hugged her for it. "I know you. You're the one that made cheerleader and had so many friends and used to make Monica hang upside down in the tree!"

"Yes." She said it sheepishly but Monica could tell she was pleased. "That's me."

"Your baby is so cute." Ann walked over to waggle one finger at Patrick. "How old is he?"

"Fourteen months."

"I'm having one, too." Ann said proudly. "Just four more months."

"Patrick's learning to walk." Sarah glanced over at Monica. "Do you want to watch him?"

"Yeah." And they all stopped to watch Patrick perform as Sarah steadied the little boy, his fat legs bowing. He teetered as he took one step and then the second. Monica realized she was holding her breath as Sarah backed away and then coaxed the child to her.

As Monica watched them together, a wave of inadequacy swept over her. She knew it was absurd. But Sarah had given so much to Eleanor and Cohen—two perfect, precious grandchildren, blood-related. It was something she could never do. It seemed to Monica just then, as she watched Patrick toddle toward Sarah's outstretched arms, that being a mother was everything. Sarah was so gentle with him and so good.

Suddenly Patrick tripped on a rock and stumbled forward. Sarah lurched forward to catch him. She grabbed him and pulled him up to cuddle him against her shoulder. He started screaming.

"He tried." Sarah shrugged and spoke between his deafening wails. "He does better inside on the carpet. I guess I was too anxious to show him off to you guys."

"It's neat," Ann giggled. "He's so little but he's so *fat*. Like a ball. I don't know how he can even keep his balance."

"We're going riding," Monica said. "Do you want to come with us? You could try Kwan."

"No, thanks," she said. "I can't leave the kids."

"I wish you could," Ann said. "It's awfully nice meeting you."

"You, too." Sarah followed them to the stables. She watched as they climbed atop the horses, and all the while, she held Patrick against her, almost wielding him like a weapon. "You two have a good time."

Monica turned to glance at her sister as they made ready to ride away. She saw something new and sad in her eyes, something that said she was very, very alone. But how could she be, with such a family?

Monica said the first thing that came to her mind. She couldn't know it but it was the one thing Sarah needed to hear. And, what was more, Monica meant it. "You are such a good mother, Sarah," she said gently, as she looked down at mother and child from her horse. "I often envy you."

"You really think I'm good at it?" Sarah asked, timid suddenly as Ann looked on.

"Yeah," Monica said. "I do."

Ann and Monica rode away from the house.

"What did you and my dad talk about at that meeting at Joy Martin's yesterday?"

The Appaloosa felt Monica tense up. It picked up its pace and Molasses followed. "You, mostly."

"Why?"

"Because we both care about you so much."

"Really?" Monica was surprised by the tiny glow of triumph in Ann's eyes. "That's why Dad went, too?"

"Yeah."

"He didn't tell me that."

"What did he tell you?" Monica asked with forced nonchalance.

"Not anything, really. He got home and Abraham had chewed off the cable connector to the TV set. He got mad again and said he was so frustrated he just wanted to go to sleep. He told me if I can't control the dog I might really have to find Abraham a new home."

"Sometimes," Monica said, "I can't really blame him."

Ann gave a tiny laugh, a little chirp like a robin. "Don't you two gang up on me or anything like that." She sounded so certain it wouldn't happen that the words speared straight through Monica's heart.

When Monica's answer came, it was soft and sad. "We won't. I promise."

They rode in silence for a while after that, each of them in her own world, until Ann started talking about math class and Mr. Samuels's word problems and Danny's detentions.

"Dad bought me a new sweater after he went to that meeting with you," Ann said. "It's really pretty."

"Ann. That's wonderful."

"It's the first maternity stuff he's bought me." She drifted onto another subject. "Sarah's nice. I'll bet she had lots of boyfriends, didn't she?"

"She did."

"Do you have lots of boyfriends, Monica?"

Monica laughed. "Oh, yes," she said brightly. For some reason, she wanted to sweep on to something else. It wasn't worth discussing. She had many men friends. She often dined with one or another of them, and went to the theater in Denver. There were several acquaintances from the University of Denver who loved to come up to Evergreen whenever the chorale or the Evergreen Players had something going. "But it doesn't mean anything—"

Ann was not to be distracted. "So, if you have boyfriends, how come you aren't married?"

"I don't know. I just never fell in love, I guess."

"My dad doesn't have any girlfriends, I don't think," Ann said, just sharing for sharing's sake. "I've thought about that sometimes, you know, how I would feel to have my dad fall in love with somebody . . . when I wasn't really certain he loved me."

Monica's heart turned to ice. "So . . . what did you decide? How would it make you feel?" For a moment she almost dared to hope as she held her breath, waiting for her Little Sister to answer.

Ann studied the sky above her. "I decided—" Ann said slowly, contemplating the subject "—I wouldn't like it."

"I see."

"He hasn't wanted anybody since Mom," Ann said, her voice full of the certainty of youth. "At least, I don't think so."

"I've been wondering about that." Monica said. "I didn't know. I didn't think so, either."

"Abraham!" Richard groaned as he kicked aside a shredded magazine and made for the ringing telephone. "You ate up my *Train Man's Digest*. You confounded mutt."

The puppy was hiding beneath the couch. Richard could see his tail poking out. And it certainly wasn't wagging.

"Ha!" For some absurd reason, Richard wanted to laugh. He had been laughing at this crazy dog way too much lately. But sometimes it just felt good.

"Richard here," he said when he grabbed the receiver.

"Richard. It's Monica."

It happened all over again. His pulse started whamming against his chest like a hammer. After that meeting with Joy Martin, he wasn't even sure they were supposed to be talking to each other. But he wanted to. Oh, man, he wanted to.

"Hey," he said quietly. "Ann's asleep. Do you need to talk to her?"

"No. Don't wake her up." Monica wasn't even certain why she had called. She just knew she wanted to hear his voice again, after their meeting with Joy and after the things Ann had told her today. "I called to talk to you, I think," she said, her voice timid, as if she wasn't certain she should have done it, either. But she had just been thinking about everything Ann had said and she'd been feeling so alone.

"I'm glad you did," he whispered. Then, almost involuntarily, he turned to check Ann's door. Though there was no light coming from the crack beneath it, he felt a horrible rush of guilt, just because he was feeling the things he was feeling. But he couldn't help himself. It was much too late.

"Today while we were riding, she told me you bought her a new sweater," Monica went on.

"Yeah."

"She was really happy about it, Richard."

"I'm glad."

She couldn't stop herself from asking the next question. She had to know. "So . . . why did you do it?"

He was quiet for a minute before he gave her his answer. "I was trying to do it your way."

"What way?"

"You know. Showing her that things don't always turn out bad. That sometimes good things can come, too."

She closed her eyes, wondering at his answer. Suddenly she was afraid. What if she was telling him too much? What if she was leading him in the wrong direction?

"You know what?" he said softly. "It was fun."

"Was it?"

Richard was surprised by the relief he heard in her voice. He responded lightheartedly. "It was great. They showed me what must have been hundreds of sweaters, all costing a fortune and looking so big hanging there. And they had this little pillow thing they put inside the sweater."

"What?"

"It's supposed to look like this big pregnant tummy, so when you go in there and you aren't pregnant yet—or," he amended, "you don't look like it—you tie this thing on and it makes you fat as a fiddle. I found this sweater that looked just like Ann, and when they stuck it up in there so I could see, it did look just like Ann." Richard began to chuckle and he couldn't stop. Monica was laughing, too, right along with him.

"I've never seen anything like that. . . ." she said, laughing.

"That's because you've never been in one of those stores before," he replied.

"I've never had a reason to be, but I'm glad you found it so amusing."

Richard was silent for a moment, listening to her laugh, listening to the music in her voice. It was a melody she sang in her heart as well, because she had been lucky in life, blessed with fullness and certainty. How he wanted that for Ann, too.

"While we were riding today, Ann asked me what we talked about at the meeting." This was the reason Monica had made the phone call. At least, that's what she told herself.

"What did you tell her?"

"I told her we met because we care about her so much."

"You didn't tell her about our differences?"

"No. I thought it best not to."

"Monica." He had to ask her. He knew in his heart that the meeting had been about much, much more than their differences. "Is that what that meeting was really about?"

Please, God, I didn't mean to get into this. She clutched the receiver as if she was gripping the railing of a boat, a boat threatening to pitch her overboard. "Richard . . . yes . . . no."

"It was about us, wasn't it? About what's happening, because we've become friends?" *Because we're becoming more than friends.* "Joy Martin knows, doesn't she?"

"They can't rematch Ann, Richard. Her life has had too many upheavals. She's pregnant, too involved, too dependent on me. She's too dependent on you. Things in her life have to stay on an even keel. . . ."

"I'm right," he said.

"Yes. And Joy knows," she said.

"Monica. I'm sorry."

"I'm scared, Richard. I'm pitching around for solid ground. What I want is wrong and, even if it isn't, I can't show it."

Richard felt his guts wrench up inside him. For some insane reason, he wanted to laugh at the irony. The world and God had given them something so precious, but they couldn't have it.

"You know what's crazy?" she asked. "I want you to believe in happy endings. And you want me to believe it's okay for everything not to be so easy. I began to realize some things are worth fighting for, and in my mind today, there are all sorts of possibilities that weren't there before. Things I never even looked at before or wanted to see."

"Like what?" he asked, wanting her to continue.

"Like Ann. Like both of us fighting to help her in our own separate ways. You're pushing her to find what she needs. And I'm like a coach trying to be a player, trying to do it for her. . . ."

"Bingo." He slammed his fist against the table. The lamp wobbled violently on its base. Abraham ran out from under the sofa into the kitchen to find another hiding place.

"Joy helped us, then."

"Yes," he said. "In one way she did. But in another way . . ." He stopped then, waiting, his heart in his hands, for her to finish it.

Her words were soft but he probably could have used the Richter scale to measure their impact on him. His blood raced. "She didn't."

"No," he said. "I didn't think so, either."

She waited then, wanting to say more, to be honest with him. "You are an attractive man, Richard, when you aren't so angry at things. I've thought it . . . felt it . . ."

"For how long? For as long as I've been thinking the same about you?"

"Maybe longer."

"No," he said. "Not longer. Because I've felt this way almost from the beginning."

"Richard," she said. "Listen. What we're thinking of, speaking of, cannot exist. It has everything to do with what Joy said the other day. About stability for Ann. About her self-esteem. That's the only important thing now."

He put it in his own words. "There isn't a way." They both understood what he meant.

This is it then, Richard thought. *Another trade-off in my life. As always, worth it. As always, painful.*

The silence hung between them like a barrier. They had gone as far as they could go and they both knew it. Neither wanted to say anything more.

At last it was Monica who was brave enough to speak. She was desperate to change the subject. Now that they had voiced it, the quiet knowledge of their mutual attraction hung in the air, forming a strong current between them.

"Ann and I spent a long time together this afternoon. Did you just get in from the station?"

"Yeah," he said. "I had another long day there today." Before he knew it he was chuckling. "And then I walk in here, flip on the light and find out this crazy mongrel has been chewing again. I've been wondering why God put teeth on perfectly good, cuddly little puppies."

Monica laughed with him. It felt wonderful to take the edge off the tension of the past days. "Probably for the same reason he put teeth on perfectly good, cuddly little sharks."

"Nope," he said. "Your answer doesn't wash. Sharks are predatory animals. They *need* their teeth."

"Well. I guess it's going to have to remain one of those great mysteries we don't understand. Too bad."

"Yeah," he said, his voice sobering. "Too bad."

His mind was on the possibilities between them again, possibilities that could never be. *Too bad for us.*

She knew what he was thinking without him having to say it. But she had to say it to reinforce their position. "I'm going to do my best to be a good Big Sister to Ann, Richard. You'll understand if I do my best to keep from seeing you?"

"Yes," he said, hating himself for not fighting it. But he knew Joy Martin was right. "I'll understand."

He hung up the phone and walked into the kitchen, aching for her and for what they might have shared. It would have been a new life for him and Ann, if only the timing had been different. He shook his head sadly and then spotted Abraham cowering beneath a kitchen chair with his tail between his legs.

"You poor mutt," he said tenderly. "Have you been in here all this time?" He scooped the puppy into his arms. It felt wonderful to hold something, wonderful to claim a little living thing as his own. "Abe. You're a good little guy, you know. Even if you do like leather work boots. Poor Ann. If you had just chewed up the sole, too, I probably could've taken them back and gotten another pair. The sole was the only part with the forty-year warranty."

Abraham licked his hand.

He stroked the little dog's ears back, holding them together in one hand, thinking how velvety they felt beneath his fingers.

Probably just as velvety as Monica's lips would feel if the Lord ever saw fit to let me kiss her.

The princess and the pauper, tied together by their love for one fine, sad teenaged girl.

But never, never allowed to think about loving each other.

Richard set the pup down onto the linoleum and nudged him toward his food bowl. "You go on now and eat something, you crazy dog." And as he watched Abraham sloshing his velvet ears in the water bowl, he felt more alone than he had ever felt before.

Chapter Ten

"You'll be excited about these photographs," Monica stated as she handed Ann's pictures to the various members of the Jefferson County Historical Society. "They're very good."

"What is this one?" Coralee Frank asked. "Is it Hardy House?"

"No," Monica told them. "But you're close. It's one of the other gingerbread houses built in Georgetown right at the turn of the century. The mines you see are the ones around Central City. The cemetery is Central City, too. Several of the other buildings are Silverthorne."

"I cannot believe this is the work of a fourteen-year-old child," Dolores Watley commented. "She is good. Quite talented indeed."

Monica grinned. This was exactly what she wanted to happen. She was playing by Richard's rules now. She was willing to help Ann prove she could follow her dreams. "She *is* good," she said, nodding. "She's had photography classes at school. But her talent goes much further than that. She has a certain feel for composition. I'd like to give her the chance to use her skills professionally."

"You're certain you don't mind working with a child this young to put together the museum brochure?"

Monica nodded. "Positively certain. As you all know, Ann Small is my Little Sister. I'm emotionally involved with the girl. I'd love to work with her on this."

"I'm not sure," Angela Attaway commented. "These are certainly professional shots. I love the angles she got on the gingerbread trim with the sun coming through them. But what about that young man who did the Chamber of Commerce folder? You know, the young man from the *Canyon Courier*?"

"He did an excellent job for them," Monica admitted diplomatically. "I wouldn't mind hiring him. But I have two reasons I'd like to use Ann Small instead. One, he is a commercial photographer and will charge commercial rates. We can offer Ann a flat rate—say forty or fifty dollars per photo we use. But it will seem like a gold mine to this young lady."

"A good reason," someone agreed.

"Money talks," someone else said.

She almost had them. "And two, Ann Small still has the lovely ability to view things through the eyes of a child. I cannot think of a better way to portray our toys. She has such an innocent style."

"I think the child will do a lovely job," Coralee said, "with Monica's supervision, of course."

They all voted and agreed.

"Okay, Monica," Louise said in her lovely drawl, smiling sweetly. "There's your vote. You'd better let her know she has an assignment."

"She won't disappoint you with her work." Monica was so excited she wanted to jump up and down. She waited until the last member of the society had left, then grabbed the telephone. "Ann!" she shrieked. "It worked. They said yes!" She had known they would or she wouldn't have mentioned it to her beforehand. "They voted you in. You have a photography job!"

"Monica. I can't believe it! Things like this just don't happen to me."

"Well, guess what. They do now."

"They really want *me* to do it?"

"Yep. They think you're terrific. Just like I do."

"Really?"

"And they're going to pay you."

"Money? But it's just something I like to do. . . ."

"Money, Ann. At least forty dollars a photo. And I know I need at least eight photos just to start."

Ann was flabbergasted. She was calculating figures inside her head. "Dad's gonna die, Moni! That's enough money to keep Abraham in Puppy Chow for a whole year. I can't believe it!"

"It is a very good start, little one." She wasn't under-mining Richard any longer. She was using his strate-gies. Ann would, after all, have to find her own way. It was her own path to choose.

"I can't believe I can make money just like that." She snapped her fingers and Monica heard the little pop-ping sound over the phone. It made Monica want to laugh. "Like magic. Dad is gonna die."

"You said that already."

"When do I start, Monica?"

"Whenever you want to. Maybe even tomorrow after school."

"I want to start *now*."

"We'll have to get you some film, Ann. And I need time to dust the exhibits before you photograph them. Especially the trains . . ."

"Moni." Ann had just thought of something won-derful. "I want my dad to come, too. I want him to see everything. I want him to see the museum and the trains and me taking pictures and what I really can do when I behave like an adult. Oh, Monica. Can he come?"

Monica froze. She didn't say anything.

"Moni? What do you think?",

She forced herself to say anything, something, while her insides reeled. "You really want that?"

"Oh, yes."

I would give anything to see him.

I would give anything not to see him.

Only Monica knew what a victory it would be, in Ann's eyes, to share this with him.

Ann didn't understand Monica's hesitation. "Can't he come, Monica, *please?* I wouldn't let him get in the way or anything. I promise he won't be any trouble."

"Why—" Monica said wildly, trying to laugh "—do you sound like you are talking about a child or Abraham instead of your father?"

She should have known it would come to this. She should have *wanted* it to come to this. Richard was hoping to become more and more involved with his daughter's life. Ann was now reaching for him, too. Monica wanted it for them. They were working toward a time when they would be together, without her. She should be proud and pleased that she was helping bring them to that.

The thought seared through her, tortured her with pain.

"You know what? If he sees me taking pictures and he knows I really can do it, maybe he'll think I should stay in school, too. With or without the baby. I think it might really do it, Moni!"

Monica couldn't contest any of Ann's arguments. She knew Richard had to come. It was worth everything it would cost her to see him again.

"All right," she whispered softly to the petite teenaged girl she loved so dearly already. "If you can handle working as a professional photographer with your dad looking over your shoulder, go ahead and bring him."

"Ann I just can't come kid," Richard said. "I'm really, really sorry."

What had Monica been thinking when she invited him to Evergreen?

She was testing him. That had to be it. She wanted to know how strong he was.

"Oh, Dad," Ann pleaded. "It's gonna be so *neat*. I want you to see where I'm working and I want you to see the trains." She was tugging on his shirt. She was tugging on his heart, too. If only she knew how desperately he wanted to come. He could hardly bear it.

"I can't," he said stoically. He didn't look at her. "Can't get away from the station."

"You can. You've been doing it all the time lately. Just get Mr. Hill to be there instead. I have to do it when there's light outside. We'll be back in time for you to go in and work the last train if you need to."

He crossed his arms. "Impossible. Absolutely not." He couldn't consider it.

"But they asked me to do it, Dad." She was wailing now, because she didn't understand. He hadn't shut her out like this for months and months. "They *voted* on me to come."

"That's fine, Ann. They didn't vote on me. Do a great job by yourself."

I'd give anything to be there.

I'd give anything to see Monica again.

I'd give anything to see Ann winning at something.

"Dad. I think this is going to be the only time in my life I'll get to do something I've dreamed about." Suddenly she was just talking to him, doing her best to be rational, to behave like an adult. It was breaking his heart listening to her, knowing how badly she wanted

172

to share it with him. Months ago he wouldn't have thought it possible. Her voice was faltering as she finished. "It's just something I wanted us to do together."

Confound it. "I will not go with you, Ann. Do not ask me about his again."

There was no way to describe the desolation he saw in her eyes. "This has been really stupid, Dad," she shouted. "You really faked me out. All this time, I thought you were really starting to *care.*"

"I *do* care." He was frantic suddenly, trying to make her understand, but he couldn't. "I *do* care."

"You don't want me around." She spat the words out at him and her eyes were full of venom. "You've never cared about me."

It occurred to him that this was exactly what he and Monica were sacrificing for, so Ann wouldn't doubt herself, wouldn't doubt his caring for her. But it was happening anyway. Months ago he would have walked away from his daughter, knowing he had lost her, knowing he couldn't change her by striking out.

He was a different man now.

He would fight for her.

"I am your father, young lady," he said quietly. "You will not talk to me in that tone. It doesn't matter if what I say is unfair. You have no right to decide what I am feeling. I love you, Ann. I've given up things for you that you do not know of. I will continue to do so. No matter what happens, I love you. That's all you need to know."

Ann stood still, listening to his solemn words. She stared at him. "You mean that?"

"Sure I do." She saw it in her father's eyes, the regret and the love.

"Oh, Daddy," she whispered and she moved toward him. And then they were in each others arms, holding on. "Oh, Daddy. I'm so sorry."

"It's okay," he told her. "I'm sorry, too."

She looked up at him again, her eyes wide and innocent and to Richard, she looked just like she had when she was seven years old. "I love you, too, you know."

He gripped her to him then, forgetting her growing stomach and the hard years and everything that had happened between them. Ann was all that mattered to him. "You know, I really want to see you take those pictures. I'll talk to Ty in the morning. I'll be there, okay?"

May 30
Dear Diary,
I think I've got one of my big dreams coming through and it feels amazing. Monica (my Big Sister) wants me to take pictures for a brochure for the museum where she works and she had to talk to all these people and they all said it was okay so now, I've got a job! It's something I always wanted. I cannot believe this is happening to me. Things this good just do not happen to Ann Leidy Small.

I went to the camera shop this afternoon to pick out the kind of film my teacher taught us to use and I told them what it was for and the man said, "Oh, you're a professional!" and he gave me a discount. I'm feeling pretty important right now. The camera I'm using is Monica's. It's terrific.

Now, on to other things. Lots is happening. Dad is getting real good. And Danny's getting to be a friend. Yesterday was the last day of school. It was really hard leaving. Everybody else was real excited about summer vacation and getting out of jail. I know it was dumb but I just sort of stood in the hallway for a while and looked and everything, and I just kept wondering if I was going to come back again. It's really sad. Sometimes I don't know if my life's all over or if it's really all just starting. Then I think about taking those pictures and I think, "Crazy Ann. You know it's just starting." But then I have a day like today when I have to tell everybody and everything good-bye and I keep wondering if it's what I want.

I know it sounds selfish but sometimes I get mad at the baby. I keep thinking, "Look now, you're ruining this stuff." Then I get mad at myself. When I see Monica's family, the Albrights, and everything they've done for her, I have to think I might want things that way for my baby, too. I might want my baby to have a real life with a family and things, instead of just being stuck here with Abraham and me. It's sort of like wishing for a fairyland to happen. If I keep the baby, I probably won't go back and stand in the same hall I was standing in today. But I might. I can't let the baby make my decision for me, either.

Now, back to the picture-taking tomorrow. I haven't even written about the best part yet.

Here it is.

Dad is taking time off from the station and he's going up there with me. I wanted him to come so bad. I wanted him to know I could really do something and that I'm growing up and that I'm a person. I had to work on him for a little while, but he said yes. He said more than that. He said he loved me. So now I know for sure.

I'm real excited to see Monica's museum. She talks about it but I haven't gotten to go there until now.

You know what? It's like I'm all full up inside, not just with the baby growing (ha!) but what's in my heart. All of a sudden, I have people who are loving me. And Dad is one of them! Yeah!

I'd better go.

Hugs and Love for always,

Ann Leidy Small

P.S. I keep thinking about what I should say to my fourteen-year-old daughter about things and today I keep wanting to say this: If you ever feel like people don't care about you or what happens to your life, sometimes all you have to do is wait. It's like you can't do things to make anybody like you or care. Because if you're making them then it doesn't end up being right, anyway. Maybe that's kind of what happened with me and Danny.

Hugs and Bye.

A.

As he walked into the Jefferson County Antique Toy Museum with Ann tugging at his arm, Richard had absolutely no idea what he was going to do when he saw Monica. He had been conscious all afternoon that he was doing this for Ann.

"Hey, you guys, come on in!" Monica called when she heard them enter. "I've got to get this train back on the track." When he heard her voice, he wanted to cry out, it sounded so good to him and it had been so long since he had talked to her.

"Dad's here," Ann called back. "He'll get your train on the track. They pay him at the station to do stuff like that."

He couldn't help but notice how Monica's voice softened then. "Good. I'm glad you brought him."

This is ridiculous, he thought. *We're two grown people.* He hadn't felt this inadequate since he used to sit in class waiting for Carolyn to walk into the room. Carolyn had ended up marrying him, he reminded himself with a boost to his self-confidence. He hitched up his belt, dug his thumbs into his back pockets and strolled into Monica's museum as though he owned the place.

"Hi," Monica said, looking up at both of them. She was on her knees, eye level with the tiny tracks and a quaint replica of a snow-covered alpine village. Then, as if that didn't seem enough, she added, "Hello, Richard."

He hated himself. She was staring up at him and it happened again. Just seeing her took his breath away.

There was a question in her gray eyes, as if there was something she wanted to ask of him, something she didn't dare voice.

"Oh, just *look* at everything!" Ann lay her satchel down on an antique school desk and skipped around the exhibits. "I can't *believe* all this stuff."

Richard held his breath. It was the only thing he could do as he stared down at Monica.

"I'm glad you came," she said simply.

He had to ask it. "Are you?"

She nodded. She reached up with one small hand so he could help her stand up. "Ann wanted you to come so badly, to share this with her. It's an excellent opportunity for her to find out what she can do."

"I know that." He held her eyes with his and they spoke volumes. He wanted to let her know why he had really come. "She said you invited me. Even so, she had to work pretty hard to talk me into it. Poor kid."

"Yes," Monica said. "She coaxed me, too." Everything they were saying had a double meaning. "It was so important to her."

She had sacrificed for this, too, then.

"Ann takes such lovely pictures, Richard. I wanted a photographer who could see the exhibits through the eyes of a child." She was covering for herself. She had been frightened of this all day, just thinking he might be coming. But deep within her heart of hearts, she had been praying for him to be there.

Ann was in the other exhibit room. They could both hear her moving from station to station on the ancient plank floor.

"Guess we'd better see about that train." His voice was matter-of-fact. His eyes were searing through her, asking her a hundred different questions, telling her a hundred different things. "What did you do to make it jump the track?"

"It happened when . . . you . . . walked in," she said. "I just . . . knocked it away. . . ."

He gave her a lazy, devastating smile, wordlessly acknowledging what she had told him.

None of it has changed between us, then.

"I'll see what I can do," he said.

When Richard turned to the trains, it was the first time he had taken his eyes off her since he walked into the room. He lifted an iron caboose from the track.

"The chimney really smokes," she said. "It's a wonderful little caboose."

"A caboose that represents train life the way it used to be," he said, suddenly grinning, as if the trains had rescued him, or he had found an old friend. "The brakeman used to live in his caboose. See here?" He pointed to the tiny cubicle above the car. "They used to cook there. And they kept it warm with a coal stove. My dad told me all sorts of stories when I was a little boy. Those brakemen used to take so much pride in their cabooses. Used to paint them bright yellow or bright red or bright green. You'd know them by their numbers. You'd pass them on the siding and you'd see number 401 and you'd know there was Joe Jenkin's home sitting there. . . ."

Monica smiled. "Sounds like something you've thought about."

"I have," he said, looking at her again, his huge fingers encircling the tiny car as if it was a treasure. "When I was a kid, I used to dream of living that way. Just hitching up to the next train and taking everything I owned someplace far away."

"Do you still wish you could do that?" she asked softly. She was seeing yet another facet of him, a facet that endeared him even further to her.

He shook his head. "Naw," he said. There wasn't a trace of doubt in his voice. "I tried it for a while. It isn't as glamorous as it sounds. It didn't take long before all I wanted to do was place my feet on a floor that wasn't clattering over the tracks. I always wanted to come home to Ann and Carolyn."

He stopped. Their eyes locked again and held.

"You loved Carolyn a lot, didn't you?" she asked.

"Yeah," he said. "I did."

He knelt down beside the train display and set the wheels of the caboose upon the tiny thread of track, carefully wheeling it back and then forward again to make certain it was steady. He talked to it as if it was a child. "There you go."

He didn't look up at Monica again. He placed one hand on either side of the tracks, his arms spread wide, his fingers splayed against the platform. When he spoke, his voice was full of wonder. "Look at this. Just look at this."

She stood above him, wanting to laugh, wanting to cry. As she watched him, something was filling her, something tender and ablaze. She had never seen him like this before. Without his hardened edges, his face was hauntingly handsome, a youth's face. She would have given anything at that moment, everything, to explore its textures with her fingers, her lips. "It's pretty incredible, isn't it?"

"I've never seen anything like it."

She bent beside him and pointed to the working waterwheel beside a replica of an old gristmill. "We visited this mill in Virginia the summer Sarah and I turned nine. It was built of river stones. Dad worked on the model for nine months. Each night, he'd let us put a few more stones on the walls. Under his expert guidance, of course."

"I wish," Richard said quietly, "that my dad could see this."

"Were you and your dad close?"

"Yes," he said enthusiastically. "We were. We had some rough times when I was a teenager but, generally, things were good. We got along just well enough to drive Mom crazy. He was gone a lot, though. He worked the Southern Pacific trains for forty-four years."

"So, in a way, you followed in his footsteps."

"Ha!" he chuckled. "You could say that. He used to have a model railroad. It wasn't as elaborate as this one but it was special. He kept it on his workbench in the basement. Wouldn't let me touch it until I was eight years old." Richard's eyes narrowed mischievously. "He was always gone and Mom was always out back weeding the garden. I started going in there when I was five, driving his trains real slow so they wouldn't make any noise."

"Dad," Ann said from behind them. "Shame on you."

"I know," he turned and winked at his daughter. "I was horrible about it. You shouldn't be listening to this."

"Yes I should be," she said, her eyes twinkling as she teased him.

"On my eighth birthday," Richard went on, "he took my hand and led me into his workshop. He pulled out his stool so I could reach that confounded train. He set the control down right in front of my nose and said, 'Time to start driving trains.'" He was laughing out loud now, a rich, full sound that made Monica want to chuckle, too. "Dad was all nervous and everything, scared to death I was gonna drive that thing right off the track. I started it going around the track and let it pick up speed and there it went, lickety-split, without a problem at all. Dad hugged me and told me it was in my blood, that I was going to be a train man for sure. Poor Dad. He'll never know I had been practicing on that train for three years before he let me drive it!"

Ann came up from behind him and hugged him. Monica watched them as the warm realization swept through her—she had never seen Ann embrace her father that way. "Dad. Think about it. Of course he knew. He probably knew it for the whole three years. He never would have just set you up and let you drive them unless he did. Dads always figure everything out."

"No," Richard shook his head slowly, thinking about it. "He couldn't have."

"I'll bet he did."

"Ann, you hush," he said. But he had a funny little smile on his face as if he half believed her. Then he hugged her again. "Confound it," he said, grinning. "I wish I had asked him about that before he died."

Ann was dancing around behind him. "Now you'll never know. . . ."

"Where are his trains now?" Monica asked.

"Mom's probably got them in storage. She put all that stuff away when she moved back to her sister's in Nebraska."

"Maybe you should talk to her about it," Monica suggested. "Maybe you could get them out, set them up."

"I probably should also tell her she's going to be a great-grandmother."

"Might be a good idea," Monica nodded. "Now, do you want to drive this train?" She scooted the transformer toward him.

"I'd love to," he said, "if there isn't a law against me driving museum property."

"While you kids play with the train," Ann called to them as she shouldered her camera, "the professional photographer is going to work. I have some ideas for the doll display."

They both waved her off.

"Yes." Monica picked up the conversation where they had left off. "Only museum personnel get to do this. But—" she was half grinning again, kidding him "—that rule doesn't take into account experts like yourself. Experts with years and years of practice . . . even before their eighth birthday. . . ."

183

"Thank you, ma'am," he saluted her, "for taking all that into consideration."

"Drive the trains, Small. Don't get sarcastic with museum personnel. You never know what might happen."

Their eyes met again.

He was the first to look away. He was a little boy again, driving the trains, as he pushed the throttle forward and the train picked up speed. She stood and watched him as he switched tracks and made the model race through tunnels and across miniature suspension bridges and beneath a tiny waterfall. Every time he lost a car, he knew exactly what to do: he slowed the little engine down and then backed the entire row of cars slowly into the connector, bumping it until it latched again.

As she watched him, the top of his head bent slightly over the mass of tracks, covered with the same dark unruly curls as his daughter's, he seemed even more vulnerable than Ann. His hair glinted like cognac in the lights. He had a funny little cowlick at the back of his head, slightly to the left. Monica could imagine how his mother must have fought to keep all those curls orderly when she helped him dress for school or for church on Sundays.

The need Monica felt to touch him overpowered her. She would have given anything to smooth her hand across his dark hair, to spin a thumb inside one curl, to tame the cowlick with her own fingers.

As if he sensed what she needed, he set the train controls down, got slowly to his feet and stood beside her.

Her voice, when it came, was scarcely more than a whisper. "Richard. All these months. All the things that I've said to you. I had no right . . ."

"No." He cut her off, his voice gruff as he stood a head above her and gazed down. "Stop it, Monica." Still, his voice was soft so Ann wouldn't hear. "Don't say it. Can't you see? If you hadn't been brave enough to disagree with me, who would have been? All this time—these days, these months—you've been leading me, and God knows I've needed someone to set an example . . ."

For so many nights he had sat alone, thinking how thankful he was to her for that. For that and for so much more. It was an awe-inspiring thought to him. She cared enough about him to give that much of herself when she could expect nothing in return.

"There are so many little things she needs that she's getting from you now," Monica said. "You've trusted her enough to let her keep that crazy dog. You've made her trust you enough that she's reaching out to you . . . hugging you. . . ."

"You noticed her hugging me," he said.

She nodded up at him. She looked so beautiful to him and she was standing so close, he could hardly breathe. He had to force himself to do it, something that should have been an unconscious action. Air in . . . air out . . . air in . . . air out . . .

"It means so much to me to see it," she went on. "I know it means so much to Ann to suddenly become so certain of the things you feel for her."

His arms took on life of their own. They rose,

crooked at the elbow. His hands brushed her skin, a whisper of a touch. Desperately, almost fiercely, he grasped her arms with his big hands.

"You've given her so much, Monica," Richard admitted to her at last. "So many of the things I *couldn't* give her. I used to be so angry because of that. . . ."

From the other room, they could hear the faint clicks of the camera as Ann worked with it, apparently engrossed in her task.

After all this time, they clung to one another, needing each other, each of them amazed at that discovery.

"Monica. We can't—" he breathed.

"Richard. We mustn't—" she breathed.

"You mean so much to me," he said, his words rough with emotion, as if they were being gouged out of him.

"You may never know all the things you've added to my life," she told him earnestly, wanting him to understand what a gift he and Ann had been to her. "Now I can feel what is right." *Strange when before, I used to think everything was right. Now I can appreciate the texture so much when, before, I thought everything was just smooth.*

She could scarcely hear his words when they came. Even if she hadn't heard them, she would have read it in his eyes. "I need you as badly as Ann does."

She stood helpless, frozen.

He stood a breath away from her, his eyes pleading with her. It was the little-boy part of him that tormented her now, the way his lashes shadowed his cheeks, the way the short sleeves on his blue linen shirt dangled open above his elbows, the way he had laid himself totally open to her.

She fought to say the words. "Your daughter doesn't need me, Richard. She needs you." She whispered it, knowing any minute Ann might find them out.

His whisper matched her own. "I want to kiss you."

And I haven't wanted to kiss anyone in a very long time. Not this way.

She closed her eyes. More than anything, she wanted to lean forward, to admit defeat and rest her forehead against the lean plane of his chest. But she knew if she touched him she would be lost. Instead, she met his eyes again, knowing what she had to say. "Ann is finding herself finally. And she is finding you. It's what you've wanted all along."

Emotion pounded inside of him, powerful and acute, surging through him like a cresting tide. He wanted to hold her forever, wanted to shield her from the pain of their impossible situation with the strength of his arms. "Why do we both have to be so *confounded strong?*"

Monica steeled herself. *Oh, Father, please help us do the right thing for Ann.* "Richard, you don't—"

"I do." It was easy, then, to lay it all on her. "Don't tell me what I do or don't want, Monica."

"Dad!" Ann called just as she stepped through the door. Richard found a split second to drop his hands and back away. "I've got this great idea to try with the trains. Will you help me? If I can take one or two close-ups while the train is coming toward the camera around a curve, I can get some great motion on the back of the train. I'll focus on the front of the engine . . ." She

187

looked up at his face, suddenly worrying. He looked exhausted and sad and she didn't know why. "You okay?"

"I'm fine," he said, forcing composure. He jabbed at her with his fingers and made her giggle. "Quit trying to act like you're my mother."

"Okay, *son,*" she teased him. "Let's do this thing." She focused on the engine while Monica adjusted the overhead lights, and then Richard made the miniature train rush around the track while Ann took picture after picture. "I can't quite get it the way I want it," she lamented. "I could use a whole roll." And on the next shot, right as the train was coming toward her, she shouted, "This one! This one is going to be *it!*"

"Don't talk," Richard kidded her. "You can't focus the camera and move your mouth at the same time." He was doing his best to sound lighthearted but there was something heavy that wouldn't leave his voice.

Ann took the shot and then held the camera to one side of her face with both hands. "Are you telling me what to do? I thought I was the camera expert here."

"You're my kid," he said. "Professional photographer or not, I *always* get to tell you what to do."

"Great." Ann giggled again. And as Monica watched them, a new emotion shot through her—a piercing loneliness. She felt empty as she watched the two of them bantering with each other. She loved Ann. She didn't care to put a label on the warm intensity that threaded in and out of her heart for Richard. But whatever it was, Richard and Ann belonged to each other. They would *always* belong to each other, father and

daughter, bound by blood ties and a lifetime of memories and living.

It was something she would never share with them.

"I got it," Ann was saying. "That one was just what I wanted. But maybe I ought to take one more just in case."

"Fine," Richard said, laughing as he took the control again. "Let's take ninety million of them. Here she comes. . . ."

Together, they shot three more pictures of the train. Then Ann moved to the hobbyhorses while Richard rose, brushing his hands against his jeans with a forced nonchalance.

Monica stood in the center of the room, surrounded by old toys, all of them once treasured and given life by children. Some now were showing signs of age— the paint chipped off, the material thin and fraying. As Monica stood before Richard, her fingers twisted like knots, every inch of her five-foot-four-inch frame was aching to be cherished and touched like the toys.

Please, Father. She was praying the way she often did, right where she was standing, right where she felt her pain. *I don't want the easy way out anymore. You created me to feel these things. Why would You make me feel this way when it's someone impossible for me to have?*

Chapter Eleven

"While Patrick takes his nap, will you watch with me?" Kaylen gestured toward the blaring television.

"Honey," Sarah started out gently, and then she started laughing. "I've seen that video so many times I could *star* in it. I already know all the lines."

"I know," Kaylen gave her a little shrug that looked oddly adult for her age. "So do I. That's what makes it good."

"Love you." Sarah bent low to kiss her daughter on the top of the head. Then she scooped Patrick up and took him to his bedroom. Miraculously, he didn't fight her and went right to sleep.

Sarah took an extra ten minutes to paint her fingernails for the first time in two months. But while they were drying, Kaylen flipped off the video, climbed on top of the dryer in the laundry room and brought down a pile of birthday presents Sarah had put away after the party.

"Mommy," she said, wandering in carrying the little box Monica had given her. "Can I put this thing together?"

"Are you sure you want to?" Sarah asked, blowing on her nails as she waved her curled fingers in front of her lips. "I'm not sure you're ready for it yet. You can do it yourself if you'll wait until you're older. If you do it now, I'll have to help you or it won't be as pretty."

"I'll have you help me, then. I don't want to wait. I want to do it now."

She is exactly like me.

Sometimes watching Kaylen grow was like watching herself all over again. She had wanted everything immediately, too. A college degree. A marriage with

David. Two perfect children. A career and a life all her own. Everything, all at once.

Kaylen began to lay the little tiles out on the table in simple preschool patterns. A flower. A tree. A sun.

Sarah glanced through the instructions for mixing the cement.

"Did Aunt Monica give this to me?"

Sarah nodded.

"I love Aunt Monica," Kaylen said, satisfied.

"Me, too."

Kaylen looked sideways at her mother. "Why?"

Sarah chuckled at the question. "Because she's my *sister.*"

Kaylen looked blank.

"Just like you and Patrick are brother and sister."

"But Aunt Monica isn't a brother," she said, relying on four-year-old logic.

"No," Sarah said, smiling. "She's a sister. In my family, we just have sisters." She glanced at a photo propped up against the mantel, of both of them standing barefoot by the corral, their legs tanned the same gold-brown by the sun. They had been seventeen that year.

How alike we were, she thought, and how different.

"I'd like to have a sister," Kaylen said.

Sarah eyed the vivid photo and let it transport her back fifteen years. *I had just been named valedictorian. We were going out on the horses, celebrating together.*

She was always so willing to celebrate my successes.

"My sister and I were very different," she told Kaylen. "She was always quieter than I was. She was a few months older, but she was always the one who thought about things, waited and watched, let me be the leader." Sarah smiled a faraway smile, just remembering. "When we went swimming, I'd always dive in headfirst. Monica would always test the water with her toes."

It was the same way they were living their lives now. Sarah had jumped into everything headfirst while Monica waited, moving ahead slowly.

"We always knew we were going to want different things," Sarah said.

It's okay, isn't it, to love each other and want different things? But maybe the things Monica and I want aren't so different anymore.

She gazed at the two wiry teenagers they had been, ponytails pulled high and bouncy, hers dark, Monica's as light as dry, baled hay. Now Monica was beautiful and professional and respected, and she still had everything to give.

But to whom?

"Mommy?" Kaylen asked just then. "Can you fix this flower? I don't like the way it looks."

Sarah began jostling the tiny tiles. "How do you want it? Like this?"

"No," Kaylen told her. "Like a daisy. Make the things stick out."

"Those are supposed to be petals." Sarah bent over her daughter's handiwork, rearranging little details, while Kaylen nodded. The work with her hands proved therapeutic. A realization came mushrooming up inside of her while she sat, designing flowers. *Maybe that's why I feel jealous of Moni sometimes. Maybe it's because I see her giving so much . . . to her job, to her new Little Sister. Maybe I wish somebody could see me giving of myself like that, too.*

"You think the petals look good like this?" she asked her daughter.

"Oh, yes," Kaylen exclaimed. "Yes. Yes."

"Here, you pup," Richard called as he placed the bowl of chow on the floor. He stood a moment, waiting to hear Abraham scampering toward him. "Come on, Abe! This is dinner!"

When the dog didn't respond, Richard went to Ann's room and tapped on the door. "Have you seen Abe?"

"I don't know where he is," she called back. "Open the door, Dad."

He turned the doorknob and smiled. Ann was sitting cross-legged on the floor, absently massaging her big stomach in circular motions with her hands.

"What are you doing?"

"Relaxation exercises."

She did it again while he watched. One deep intake breath for four counts. A round O with her mouth. Her cheeks billowed out, flexing with the air, as she blew out for four more.

He thought again how pretty she was. How young and vulnerable she looked as she sat on the floor, palms up, practicing for labor and the birth of her baby.

"I look at you sometimes now and it's easier to think of you having a baby," he said. "But I still have a hard time seeing myself as a grandpa."

"Do you?" Ann turned huge eyes toward him and he swallowed hard.

"Yeah." He studied the face he loved so much. Then he pictured another face he was beginning to love. And for one horrible, lasting minute, he resented his daughter for the choice he and Monica had had to make. Though he tried to quell the thought, it was like a seed growing within him.

"Why are you looking for Abraham?" Ann asked.

"I wanted to feed him. He isn't coming when I call."

"I don't think he's chewed up anything in here lately. Usually, when he does that, he hides pretty close to the evidence."

Richard cocked his head, scowling at the idea of Abraham chewing. "I don't know where he is."

She lifted an arm to him so he could help her up. "I'm not so good at getting up off the floor anymore."

"That's okay," he said. "You've got good reason." He took her hand and tugged. He watched as her coltish legs unfolded. Then, with a grunt, she was standing beside him. "I'll help you look for him, Dad."

For the next few minutes that's what they both did, calling to Abraham in every room, trying to coax him out.

"Dad," she said at last. "I'm worried something's happened to him."

"I know," he said. "I'm concerned, too." But suddenly, he stopped short and chuckled. "Well, I guess I'd better not leave towels on the floor anymore, either."

"Oh, *no,* Dad. Did he eat them?"

"No. He's made a bed."

She came into the bathroom where the little puppy lay curled on the pile of terrycloth. As they stood together watching Abraham, Richard realized this little dog from Danny had become a precious gift to both of them—something for them to share.

"Oh, Dad, he's so cute," Ann said. "He's just been sleeping." But when she bent to scoop him up, he felt hot and limp and he didn't lick her hand.

Richard saw it, too. "He isn't acting right."

"No. He isn't."

"Feel his nose."

She placed two fingers on his button black nose. She could feel his breath as he sniffed at her. "It's hot."

"And dry?"

"It's dry."

"Here, little fellow," Richard said with an abundance of love in his voice. He took Abraham from Ann and held him tightly, next to his torso. "Let's have a look at you." Gently he scratched the two little silken ears and peered into two sad, trusting eyes. "Something's up," he said quietly to Ann. He didn't want to scare her or the puppy. "We'd better get this little guy to the vet's."

He didn't have much money left in his monthly budget for things like this. Maybe the vet would let them pay later. He couldn't worry about that now.

He telephoned the nearest veterinarian. Ann brought one of the towels for Abraham to lie on so he would be more comfortable in the truck. The traffic was very heavy and it was 4:25 when they finally pulled up in front of Dr. Garrity's office, only five minutes before the office closed.

Dr. Garrity examined Abraham quickly. Then he informed them that their little dog had the flu.

"He'll be okay," the vet reassured them. "He'll probably run a fever and act sluggish for another forty-eight hours. If he isn't any better by then, ring me and I'll take another look at him."

"But how can a dog get the flu?" Ann asked.

"Same way you can. He's gotten himself close to a germ somewhere that pounced on him."

"But isn't there something I can do to make him feel better?" She was standing by her father, clutching his hand like a little girl. "I want to help him get well."

The doctor smiled down at her. "Since it's a viral infection, I can't give him any medicine. But I'm guessing he isn't eating. Has he been getting liquids that you know of?"

Ann shook her head and Richard did, too.

"We haven't seen him at his water bowl," Richard added.

Dr. Garrity handed Ann an eyedropper. "Chances are, if he hasn't been drinking anything, he could get dehydrated before this thing is over. Take some time with him and hold him in your lap if he doesn't fight it. Dribble some water down his throat with this. That will keep me from having to give him intravenous fluids if this thing hangs on very long. If his little body has a good supply of fluids, it will make him stronger *sooner.*"

"Okay," Ann said, nodding. "I'll do it."

When they left, Dr. Garrity's wife, who was managing the front desk, agreed to send them a statement.

"You just get that little guy well," she called out as she waved them off. As Richard held the door open for Ann, he felt as if everybody in the world was caring for them. It was a frame of mind he had forgotten.

All that evening, as he sat beside Ann and the little dog, Richard couldn't shake his unfamiliar, unexplainable surge of well-being. He would have given anything, as he knelt beside Ann and gave Abe a friendly scratch on the rump, if he could have shared his feeling with Monica.

Richard went to bed just after eleven. He generally went to sleep just after ten on a work night, but Ann didn't show any signs of going to bed and he guessed she wouldn't. He guessed she was going to sit up with Abraham long into the night, just worrying about the pup and trying to help him.

He kissed her good-night and went to his room and then, as he lay in bed thinking of it, it struck him what a good mother Ann would make. Someday. If only she could have had the chance to wait until someday.

June 5
Dear Diary,
Well, I've found time to write again and it's in the middle of the night. I'm tired and I should be asleep but I can't help it. Abraham is sick. I'm staying up with him so I can help him.

He's got a fever. His nose is hot. The doctor thinks he might get dehydrated. I'm feeding him drops of water because nobody knows if he's been drinking.

197

Seems like I also do a whole lot of thinking at night. Like when I'm awake like this. Or like when I'm in bed waiting to fall asleep. I've been feeling lots of things about myself. And tonight I've had lots of time for thinking things! Ha!

Now. Where do I start? I suppose with Abraham being sick. I've been thinking about a baby and I know I'll have nights like this one with the baby, too. Probably lots of them at first when it's hungry all the time. And probably some, later, too, when it's sick.

I used to think it was bad for me to even think about not doing these things. But I've decided tonight that maybe it's okay to question things. I guess I'm a little scared sometimes but I guess I'm thinking that being scared is okay sometimes, too. And that maybe wondering if you can really do something is okay, too.

It's like, holding Abraham and looking at him, he is a little alive thing. Then I try to picture the baby. I feel it moving around all the time inside my stomach and then I think that a baby is so much more than a little alive thing. A baby will grow up to be a person. A baby will grow up to be a girl or a boy who feels things just like me.

I know this is hard to imagine but I think I already do love the baby. But then I wonder about me. I wonder if I'll be able just to be me. Maybe I shouldn't try to do it. I think about myself caring. I know I'm okay because now I know my dad really cares about me. But what if I do the same thing?

What if I forget how to tell my little baby that I love it?

I have to admit something. At the beginning, I wanted to have a baby just so I could prove things to Dad. Now I don't think I need to do that anymore. Sometimes it scares me that I don't know anymore if I want to keep the baby for the baby's sake or for mine. Sometimes I think I just want the baby for my sake. That seems sort of selfish, I think.

Do you think it's funny that I'm thinking all this?

At my doctor's appointment this month, the doctor said he had a long list of people who can't have babies and would like to adopt one.

Six months ago, I would have cried or yelled at him or something for even mentioning it. But I think now it's okay to be saying this. I've decided it's okay to decide things. I want to learn just to be honest with myself. Being Big and Little Sisters with Monica has taught me that much.

Maybe I should make a list of reasons about keeping a baby and not keeping a baby. I don't know. I'll try it. Here goes:

Giving it away:

When the baby grows up, it might wonder why I gave it away. I wonder if it will wonder if I loved it a lot or if I gave it away because I didn't.

Keeping it:

When the baby grows up and, the whole time it's growing, I'll have to be working to make money to feed it. Maybe this little, new person will not know how much I love it because I'm grouchy because I just have to work all the time. You know. I feel like laughing because I'm writing this and it's just like with Dad and me. Only now Dad's finding ways to show me that everything's okay.

Diary, just between us, I'm wondering if either thing will be best or worst to choose. Maybe there isn't a right or wrong way to do it. I just have to do the best I can to make everything turn out okay for everybody.

See, I told you I was thinking about lots of things.

I think I'll stop writing. Abraham's asleep again and it's two-thirty in the morning. At least I don't have to go to school in the morning so I can sleep late.

More later, I promise.

Good night (or good morning!),
Ann Small

Danny readied himself for the kick as the soccer ball rolled toward him, a round blur of black and white against the grass of the playing field. He ran toward it, mentally lining his shoe up for the stroke. He hit it squarely with a smack against his instep. The ball shot straight into the goal.

Jeff Walker grabbed the ball and brought it out again. "Good shot, Lovell. How come you always make it in the first time?" he shouted pointedly.

"Shut up, Walker," Danny hollered back at him. "I don't want to hear it."

Jeff dribbled the ball with his feet, giving it short, controlled kicks toward the opposite end of the field,

200

then back again. When he brought it into range, he gave it one determined thwack toward the goal. Luke, the friend who was playing goalie against them, picked up the ball and tossed it back. "Sorry," he shouted. "You're going to have to do better than that, Walker."

Jeff threw his hands up and turned away. "Tough luck. I tried." He grinned at Danny. "Just ignore Luke. He's got a female. He's going out with Rachel Carson tonight."

Danny got to the ball and prepared for another shot. "That's something to brag about?" He didn't mean to sound sullen. He couldn't deal with any of this stuff right now. All their chattering about girls and which ones would climb into the back seat with them seemed trivial and stupid. He would never have betrayed Ann by talking about her that way. And it wasn't because they hadn't tried to pry the gory details out of him.

Nobody his own age seemed to realize how complex it all was.

For that matter, neither did his mother.

Even though she had apologized for suggesting he just break up with Ann, she did not understand how much he wanted to do what was right.

"You're young and idealistic," she told him. "You will probably change your mind."

"No," he had told her. "I won't."

Motion on the soccer field brought him back to the present. "So, Luke is gonna have a *great* night . . ." Jeff came running toward him. "A *great* night with *Rachel Carson*."

Danny turned around and shot. Luke, who was

momentarily distracted by talk of his upcoming date, missed the ball.

"Another score!" Danny shot both of his fists into the air in a clench of victory.

Luke shook his head and pitched the ball under-handed back to Danny. "You win. Let's go. I'm hungry."

"Ah." Jeff jabbed Luke in the ribs with his bony elbow. "It's almost time for the chick."

"Just drop it, Walker." Luke walked ahead of them off the field. But after Jeff left, and he and Danny were waiting in his truck in the drive-through at McDonald's, he brought it up again himself. "Yep," he said nonchalantly, after he had leaned out and given their order. "I am going out with Rachel tonight."

"She's pretty cute," Danny said, not knowing what else to say.

"Yeah. She is." Luke was staring at a picture of Ronald McDonald. "Yeah, I was thinking. Maybe you can give me some pointers on how, you know—" He turned back to face Danny and he was bright red. "How to . . . get started. . . ."

Danny wished he could take back what he and Ann had done. Not only because of how everyone looked at him but because, now, he knew all the reasons it had been wrong. In a way, he figured he deserved all this.

"I mean—" Luke was still struggling "—I'm always gonna need to know these things, although with Rachel I've heard it isn't *too* much of a challenge."

Danny was silent for a while. When at last he decided what to say, it was both out of honest concern for his friend and because of what he and Ann were going through. "Luke. You've got to be careful. I just—" He didn't know how to say the rest of it. More than anything, he didn't want to sound corny. His friends meant an awful lot to him. He didn't want to be ostracized from their group. "Well, when you do it, it should just—" He faded out. He thought about it again. When he spoke again, he was certain at last of what he should say. "I don't want to happen to you what happened to Ann and me."

Luke looked at him as if he was crazy. "Don't worry. I'm not that stupid. I'm not going to get her pregnant."

"I wasn't talking about that."

"You could have fooled me."

"Don't *you* be stupid," Danny said. "Think about it. I'm not going to tell you to go for this. I'm going to have to pay a lot because of what Ann and I did, Luke. I'm going to be somebody's father."

"And that's *your* problem."

"But even if it wasn't, there might have been another one. What I'm saying is there's just no such thing as going out and doing this. Take my word for it. I've thought about it a lot. Sharing something like that, in the long run, will *matter* to you. Even if Rachel doesn't get pregnant, what you do with each other is going to hurt somebody."

"If I had wanted this opinion," Luke said, "I would have asked my father."

"Well, you didn't. You asked me. There's a whole lot more here than just hitting on Rachel Carson and then bragging to everybody."

That's not what I see in my dad's *Maxim* magazine."

"Sharing something like that has strings attached to it. The magazines don't tell you because they want you to buy them."

"Oh, man," Luke said. "I can't believe you're telling me this. You really think it's that important?"

Danny pitched a ten-dollar bill at the girl in the window. "I'll pay for the hamburgers, okay?" He was glad he'd had the courage to say it. Luke was his friend, after all. "Yeah, I think it's that important."

"This conversation is going to stay just between you and me," Luke said just before he chomped into his burger. "If anybody at school finds out you *talked me out* of hitting on Rachel Carson and that I *let* you—"

"I know," Danny said, grinning back. "They'd laugh at us for the rest of their lives."

Chapter Twelve

Monica stuck her head in the front door of the little town house. "Ann? What's up?"

Ann hurried into the front room. "Hey, Sister." She kissed Monica hard on the cheek. "Thanks so much for coming over. Dad's at work. I just needed to talk, you know?"

"Okay," Monica said softly, the same feelings of relief and letdown washing over her again. It happened every time she came, every time she thought there might be a chance she would see Richard. "What's going on?"

"I wanted to ask you something."

Monica sat on the sofa and crossed her hands. "Okay."

"I want to know how you feel about being adopted."

"Oh . . ." Monica gave her a little smile. Then she held out her arms to the girl. "Are you thinking of putting the baby up for adoption?"

"Just thinking about it," she said. "I want to make good choices."

"Oh, Ann," Monica said, uncertain of how to begin, wanting to give good answers, too. "I want to tell you the right thing."

"I want to know how you felt when you found out. I want to know if you ever wondered if your real mother had loved you or not."

"You know," Monica said, "Eleanor and Cohen made certain I knew it from the very beginning. They didn't talk about me being adopted like it was a bad thing. They always told me how badly they wanted me, what a miracle it was when the social worker called and said there was a baby. . . ."

"They did it the right way," Ann said.

"Yes," Monica agreed with her. "They did. They told me the truth from the very beginning."

"Did you ever think about your real mom?"

"I did," Monica told her. "When I finally got my master's in fine arts from University of Denver, I drove to Nebraska to meet her. It was the way I rewarded myself."

"Did you have to search for her?"

"No. Eleanor and Cohen knew who she was. They told me how to find her. The laws about adoptions have changed so much. Everything used to be very secretive.

I might have searched for years and never found her. They didn't want me to go through all that."

"What did you do? What did you say to her?"

"I walked up to the screen door and stuck my nose in and introduced myself—" Monica said, laughing "—and half expected her to chase me away with a broom. But she didn't."

"Did she cry?"

"Yes. And she gave me a cola and showed me pictures of my two half brothers. They looked like me, Ann. It was incredible."

"Was she sorry?"

Monica stared at her hands for a moment. Then she answered as honestly as she knew how. "I don't think so. I told her all about Eleanor and Cohen and growing up with Sarah. She told me it made her happy to hear that I had been happy. She told me she still thought about me. Then I came home to the Albrights' again. That's my real home—where all my memories are. That's where I really belong."

Ann settled beside Monica on the sofa and gave her a little squeeze. "Don't tell anybody I asked you all this stuff, okay? I'm just . . . thinking."

"I won't." Monica squeezed her back.

"Hello. This is your father calling," Richard said in a funny, professional voice over the telephone. "I have my calendar in front of me and I can see that next Tuesday is going to be a special day."

Ann started giggling. "Next Tuesday is June eighteenth."

"I know that. Do you know that?"

"I know that," she said, giggling.

"Why do you think next Tuesday, June eighteenth, is a special day?"

"Because—" she sang out in a lovely melodic voice he was only now growing accustomed to hearing again "—it's my birthday. I'll be fifteen."

"Ding . . . ding . . . ding . . . ding . . . ding . . ." He made a hilarious bell noise. "You are correct. You are a winner. And *because* you are a winner, you will be the recipient of one perfectly executed birthday party."

"Oh, Dad, *really?*"

Ann hadn't had a birthday party since Carolyn died. Richard had been considering this for days. And, as he sat staring at the dusty photographs on his desk, he had the terrible feeling this was going to be the last birthday she would celebrate as his child. After the baby came, she would be a mother herself and a woman.

"Yes," he told her. "Really. Let's do something *good.*"

Ann was laughing. "I'm so excited, I can't even think of anything."

"I can."

"Well, what is it?"

He was silent on his end and she could hardly stand it. She was practically jumping up and down and he was teasing her.

"I can't wait any longer."

"We-e-l-ll," he drawled. "I was thinking about taking you out to dinner . . ."

"Yes?"

"And I know Mexican food has been sounding good to you lately with the baby coming and all . . ."

"Go on . . ."

"I thought maybe we'd eat Mexican food . . ."

"Dad," she screamed at him, but she was laughing at him, too. He was dragging it out forever. She hadn't had a real birthday party for so long ago, almost since before she could remember. "You are driving me bananas." He was doing it on purpose and she knew it. She was playing along with him, too.

"Bananas. Do bananas sound good? I was thinking it would be fun to . . ." He trailed off again and, this time, over the line, she could hear him chuckling. "I don't know . . ."

"Daddy!"

"Okay," he said. "Okay. I'll tell you."

"It's about time."

"I was thinking about escorting you to Casa Bonita."

"Casa Bonita?!" she shrieked. She had wanted to go to Casa Bonita for a long time but they had never been able to afford it. It was a huge restaurant built underground, with many rooms, all decorated to seem like Acapulco. "Dad? Are you sure?"

"Positive."

"Dad. It would cost us money and . . . I . . ."

"I think it's high time we splurged a little, don't you? Besides," he said, sobering somewhat "I'd like to celebrate the day you were born into our lives . . . my life."

"It'll be *wonderful,*" she said, and he could tell that she meant it. He loved hearing the joy in her voice. It was something so new, so right, so strong. But then she paused. Her words turned wistful and he would have given her anything when he heard the longing in her voice. "Can it be like a real party? Can I invite a friend to come?"

He knew she had been making friends in her childbirth classes and at some of the Big and Little Sister activities, too. He didn't know who she had in mind. He didn't think anything of it when he answered her. "Sure. That would be fine. It's been so long since we've had a party."

"Good," she said matter-of-factly. "I want to invite Monica."

"Oh, Ann." He felt as if he was standing on a wooden platform and the planks had just been yanked out from under him. "I just don't think we can do that."

Her voice fell in direct timing with the plunging of his heart. "But, why? You said it would be okay."

"I know that, but . . . I thought a friend your age . . ."

"I don't have any friends my age. Dad," she said reasonably. "I don't understand why you fight when I want us to do something with Monica."

He would never be able to answer that question for Ann and make her understand. Never.

"Have you decided you don't want me to have a Big Sister?"

"That isn't it."

"I don't understand then."

"You teenagers think you have to understand everything."

It didn't work. He was so desperate he was trying to make her angry and throw her off the track. But she had matured enough and they had grown close enough that now she was relentless. "Are you angry at her, Dad? I know you used to be. I think that's why you two went to that meeting with Joy Martin."

"You took me by surprise, that's all. You were talking about friends and I assumed it was some girl or something from childbirth class or school." And, as he said it, he knew he couldn't say no to her, not when it mattered so much to her. Not when he had promised her a party for her birthday.

"I didn't mean to."

He had no choice. To do anything else would be to admit to his daughter that something had happened between him and Monica. He let himself imagine what it would be like, at the party with Monica, watching her golden hair and her radiant face across the table as they sang "Happy Birthday" to Ann. What it would be like when she looked up, smiled at him. . . .

It was going to kill him.

"You know," he said slowly, as if he was reasoning it out and deciding everything would be okay. "I'm sorry I reacted so quickly. I suppose it would be okay. Especially after everything she's done for you—getting you the photography job and everything."

Monica had let Ann bring the pictures for the brochure home so he could see them. They had turned out nicely. And just a few days ago, Ann had brought home a dummy layout for the brochure.

Every time Ann saw Monica and talked about her, a huge, cutting pain gashed his heart. "Moni thinks the pictures are good. Moni thinks I should eat beets for the baby. Moni thinks I should start a portfolio. Moni thinks I look best in peach eye shadow."

Monica was changing them all.

"I'm going to call her right now and tell her she's invited to my party," Ann said. "She's really going to be excited."

"Yes," he said. "I'll hang up so you can call her."

Monica closed her eyes against the memories of Richard that Ann's words evoked in her. The memories toyed with her now just as they did every night, a long way past bedtime, while she lay atop the blanket unmoving, trying not to wish for him.

She hadn't had one decent night's sleep since he had brought Ann to the toy museum.

"I can't believe he wants to have a party, Moni! Momma was always the one who did it before. I remember, a long time ago, my mother made us all ballerinas. She made skirts out of net and everybody got to wear one home. . . ."

Monica thought of Richard's curls, tousled richness she wanted to run her fingers through, wanted to bury her face in. She thought of his forearms, the way the muscles lay tight beneath his skin—she had noticed them while he was driving the little train. She remembered the delight in his eyes, delight that played with her senses, taunting her.

Because of their excellent restraint, she barely knew what it felt like to hold him. Even so, she remembered every detail of comforting him when Ann had gone away with Abraham. She remembered his tangy man smell, his solid bulk against hers, the steel of his arms, the gentle way he expressed his new caring for his daughter.

If only. If only.

"Will you come?" Ann asked.

She couldn't do it. She couldn't sit across the table from him and act merry while she tried not to meet his eyes. It would be impossible not to become lost in those eyes, not to notice he was a beautiful, virile man. She would look at him and her own eyes would speak a thousand words to him, even if she didn't utter one.

And, all the time, Ann would be sitting between them.

"It's next Tuesday. June eighteenth. I'll be fifteen. *Fifteen.*"

Ann was still so young. She still had so very far to go. "I wouldn't miss your fifteenth birthday party for anything," Monica said and her voice was so low Ann could hardly hear her. "I wouldn't miss it for anything."

They met at half past six on Tuesday, June eighteenth. Richard saw Monica waiting for them as soon as he parked the Dodge and started walking hand in hand with Ann across the parking lot toward Casa Bonita.

"Hi, you two," she called out as she waved. She was sitting beside a huge fountain, the water dancing just behind her. A group of children were pointing at the plume shooting into the sky and were pitching pennies into the pool.

"Hi, Moni!" Ann dropped her dad's hand and ran to her.

Monica stood. She saw Richard pause. "Hey, kid." She hugged Ann. "Happy birthday."

"Thanks. Oh, *look* at this fountain!" Ann started digging in her purse. "I want a penny. I want to make a wish." The water came slapping down just beside them. It sent up a cooling spray.

"Here." Richard was standing beside them now. He pulled a penny out of his pocket, held it there between his thumb and forefinger. "It's your birthday. I'll pay for the wishes tonight."

When Ann went to the fountain, he turned to Monica. A moment passed. A lifetime. Her eyes were a fairy's eyes, magically binding him. He was held spellbound, unable to turn away from her.

He pulled another penny out of his back pocket and held it toward her. "You want to make a wish, too?"

She stood, silently holding him with her eyes and with her heart. She reached for the penny. Her fingers grazed his. For one eternal, tantalizing moment, she paused.

It was everything Richard could do to keep from grabbing her hand and pulling her into his arms.

"Yes, I'll make a wish," she said softly.

"Can you make it for both of us," he asked, "with the same penny?"

"I think I can," she told him.

The coin was still warm from his fingers. She turned from him, held it for a moment, then closed her eyes and pitched it in. It hit the water with a little splash.

She didn't turn back to him.

"You look pretty tonight," he told her. "Beautiful."

She gets more and more beautiful every time I see her.

Ann was coming back toward her. "This is some place for a party, Little Sister," Monica said, reaching out a hand.

Ann took it, then reached for Richard's hand too. "Let's go in," she said. "I can't wait any longer."

Richard had to force himself to move. He had to force himself to smile down at his daughter. "This is going to be *some* shindig."

"Yeah," Monica said with exaggerated enthusiasm. "You've even got *presents*." She held up the canary-yellow shopping bag she was carrying.

"Oh, *amazing,*" Ann said, giggling again.

Monica knew she had spent too much on the gifts. Joy Martin had encouraged her many times to spend time with the girl and not money. But this was different. This was Ann's birthday, a time in her life that might never come again. Monica wouldn't acknowledge it, but she was feeling guilty. She had bought the gifts because she cared for Ann. But there was the possibility that perhaps she was trying to buy forgiveness for herself, too, to purchase it by purchasing Ann's heart.

Richard looked down at her and grinned. "We're all ordering the all-you-can-eat thing," he said. "We're going all out on this celebration."

He looks too good. He looks too handsome. Too tan. Too mischievous and too totally, wonderfully right.

Did he look this way the first time I saw him? Why didn't I notice it then?

If she'd brought too many presents, it was to make up for this.

214

"Order me the all-you-can-eat thing then," she said, grinning up at him like an imp. "Are you sure you want to do that to all of us?"

"Yeah." He grinned back. "I'm sure."

"You weren't supposed to bring me any presents, Moni," Ann said. "You coming to my party is present enough."

"Don't boss me around," Monica winked at her. "I'm the Big Sister, remember?"

"Yeah. I remember. But I can't wait until I grow up and get to be somebody's Big Sister someday. Then I can boss people around."

Richard moved forward and opened the huge double door. Monica took Ann's hand again. The three of them entered Casa Bonita, linked by fate, faith and their own feelings. Mariachi music swelled to greet them, and somewhere in the distance another fountain pattered gently.

"I cannot eat another bite. Make me stop, somebody, please." Monica pushed herself away from the table. "I've never seen so much food in all my life."

They had eaten it all. Enchiladas. Tacos. Tamales. They'd had a second course of quesadillas and guacamole and *chili rellenos*. Ann was on her third sopaipilla. Still, the waiter kept stopping by to see if they wanted more. Richard kept raising the miniature Mexican flag on the table that signaled him to bring another course.

"Stop raising the flag, Dad," Ann groaned as he did it for the fifth time. "Don't make them come again."

"He can't want this much to eat," Monica whispered to Ann from behind a hand. "I think he just likes raising the little flag."

"Dad. *Stop.*" Ann giggled after the waiter brought three more tamales. "This is getting embarrassing."

Just as Richard started in on the new plate, an artist came to their table carrying chalks and a wooden easel. "Perhaps you would like a caricature of the two lovely ladies, sir?"

Monica was shaking her head but Richard was laughing. "Yes," he said. "A portrait is a nice idea."

"Richard . . ." Monica couldn't keep from smiling. "You don't want this, do you?"

"A caricature of both of you?" He winked at Ann and then widened his eyes in feigned innocence. "How could I resist?"

"Hold still, please," the artist instructed as he poised his easel. Monica and Ann wrapped their arms around each other and tried their best to look glamorous. Richard leaned back and watched them. *It's good to know,* he thought, *how much they love each other.*

They joked and giggled the entire time the artist was drawing. Fifteen minutes later, he held up the completed sketch and let them examine it.

"Agh!" Ann shrieked. "I look like an alien."

"You do not," Monica chuckled. "You look wonderful. *I* look like the weird one."

"You do not."

"You both look lovely," Richard said, grinning mischievously as he paid the man. He took his drawing and stashed it beneath the table. Then he began eating another sopaipilla.

"Dad," Ann said, laughing as she leaned across the table toward him. "Are you going to eat until they have no food left in the kitchen?"

"Maybe," he said. "This place is great."

Monica couldn't resist teasing him just a bit, too. "You keep eating tonight, Mr. Small, and they'll have to raise their prices."

He raised his eyebrows at her.

"And you'll have to change your name, too," Ann chimed in, "because you won't be Mr. *Small* anymore."

He almost choked on his dessert. "Thanks a lot, guys."

"No problem," Ann and Monica chorused in unison. They looked at each other and Ann giggled.

Monica couldn't help it. She giggled, too.

"All right," he said, frowning. "Teasing me is one thing. Laughing at me is another."

Monica met his eyes again. Again, she felt the almost unbearable tugging in her heart. Her feelings refused to be extinguished. A stubborn, soft fire burned within her for the lovely, practical man who sat, scowling, across the table. "You're awfully good at letting us poke fun at you."

He smiled gently at her, allowing her eyes to hold his for a fraction of a second too long. "I'm awfully good at a lot of things." Suddenly it was there again, thrumming between them. He felt his breath catch somewhere between his lungs and his throat. Her eyes were gray opals, burning into him, their patterns of light and brilliance constantly changing as she searched his face.

A diver appeared on a rock ledge just beside their table.

"He's gonna jump!" Ann shrieked.

The muscular youth made a perfectly executed swan dive into a crystal-blue pool two stories below them.

Monica was thankful for anything to think about besides the way Richard had been looking at her. She couldn't bear it. "They make this place as reminiscent of Acapulco as they can," she commented.

The diver climbed back up onto the ledge to dive again. Ann's eyes were huge. "That guy is *cute,*" she said. She poked Monica in the ribs. "Just look at those muscles."

"Yes," Monica agreed enthusiastically, joining in mostly for Ann's benefit but enjoying herself nonetheless. "Very nice muscles."

Ann couldn't resist teasing Richard just one more time. "I used to think Dad would look like that in a swimsuit. But after seeing how much he's eating tonight, I guess not, huh?"

Monica didn't answer. She couldn't. The thought of seeing Richard with so much bare, wet skin sent her senses skidding out of control.

Wordlessly she watched the youth make his next two dives.

Richard's feelings had run the gamut during the past months. Want. Need. Acknowledged love for his daughter. A deep, burning caring for Monica he didn't want to classify. And a new one, one that angered him because he knew it wasn't fair—resentment toward Ann because he knew he had to push Monica away. But the feeling he was feeling just now was totally unexpected.

The two women he cared about most in the world were ogling the diver.

"You think that kid looks good in trunks?" he asked. He was jealous. Hm-m-m. This was a new thought for Richard. One hundred percent, full-fledged, green-with-envy jealous. Monica raised her eyes to his and his eyes fixed on her lips.

He pictured her face only inches from his own, imagined her satin hair in his hands, the anticipation of the taste of her mouth, the smell of her.

Even as he imagined it, he was living it, needing Monica.

As guilt closed in on him, he shot a look at his daughter. Sweetly, Ann smiled back at him.

Richard felt a knot of painful anticipation clench like a trap inside his chest.

He swallowed. Hard.

"We'd best be opening up your presents," he said.

"Yes—" Monica agreed softly as her eyes delved into his own. "Let's."

"That's great with me." Ann was practically bouncing up and down in her seat.

"I'll go first." Monica pulled the shopping bag out from beneath the table. She dumped it out on the table. The pile of presents seemed huge and, suddenly, she felt guilty again. Richard couldn't possibly have afforded this much.

"It's all good stuff," she told him awkwardly. "You'll see."

Ann tore open the packages one by one. There was a pair of hot pink canvas sneakers, a bottle of nail polish to match and a pair of clunky wooden earrings that Monica had known Ann would adore. In the next box, all wrapped up together, was a pair of white denim pants, a hot pink Shaker sweater she knew Ann could wear after the baby came and a tiny hot pink designer purse to match.

"Oh, Moni." Ann launched herself out of her chair and hugged her Big Sister so tightly she could scarcely breathe. "So many things. You goofy. I've never had stuff like this in my entire life."

She *had* done too much. Her eyes met Richard's again as she hugged Ann close. He didn't look angry. He only looked a little sad.

"Here, Ann." He handed her one small box. "Here's the one from me."

She took it from him and opened it slowly, slicing each piece of tape with a nail and carefully unfolding the wrapping. She made the one little box last forever. It was then Monica knew it for certain. Richard and Ann's relationship was a treasure, too. A fragile, precious, irreplaceable thing. She couldn't let anything she wanted threaten what they were learning to share.

Ann set the folded paper beside her on the table. She lifted the lid on the little box and peered inside. Tears began to roll down her cheeks. "Oh, Daddy. It's so *beautiful*."

"Do you like it?" he asked gingerly. Monica could tell he was uncertain about it. She felt her heart go out to him one more time.

Ann used two fingers to pick it up out of its cotton nest. She held it high so Monica could see it. It was a beautiful dainty bow pin, fashioned out of pastel tartan plaid. A tiny gold locket dangled from it, a locket engraved with a scripted initial *A*.

Ann pinned it to her denim jumper. Monica could see her hands trembling. When she finished, she ran around the table and plopped in her father's lap to hug him. "Daddy. Thank you . . . so much . . . it's so pretty. . . ."

"There's room for two pictures in there," Richard told her proudly. "Open it and see. One on each side."

She pulled the tiny heart up from her breast and snapped it open. "Oh, *neat,*" she said, studying it carefully before she closed it with a little click. "I know just what pictures I'll put in here. Pictures of the two people I love most in the whole world." She encircled Richard's neck with her arms while she beamed across the table at Monica. "I'll have a picture of my special Big Sister on one side—" she turned back to Richard and draped one possessive arm across the width of his broad shoulders "—and a picture of my dad on the other."

Chapter Thirteen

"Do you ever wonder whether you love Monica and me the same?" Sarah asked.

Eleanor's hands froze, poised just below the surface of the dishwater. "What sort of question is that?"

"It isn't a judgmental one," she answered softly. "It's

just something I think about sometimes."

"Why?"

"Because Monica and I are so different."

"You are very different," Eleanor said slowly. "I love you both *because* of those differences. I also love you for the very many things you have in common."

"Were you upset when you adopted a baby and immediately got pregnant with me?"

Eleanor turned toward her daughter and smiled, a beautiful, joyous smile that reflected all the peace she had harbored for so long, all the strength she had shared with both daughters. "No. Not upset in the least. I don't think you can even know how happy I was, Sarah."

"I don't know how you did it, though." Sarah's expression was almost peaceful now, too, and beautiful. "Having both of us running around so young at the same time."

"It was worse," Eleanor told her, almost laughing, "when you were teenagers. Just wait until Kaylen and Patrick get to be teenagers."

"Sometimes I think about what you went through," Sarah said quietly. "I wonder what it was like to want a baby so badly and then to suddenly have two."

Eleanor glanced at her daughter once more. She knew at last that she had to say it, knew that, for so long, it had been something Sarah needed to hear. "You and I are a lot alike, you know. I had this driving biological force within me that said, 'Be A Mother. Be A Mother.' I never could be very logical about the whole thing. I didn't want to wait. I wanted to be *performing*."

"You never told me this."

"We tried for eight years to get pregnant. Your father would have given up on it long before if he hadn't known how important it was to me. We were desperate when we put our name in with the social worker."

"That's what I mean," Sarah clarified softly. "When Monica came, she was your dream. Your first miracle."

"I will not lie to you," Eleanor said. "It was one of the hardest things I've ever done, taking care of the baby and being pregnant with you. I was so tired all the time I could barely move and I had to get up every two hours all night long to feed Monica. And *you* little girl—" Eleanor touched her daughter on the nose "—made me throw up all evening long. Not all *morning* like babies are supposed to, but all evening instead. By the time you were born, I had been through such an ordeal I felt like I had delivered you both."

"Like twins?"

"Like twins."

Cohen lay down *The Denver Post* and peered up over his shoulder. He pulled the pipe out of his mouth with a little pop, a breaking of suction. "Only it was better than twins, Sarah. And worse than twins. All of these ladies were bragging to your mother one day, saying they had been in hard labor for forty-eight hours and stuff." He jabbed one finger at Eleanor and gave Sarah a wry grin. "I just told them all to quit talking, that was nothing, that your mother had been in hard labor for ten months."

"Mommy!" Kaylen's shrill voice sang out from the bathroom. "Come help me."

"What's your father doing?" Sarah called back, echoing her daughter in exactly the same singsong voice.

"He's busy drying off Patrick and he won't dry off me and I've got goosebumps and I'm dripping water all over Grandma's floor."

"She's in dire straits, poor thing." Sarah hugged her father, then tossed her tea towel over the back of one of the kitchen chairs. "I'm coming," she called out.

When she got to the bathroom, David and Patrick and Kaylen were all huddled together in a little group, grinning at her. Kaylen had one of Eleanor's huge, plush bath sheets wrapped around her and another one draped over her head. David was perched on the commode, holding the baby.

Her husband smiled up at her, a we're-in-this-together smile that made Sarah remember why she had married him. A warm surge of gratitude for him welled up, filled her.

"You shouldn't have come so quickly," he said sheepishly. "This is my project. I have everything under control."

"Yeah, Mommy," Kaylen said, clutching her towel around her little tummy. "Daddy has everything under control."

Sarah let out a little laugh and then she smiled at all three of them, perfect, precious gifts all her own.

"Da . . . da . . . da . . . da . . . da . . ." Patrick warbled.

She leaned over the baby and gave David a long kiss on the lips. "I love you, you know," she told him.

"Umm," he said, closing his eyes and enjoying it. "Do that again."

She kissed him again and then went back to the kitchen. "David has everything under control," she told her parents.

Cohen began puffing on his pipe again. Eleanor crossed her arms and surveyed her daughter. "So. Tell me," she began noncommittally. "Which one of yours do you love the best? Kaylen? Or Patrick?"

"Oh, Mother." Sarah wrinkled her nose. "What a ridiculous thing to ask. I love them both the same."

"Didn't you ever worry? That you wouldn't?"

"No. Never." She spoke the words quickly. Then she thought about it. She stood there for a moment, silently drying the same plate over and over again with a tea towel. "Well, maybe I worried. Once. Before Patrick was even born. I loved Kaylen so much. I was afraid a little bit, I think. I didn't think I could love another baby as much as I had loved her. I didn't think I could even *possess* enough love to double what I felt for her." She gave a short laugh. "Since Patrick came along, I've never even thought about that again. I love him just as much. I don't remember what it was like without him. . . ."

"So . . . is everything you were feeling for Kaylen just doubled?" Eleanor asked pointedly.

Sarah stopped drying. "Yeah. More like quadrupled. Quintupled."

Eleanor hugged her close, her daughter who had been so tiny once and who now stood a head taller. "And so it was with me."

Kaylen came barreling in, all dressed, followed by David carrying Patrick. The baby was swaddled in his blanket and ready for sleep. Sarah took her son and bundled him next to her. She drank in the powdery, soap scent of him, cherishing him.

"That's how God works, you know," Eleanor continued, as they all gathered around Sarah. "He can come inside us and multiply us . . . time and time again . . . so there's always enough love to give."

Danny wanted to give Ann a gift for her birthday. He liked thinking about her. In a way, he was tied to her now, just as he had told Luke he was. Not in a bad way, but because of the baby.

They belonged . . . not together, but to each other a little bit. And to the baby, as well.

He walked through the mall by himself. He was also looking for athletic shoes. He carried his mom's credit card in his pocket and he knew how much he could spend. His mother had wanted to come shopping with him but he had nixed that idea. It wasn't cool to be seen hanging around Southwest Plaza with your mom, especially having her helping you pick out your *shoes*.

It was funny, though. Ever since Ann had started talking so much about this baby, he had started feeling differently about his mother. Sometimes he wanted to be really close to her.

"What was it like when Dad left and you just had me?" he had asked her yesterday.

She'd looked at him for a long time before she answered. "It was scary. And it was good. If I hadn't had you, I would have died from being alone."

"So you were sorta glad I was around then, huh?"

"Yeah," she said, swatting him with a sofa pillow. "Sorta glad."

"Good," he said.

"Good?"

"Yeah," he said. "I knew that. But I just wanted to hear you say it."

She eyed him. "Ann Small is lucky, I think."

"Why do you say that?"

"Because she got into this mess with you. I'm beginning to figure out you've got a pretty good head on your shoulders."

He took both hands and pretended to pull his head off. "Here. You want it?"

"No," she had said, laughing at him. "No, no, no, no, no."

Today he wanted to find Ann something that would make her feel pretty. He ended up buying her a tiny bottle of cologne.

After that he went to the poster store. Maybe she'd like something new to hang on her wall. He was thumbing through huge cardboard placards when he heard a familiar voice behind him.

"Hey, Danny. What's going on?"

He turned around, his hand holding his place in the posters. "Hey, Luke."

"You getting a new poster?"

"No. I'm getting Ann a birthday present. Her birthday's today."

"It's neat to see you two still being friends."

"Yeah."

"I . . . um . . . had a good time with Rachel last week," Luke said offhandedly.

"Did you?"

"Yeah," Luke said. "She's really nice."

"What did you two do?"

"We went to the movie and then out for frozen yogurt and then we walked around Celebrity Sports Center for a while."

Danny raised his eyebrows. "That's it?"

"I really like her, Danny. I made myself really get to know her. I asked her lots of questions and stuff. We talked about a whole lot of stuff. Maybe I'm gonna ask her to the back-to-school dance."

Danny felt this surge of something in his heart. It was something so foreign he didn't know how to express it. It felt like something solid within him, something persistent and new, an uncanny certainty of what he, Danny Lovell, really stood for. "I'm glad," he said to his friend. "You think she'll go with you?"

"Yeah," Luke said, nodding vigorously. "I think she will."

Maybe this is what it feels like to grow up.

He turned back to the posters and tried to act as if nothing magnificent had just happened to him. And as he did, he found exactly what he was looking for.

It was a huge picture of two teddy bears hugging each other. Beneath the picture was written Love Bears All Things.

"It will be a long time before I find her another present that's as good as Abraham. But this," he told his friend unabashedly, "is what I'm getting Ann for her birthday."

"Monica?" Richard's voice was soft over the telephone. "I know I shouldn't call. I just . . . it's been since Ann's party . . . I wanted . . . to know how you were. . . ."

"I'm fine," she said. "Just fine."

"Good."

There was a long silence between them.

"This is crazy," he went on. "I shouldn't have called. I was at the office and I kept wondering . . ." In truth he had been staring at the old rotary dial phone for an hour, trying to decide if calling Monica would make things better between them or worse. In the end, he had disregarded the thumping of his heart and decided he couldn't make things worse between them. Things were already bad. They couldn't see each other and they both knew it. "I kept wondering . . ."

"What?"

"If you wanted to talk to me. If you would think I was bananas for wanting to hear your voice. . . ."

"Bananas?" She laughed sadly. She had been aching to hear his voice for days. "I don't think you're bananas."

"Ann talks about you all the time," he said. "She tells me all the things you've done together. She tells me all the things you've said. I wish I had a reason to know all those little things about you, too, Monica."

"It was a good birthday party," Monica said, changing the subject after another period of silence. She wished for the very same things he wished for. But

229

they couldn't discuss it. Not now. Not ever. "Thank you for letting Ann invite me."

The next time Richard telephoned Monica, he was all business. "I wanted to talk about Ann," he said when she answered. "I was just sitting here in my office thinking about things. I was thinking about how she takes such good care of that darned puppy. She'll be a good mother someday, Monica, don't you think?"

"Yes," Monica told him. She was fighting to keep her composure. Every time she heard his voice over the telephone, whether it was businesslike or tender, her heart threatened to race out of control. "I *do* think so. I think it's a shame she won't get the chance to mature a bit before she does, though."

"I do, too. I keep thinking maybe she could put the baby up for adoption. But I'm afraid if I mention it, she'll think I'm pushing her. I'm afraid, if I do, she'll let go of that idea forever."

"Have you discussed it with her at all?" Monica asked him. "Has she brought it up?"

"No," he told her. "But I know . . . she has to think of it sometimes. I think she needs to make the decision herself."

Moni's heart went out to the man. He was becoming so wise as he faced this crisis with his daughter. "I think you're right. I know Ann. If *you* bring it up, she'll start thinking you don't love the baby. But if she comes up with it herself, it will be different."

"Oh, Moni," he said. "I want to help her. I just don't know if I can. When I think about everything she might be giving up . . ."

"You are helping her," she reminded him, "just by loving her."

"You think so?"

"I think so."

"She could do so much if she was given the chance," he said. "I was looking at those pictures she took for your brochures. They're good. It all seems so impossible if she's going to be caring for a baby. But she could finish a technical school in two or three years. She's talented enough. Maybe life doesn't have to be so cut-and-dried for her. Maybe, even if she keeps the baby, she can do some things . . . make something of her life. . . ."

"Richard," Monica whispered to him. "I'm proud of you, too, you know, for seeing the possibilities."

If only there could be possibilities for us, he thought.

"Hi," he said when he called again several days later. "Ann carries that purse you gave her for her birthday everywhere she goes. Thought I should let you know that."

"I'm glad. Oh, I saw the layout proofs for the historical society brochure this morning," she told him merrily. Every time he called it made her wildly happy. "It looks nice."

"I'm glad," he echoed her. He laughed. He was the one who had phoned her and now he couldn't think of anything to say. He had just been desperate to hear her voice again.

"I can't wait to tell Ann."

There it was. Mention of Ann again. She was every-thing that stood between them. "Moni," he said. "I know we shouldn't be talking . . . *I* shouldn't be—"

"No, we shouldn't," she told him. "But I don't know how to stop making myself feel lonely like this."

"I don't either," he said. "I don't either."

That night Monica stared out the window at the relent-less stars in the Colorado summer sky. They twinkled on, tiny spots flickering like hope, somewhere eons away.

A place she would never reach.

A joy she could never attain.

Every time she managed to lose herself in sleep, she dreamed the same horrible dream. There was a train speeding past the terminal without stopping. She was supposed to get on it but she couldn't. Ann was aboard the train, her nose pressed up against the glass. As her face blurred by, Monica realized she was an orphan, that she had no one to care for her.

Monica left her pile of suitcases on the platform and began running, running . . . waving her arms, trying her best to catch the train. As she ran beside it, hot steam billowed out from beneath the cars and she could hardly see.

She was almost there, fighting her way through the white steam, inches away from grabbing on . . . grab-bing on. . . . And as she ran, she shouted the only thing she could, the only words that came directly from her heart.

"I love you, Richard, you crazy. . . . I love you. . . ."

• • •

Richard marched into Ann's room with one more demolished work boot dangling from his hand.

"Oh, *no,*" Ann hollered. "Not again."

"Yep," he told her. "Again."

Ann looked as if she was ready to cry, until he hurried to hug her. "I pay for this pair. It's a fair deal." He was almost laughing as he sat down near her. "Abraham is a training dog. He's training me to close the door to my closet."

"That's the corniest thing I've ever heard," Ann snorted at him.

"How much longer can we endure this? How long do dogs go through this gnashing-teeth phase, anyway?"

When she looked up to answer him, she was already giggling. "I don't know. I know about as much about puppies as I do about babies." They were sprawled on the floor facing each other, just like best friends. Ann rolled forward and touched her head on the carpet between her knees as she giggled. It was amazing how limber she was even seven months pregnant. And he was with her on the floor, the same level, the same position, the same plane.

I really do like my daughter.

He had loved her for the longest time. Liking her was different. And there was something else.

I really do like myself.

"Love you, kid," he said gingerly as he kissed her on top of her head. "But you're worrying me about that baby. Shouldn't you sit up straight or something? You're not hurting the baby?"

She knew from her classes that the baby was fine. But out of sheer respect for him, a new respect she was just learning to find, she sat up straight again. Their eyes locked.

"I get scared about the baby sometimes," she said. "I haven't told you that."

"Do you?"

"You ever think we can't do it? You and me taking care of a baby?"

He smiled at her. A long time ago, he had told her he didn't want to be responsible for a baby. She was including him in the process now and it warmed his heart. "Yeah. Don't you remember? But I've changed my mind since then. If it's what you really want, Ann, I could do it with you. We could do it together."

"Sometimes I wonder if it's what I want anymore. I've talked to Monica about her being adopted. She's always been happy." She was staring up now, out the window, as she rubbed her stomach with circling hands. It was the first time she had admitted this to anyone. "I don't know if I'll get mad at the baby sometimes just because it *came*. I don't know if I'll be good enough. Or if I'll say the right things . . . or if I'll be the right person. . . ."

How very much alike we are, he thought.

"Don't worry about who you are," he said gently, inwardly amazed that he sounded so certain of something he was just learning himself. How many times had he thought about things he might have done differently with Ann, or done better? "Somehow, as you live your life, you've got to find your heart's way. Then you'll have everything inside you that you need to give to others."

Somehow you've got to find your heart's way.

How noble he sounded.

You'll have everything inside you that you need to give.

It certainly wasn't what he had done.

But my heart is yanking in two different directions.

"I've got to decide," Ann said. "I was so angry at Danny for not wanting the baby. For so long, I've just wanted somebody to belong to me."

He reached for her again, needing to feel her, needing to grasp onto the importance of her, the steadying influence of all she was now in his life. "I belong to you, Ann," he said quietly. "I belong to you."

Chapter Fourteen

July 1

Dear Diary,

I feel surrounded by people who love me. Monica hugged me last night at childbirth class and told me she cared about me more than anything in the world. And Dad and I just sat on the floor and laughed the other night. Danny brought me some cologne and a teddy bear poster for my birthday.

Dad has to work on July Fourth. There's lots of summer travelers riding the train that day. Monica invited me up to Evergreen to see the fireworks they shoot off every year over Evergreen Lake. (It should be good, huh?)

I know Moni's family pretty well. I'm excited about spending time with Patrick. He's the baby even though he's walking around already and he's almost just a plain kid.

Better go. More later.

Ann Leidy Small
(Age 15! Isn't that amazing?)

Even in Cohen's huge Wagoneer, the Albrights and Taylors were jostling for position.

"I have a tummy ache," Kaylen wailed as she climbed across Sarah's lap toward David and Ann. "It hurts too much to sit still."

"Sitting still will make it feel much better," David told her. "Shouldn't she be in her seat belt, Sarah?"

"If you park beside the golf course," Eleanor was instructing Cohen, "we'll have an easier time of it."

"She should be in her seat belt," Sarah agreed. "She unbuckled it herself."

"My tummy hurts," Kaylen wailed. "The seat belt makes it worse."

"It doesn't. The seat belt makes you *safe.* Monica? Can you reach her? Will you buckle her back in?"

"Da . . . da . . . da . . . da . . . da . . ." Patrick said, chiming in with the bedlam.

Kaylen climbed across the seat one more time. Monica did her best to reach the child. But Ann's growing tummy and Patrick's car seat were in her way. "Kaylen," she commanded. "Sit down. Ann? Can you reach the belt buckle?"

"I'll try," Ann said, reaching across Patrick. She had

been busy making funny faces at the little boy. Already they were becoming fast friends.

Kaylen reached up and in one violent motion shoved Ann's hands out of the way. "I don't want to sit here. I want to sit by Aunt Monica."

She jostled Patrick's car seat, causing him to wail as if mortally wounded. Suddenly she flopped over and began climbing across all of them. She stuck her feet in Ann's lap and started climbing over Ann's belly, using it the same way she would have used a stepladder.

"Kaylen. Watch out." Monica grabbed the girl and pulled her across the seat. "You can't do that. You have to be careful with Ann's tummy."

"Does it ache like mine?"

"No. Yours just aches because you got into the picnic basket and ate too much watermelon."

"Did Ann eat too much watermelon? She looks like it."

"No," Monica explained as simply as possible. "She has a baby growing in there. That's why you can't step on her."

Kaylen strained against Monica's arms. Cohen was doing his best to parallel park while Eleanor gave him directions. David was frowning. Sarah didn't say anything.

"I stepped on her," Kaylen reasoned, "because she was in my way."

"That isn't nice," Monica warned her. "You don't just shove people aside if they are standing in your way."

I have learned that, too.

Cohen set the parking brake and pocketed his wallet. "We've arrived."

They all tumbled out of the car and began gathering things—blankets, the picnic basket, bulging plastic bags and the Styrofoam camp box Eleanor had rigged up with a trash bag to keep their corn on the cob warm.

"There's a nice spot." Eleanor pointed to a green hill beside the golf course. "Let's go over there."

As they walked along together toward the spot Eleanor had suggested, Sarah stepped up beside her sister. "I wish you wouldn't have told Kaylen those things. It wasn't your place."

"What?" Monica stopped walking. She was astonished.

"It isn't your job to tell my daughter about the facts of life. She's much too young. She's only four years old."

"I didn't—"

"You did," Sarah stated. "All that stuff about the baby in Ann's tummy. It wasn't the right time for that."

"I don't think you have to look around and find the right time to be honest about things. You can be honest any time you want to."

"But such important things," Sarah said. "You have to be very careful with the important things."

Monica eyed her sister. "You have to be honest about the important things most of all," she answered.

Eleanor had spread out the blanket and was arranging food. Everyone was hungry and ready to eat. All the food looked and tasted delicious. A member of the Chamber of Commerce handed Kaylen a purple helium balloon. Patrick managed to smear barbecue sauce all over everything. Cohen leaned back on the grass and smoked his pipe while Kaylen danced about with her balloon. It was a relaxing time for everybody. Soon the sun set and the sky turned dark around them.

At precisely 10:00 p.m. the first skyrocket went up, shattering the darkness. After that there came another and another, with loud ear-shattering booms and great peonies of color that lit up the mountains and reflected off the water below. Red. Blue. Gold. Pink.

Every time one went off the crowd of thousands gasped in a huge, collective sigh. The display went on for almost an hour as everyone cheered and clapped. Then, at the end, a great sparkling American flag illuminated the hillside as the Evergreen Community Band began to play "America, the Beautiful."

"It was *wonderful,*" Eleanor breathed as the last sparkle faded into darkness. "The best ever."

"Oh, honey," Cohen said, wrapping his arms around her. "You say that every year."

"And I'm right every year."

David was folding the blanket and Ann was helping gather things together in the darkness. Kaylen stood beside her father. Sarah and Monica were staying as far away from one another as they could. Everyone was aware of the tension between the sisters.

Suddenly David asked one simple, terrifying question. "Who's got Patrick?"

No one answered.

"I thought you had him," Sarah said.

"I did," David said, his voice frantic. "He was sitting

with me. Then he said he wanted to go over and sit with your mother." He did say it. "Ga-ma" was one of his few words.

"He sat with me for a while." Eleanor was panicking, too. "He climbed into my lap for a few minutes, then I thought he was going to sit with you." She pointed at Sarah.

"He's gone," Sarah shrieked. "Oh, David. We'll never find him." She had let him wander over toward Monica but she hadn't watched him. She had just assumed he would get there. "I lost track of him."

By now it was almost eleven o'clock and everything was pitch black. There were still many people milling around, gathering their things to leave. The family might never find Patrick. The lake was nearby—he might have wandered into one of the little streams that led there.

Cohen took charge. "We'll separate and look for him. Go in pairs and weave back and forth. Eleanor and I will take Kaylen with us. If you haven't found him in twenty minutes, come back here. By then, we'll have to notify the police."

Even before he was finished giving instructions, they were going. Ann and Monica went together. They zigzagged back and forth, never losing sight of one another, searching through the groups of people who remained, asking if anyone had seen the child. Other people began looking for Patrick, too. And the entire time they moved back and forth, Ann's mind was screaming out to her. *Sarah's such a good mother . . . this isn't fair! What if I gave my baby to them . . . he would be happy and have everything that the Albrights gave Monica. . . . Will this happen to me someday? Sarah is a good mother just like Dad is a good dad . . . why is it so easy to do the wrong thing?*

She was crying and she didn't even know it. As she zigzagged away from Monica, she thought she heard a baby crying, too. Maybe she was imagining it. She stopped, listened.

Ann saw a group of people ahead of her. Someone was holding a flashlight. A sliver of light sliced through the darkness toward her and, when it passed her, she saw that one of them had a baby in his arms. The crying was real.

"Where do you belong, little guy?"

"Can you tell us who your mother is?"

"Do you suppose his mother went off and left him?"

"Da . . . da . . . da . . . da . . . da . . ."

"Patrick!" Ann hollered, and then she raced forward to make certain it really was him.

"Are you his mother?" somebody asked.

"Why is he out toddling around all by himself in the middle of the night?"

"I'm not his mother," she said calmly now, even though, in the beam of the flashlight on her face, they could see tears streaming down her face. "I'm a friend. His mother is looking for him. Patrick. Come with me."

She held her arms out to him and he lolled toward her, arms outstretched.

"Moni! *Moni!*" She called again, but not too loudly because she didn't want to frighten Patrick. "I found him!" But she couldn't find Monica, she was so excited, and she was stumbling around in the darkness with the baby. After the beam of the light from the flashlight, everything seemed blacker than before.

Ann turned back to the group with the flashlight. "I can't find my way," she told them, and they offered to escort her back. They all wanted to see the little boy reunited with his mother.

As they approached, Ann could see the others in the flashlight beam. Eleanor and Cohen hadn't returned yet. Monica was waiting for Ann. David was holding Sarah gently while she cried. "I'm never going to find him . . . never. . . ."

"Da . . . da . . . da . . . da . . . da . . ." Patrick called out from Ann's arms.

They all looked up and saw him with a group of strangers and with Ann leading the way.

"Oh . . . *Patrick!*" Sarah squealed as she ran toward him. David was right behind her. Ann handed the baby to Sarah and she held him against her. "Oh, Ann, thank you," she cried.

Sarah, Ann and David walked back together as Ann made little clucking sounds at the baby and wiggled her fingers at him. Sarah thanked Ann over and over again.

Monica was waiting for them.

"He's okay," Sarah cried to her sister as she nodded her head in triumph. "Ann found him. He's really, really, okay. Not even a scratch. . . ."

"I'm so glad," Monica whispered with tears in her eyes. No one even noticed which sister moved first. Suddenly they were in each other's arms, with the baby boy between them.

• • •

Monica's heart was clanging like a jackhammer as she waited on the phone that night for Richard to answer her question. She sat bolt upright with Ann right beside her.

Ann'll know. She's got to see it. How can anyone sit beside me and not see what the sound of his voice does to me?

His voice was warm and rich, a friend's voice, the voice of someone who could have become much, much more.

Tender torture. That's what it was every time she had to contact him for Ann's sake.

"I don't know," he said. "I didn't think about her spending the night up there." He sounded wistful, alone.

"We'll only do it if it's okay with you. It's just been such a traumatic evening for us." Monica knew she was rambling but she couldn't help it. Every sense in her body was aching for him. She had to cover it . . . for Ann's sake. "We aren't at my house. We're all staying at Mother's. We all just wanted to be together."

Sarah was sitting beside her, too, both she and Ann sprawled out on the tall four-poster bed that had belonged to Eleanor when she was a girl.

"I don't want her to be any problem," he said hesitantly.

"It isn't a problem," she told him. "She can wear one of my old nightshirts."

He was silent for a moment. At last he consented. "If you're sure Ann won't be imposing on anyone." She knew he was covering for himself, too. He didn't want Ann to be away. She could tell by the sound of his voice he was already lonely, thinking of Ann not spending the night in their house in the room next to his.

You sound so alone, she wanted to say. And she would have, if not for Sarah and Ann sitting there, cross-legged now on the chintz coverlet. It would never do for them to hear her being personal with him.

"I promise she isn't imposing," she said instead. "I'll have her home in the morning."

"I suppose . . ." He sighed. "That will be fine, Monica." He was speaking so formally to her, so properly. It was absurd. She wanted to laugh crazily but she didn't.

"Good," she said. And then she couldn't quite bear to let him go. "You would have been so proud of her, Richard," she told him. As she did, she finally turned and grinned at Ann. "Everybody was running around and panicking, and it was so dark. There were little streams running everywhere and the lake was nearby and there were about a thousand people. And your daughter just went right out there and found Patrick."

"I'm . . . feeling very proud of her, indeed."

"I wish you could have been there."

"Me, too," he said softly. She would never know how desperately he had wanted to be there.

There was a lull between them.

"Sarah is so grateful to her," Monica said.

"I'm sure she is. Ann needed something like this, you know." He was smiling now. She could hear the change in his intonation.

"Yeah. I know." She hesitated. "I'd better let you go."

"That's fine," he said, almost sadly. "Good night, Monica."

After she hung up, she, Ann and Sarah sat together on the bed for a while. They talked about Patrick. Sarah talked about being a mother. They giggled about funny things kids do, until Ann started yawning. After all the excitement, she would have been tired anyway, even if she hadn't been pregnant.

"What do you say?" Monica asked her, tousling her curls. "You ready for a nightgown?"

"Yeah," Ann admitted. "I really am exhausted."

Monica dug an old cotton shirt out of the drawer and Ann donned it. "Night," she said as Monica kissed her.

When she left, Sarah and Monica were left alone.

They sat together on the bed.

It was Sarah who finally broke the silence between them. "I have to tell you . . . how sorry I am . . . for getting mad. . . ."

Monica stopped her. "No, I'm sorry. I didn't have any right to talk to Kaylen about babies. . . . I just . . . take over sometimes."

"Maybe," Sarah said "we were both wrong. It's okay, anyway. Kaylen needs a firm hand. I feel like I've neglected her a little since we got Patrick." She smiled a sad little smile. "She *was* being very naughty."

"Yeah," Monica said, "but I shouldn't have—"

Sarah stopped her by touching her arm lightly. It almost wasn't a touch. It was just a movement of air across Monica's skin. It was the first time Sarah had reached out to her since Ann had found Patrick at the lake. "My own daughter listens to you better than she listens to me."

"But I'm her aunt. I'm just a novelty when I'm around. I think that's okay, don't you?"

"No," Sarah said. "It isn't okay. And it's more than that. It's one more thing in your life that's *right*—when I look at my own life and see everything wrong."

"Is that what it is then? Is that what's been wrong between us—what's right with my life?"

Sarah was weeping now, soft enveloping sobs that made Monica feel like the elder sister, more nurturing than she had ever felt before. "It isn't what's wrong between us, Monica. It's what's wrong with me."

"I don't want to lose you," Monica whispered. "Not as a sister. And not as a friend."

"You haven't," Sarah answered. "You really— haven't."

"I thought maybe it was because I was the adopted sister. And because you are the real one." It was something that had been on Monica's mind forever. She had to voice it now that they were being honest with one another. "It was the only thing I could come up with."

"Oh, *no!*" Sarah reached out to her and gripped her arm tightly. "Not that. Mom and I talked about that some. I just . . ." She paused, took a breath, girded her courage, knowing she had to start somewhere. "Moni. Look at your life. Look at what you've become. You took Dad's old trains and made an entire *museum* out of them. You've made everything good and you've kept everything easy."

"No," Monica said. "I haven't."

"You've got all this time to yourself and you're doing volunteer work and you're changing Ann's life. . . ." Here, Sarah couldn't help it; she had to start laughing at herself. She was still hurting, but it seemed somehow funny, too. "You're never late to church on Sundays and your makeup always looks perfect, and every time I see you, you have on an outfit I've never seen before. Your panty hose never wrinkle at the ankles—"

"Sarah!" Monica was crying now but she was laughing, too. She was relieved and sorry, and she couldn't help thinking of all Sarah's blessings, all the things she had been longing for in her own life. Sarah had David and the children. It was everything Monica wanted and couldn't have now. A life, a love, with Richard Small. "If you'll quit feeling this way, I'll give you every pair of panty hose I've got."

"No," Sarah giggled through her tears. "Oh, no! It would never work. They would all have runs in them before I stepped out the door. That's just how my life is."

"But—" Moni had to say it. The words, when they came, were almost just a breath, they came so softly. "Think of your treasures. Think of all the people who love you."

What I would give . . . just for that.

"It's so hard to explain," Sarah said, analyzing herself for the hundredth time. "I love being a mother. I wouldn't trade it for the world. But it's the little things. Last week we bought Patrick his first real pair of walking shoes. Then there wasn't enough money in the budget for me to get my hair trimmed. I would not have traded Patrick's shoes for my haircut. I *wanted* him to have those pretty, white leather shoes. We were so excited, we took pictures and everything. It was better and made me happier than getting *anything* for me. But . . . I'm never *first* anymore. Sometimes I just miss being first . . ."

"You are a good mother, Sarah."

"They are so precious," Sarah said. "Such individuals. Tonight, when I thought I might have lost Patrick, I wanted to just sink down somewhere and die. If he was gone now . . . if I didn't have another chance . . ."

You always have another chance, Monica wanted to say. But she didn't because it wasn't true. Sometimes, the chance never did come.

"You know what?" she asked instead. It was ironic really, thinking how much she and Sarah loved each other and thinking of how different their lives had grown to be. "Richard and I were talking about this once . . . a long time ago. . . ."

Sarah looked confused. She had stopped short and was staring at her sister. "Richard?"

"Ann's father."

"Oh." Sarah still studied her face. Monica realized she had said his name with too much familiarity. She had blown her cover.

"An easy life isn't always the best life. He and I . . . we did this, too—we compared our lives. In a way, he accused me of some of the same things."

"I didn't know that you knew him that well," Sarah said, watching her.

"Living with Mom and Dad, I always saw things as

black and white . . . right or wrong . . . and maybe I've grown past that."

Richard has taken me past that.

Sarah was still eyeing her, sizing up the bleak expression on her face. Today when she had confessed so much to her sister, she had meant most of it as praise for Monica. She had never seen such a lost expression on Monica's face. And the way she had said the man's name. Richard. As though he were a treasure. "What makes you think that?"

Monica's eyes filled with tears. "Doing something the easy way usually means doing it alone."

"You're right."

"Look at everything that's happened to Ann, Sarah. Being her Big Sister, being a part of her life, has been monumental for me. Being with her, supporting her, while she makes such difficult choices . . ." She trailed off.

Sarah prodded her. "You sound as if there's more."

"There is," Monica said. "Much more." She gave a desolate sigh. "It's Richard, and I don't . . ." She stopped again.

"Monica. That's it, isn't it? You *like* Ann's father."

"Shh." Monica grabbed Sarah's wrist. "You mustn't say it. If Ann was to hear . . ."

"But I don't understand," Sarah whispered joyfully. "It could be wonderful. Just like the fairy tales we used to act out. Monica, the three of you could be a family."

"But there are other parts to it," Monica told her in a hushed voice. "I should never have let myself start feeling this way. I didn't understand how bad it could be at first. I've worked so hard to gain her trust and friendship. If something happens between Richard and me . . . if it doesn't work out, if I have to leave her, too, or if she thinks I'm taking her father away . . ."

"You have to be careful, then," Sarah said matter-of-factly.

"I've never been reckless," Monica said. "Not ever in my life. Everything's just been *there* for us. . . ."

"Everything's just been *easy,*" Sarah amended.

"Right. And there's more than that. The main reason Ann needed a Big Sister is because she and Richard weren't close. He was scared to death of her when she started growing up. I've watched him change with her, Sarah. I've watched him reach out and give everything he's got just to try with her. And I've watched her learning to trust him again. I can't stand in the way. I can't take that away from them again. If something happened and Ann thought it was because of me . . ." She stopped. She couldn't even say it. But Sarah knew her well enough to guess the rest of it.

"So," Sarah said, "you love him."

"Don't say it." Monica's voice broke. "Just don't say it."

"Oh, Sis." Sarah gathered her into her arms and again they held on to one another. "I am so sorry."

"It's all so impossible, Sarah. If I had met him somewhere else. Some other time."

"But would you have still loved him if you hadn't seen all the sides of him you've seen?"

"I don't know. It's been such a precious time for us. Such a difficult time."

"But what about someday? What about after Ann is grown up or married or involved with the baby?"

"I've thought about that. But I don't want to wait until Ann grows up or goes away to start my own life. The worst thing I could ever do is resent her." She stopped and sniffed and rubbed away tears with a tissue. "I love her, too. I love her too much for that."

Sarah clung to her hand. "Oh, Monica."

"So you see, I've been sitting around wanting so desperately what you have. . . ."

"I didn't know."

"There are days I would give anything not to have to go to Ann's house to get her . . . not to risk seeing him . . . not to have to pretend around them or act like I don't care. . . ." Her eyes squeezed shut then and the sparkling tears that had been threatening to fall did so at last.

"Moni. Oh, Moni . . ." Sarah leaned forward ever so slightly and, as they sat there atop the bed where they had spent so many hours talking about boys when they were teenagers, they looked like two strong willow limbs bent together. "Do you think he feels the same way about you?" She had to wonder whether he was hurting this badly, too. She thought of David and of how much they had shared and how badly they had wanted one another. And how grateful she was to have him, no matter how hectic their lives together had become.

"Sometimes I wonder about it, too. We held each other once, a long time ago, before either of us realized what it could do to Ann. He looks at me—"

"He looks at you and you know he loves you."

Monica was nodding her head.

Sarah had to continue. "But you've never asked him."

"I haven't the right to ask him. I don't even want to *know*."

Sarah took her hands and grinned. "Same way I did."

"Thank you," Monica told her, "for loving me in spite of myself. In spite of everything that's right and everything that's wrong. . . ."

"Hey," Sarah said, and she sounded certain now, and happy. "That's what sisters are for."

Chapter Fifteen

It was the wee hours of the morning. Richard sat alone on the back deck, the legs of his pajamas blowing slightly in the night breeze.

Even Abraham was asleep.

He thought of Ann sleeping somewhere in the mountains, without him.

This is what it will be like when she's gone, he thought without emotion. *I won't have anything left. When I might have had everything.*

He studied the stars above him once more. Then he stood to go inside.

It was almost four-thirty when he glanced at the clock. He fixed himself a bowl of cereal and munched them. At the sound of his crunching, Abraham wandered in, bleary-eyed.

"Guess I'll get to the station early this morning, huh,

pup?" Absently he bent to scratch Abe's ears. Then he dressed, left a note for Ann to phone him when she got in, and drove to the station.

He had four hours to do paperwork before things even started to get busy. He should have zipped right through it. But he didn't. Often he caught himself staring at the sketch of Ann and Monica he had framed and propped against a lamp on his desk.

It will be over for me when Ann's gone. If I could only capture everything just the way it is now and save it. . . .

He shook the thought out of his head. He hadn't been so melancholy or felt so helpless since Carolyn had become ill.

How he missed Carolyn.

We should still have had years to share. We could have watched our grandchildren grow together.

"You would love Monica, too, you know," he said to Carolyn. Perhaps, from somewhere far away, she could still hear him. "She cares so much for Ann. It would do you good to see them together. It's been so hard . . . for me . . . but I've tried. . . ."

He felt tears of emotion welling in his eyes.

He buried his face in his hands.

The telephone rang at 10:00 a.m. It was Ann telling him she was home. "Monica brought me down," she said cheerily. "She had to work today. We had a good time."

"I missed you," he told her.

After the connection with his daughter was broken,

he stared at the telephone forlornly. Nobody would know, would they? Ann was home. Monica was in her office. He could talk to her so easily. . . . Just talk to her, see how she was doing. . . .

He waited thirty minutes, then dialed her number at the museum.

She answered and he lost all his courage.

"It's just me," he told her.

"Hi," she said, so quietly he almost couldn't hear her.

"I just wanted to talk. To see how you're doing."

"I'm fine," she said. "Thanks for letting Ann stay last night. We had a good time. We didn't stay up too late. She was pretty tired after she was such a heroine."

"She called a while ago to tell me she was back. She told me about it. She told me you had to work today."

"I just got here."

"I should let you go then," he said.

She was silent.

It wasn't enough. Talking to her only made it worse. He wanted to see her. He wanted to touch her.

"You sounded so lonely last night when we talked," she whispered.

"Monica. Can I see you?" he asked desperately. "Maybe we can just go to lunch or something. I know we shouldn't but . . . it wouldn't—"

"It would," she said. "It would hurt."

"I want to see you." His voice over the phone was a stranger's voice, gruff with need as he spoke to her.

"What about Ann?" She cast her eyes around frantically. Her heart was in turmoil. *I cannot escape this. I cannot escape what I'm feeling for him.*

"Ann isn't here."

"Maybe not lunch," she said. "Maybe . . . we could talk. Would it be bad? I could just come to your office." She wanted to see him, needed to see him, needed it even more than she needed to live or to do what was right.

"Yes," he said. "Come here."

She didn't know it but, phone in hand, he was pacing the floor like a caged cat. That's exactly how he felt—as if every direction he turned he faced steel bars, obstructions, a million reasons to keep him from her.

"Please," he said again. "Come."

"I'm afraid," she told him frankly. *Afraid of what I'll want when I'm in a room alone with you.*

"I have to resolve some things about you . . . for myself . . . by myself. . . ." She couldn't know how paralyzed he was feeling without her, how totally lost. He felt as if his emotions were being mangled—shattered from hurting her, from wanting constantly to be near her.

"I'm coming," she said. "Richard, I'm coming now."

While he waited for her, he thought of everything Ann had told him on the phone. It was so painful learning about Monica secondhand. "Monica and Sarah had this big hole dug in the side of the hill. It was their cave and they used to sit in it and make mud pies. . . .

"You should see Moni's old room. It has all white furniture with flowers on it and it smells so good . . . like a garden. . . .

"Moni has this funny stuffed horse with big pink flowers all over it. It's named Anastasia and she slept

255

with it and she loved it so much its mane and tail came off. Now Mrs. Albright keeps it in a basket in the den and they won't let Patrick or Kaylen *play* with it and it doesn't match anything. . . ."

Monica arrived at Denver Union Terminal forty minutes after he had called her. She knocked timidly on his door. He didn't call out because he knew it was her. Instead he hurried to it and let her in without speaking. For long moments they stood together, searching each other's faces, before he stepped away.

He felt as if he had been rescued. "Thank you," he said breathlessly as he leaned against his desk and grasped at the edges of it to keep himself steady. "Thank you for coming." He wanted to call her what Ann called her. "Moni . . ."

"I wanted to come," she whispered. "I always want to come. I never want to come."

He smiled sadly at the paradox she described. It was a paradox they both lived and he understood perfectly. "I know."

She glanced at his desk and saw the drawing of herself there. Herself and Ann. Together. "I shouldn't have done it."

"I'm glad you did. I didn't have any right to ask you." He stopped, just stared at her again, thinking how very beautiful she was.

"I admire you for so much, you know," she said, searching for something to say, anything to begin the conversation between them. "When I think of what great strength you've shown to pull yourself back to your daughter."

It was the first time in his life anyone had said anything like that to Richard. When she said it, the great strength welled up within him. It was as if she were the one giving it to him. He picked up the sketch and studied it. Then he lay it on his desk and moved toward her.

"I don't think you know how much you've taught me," she said quietly.

He wanted to laugh in disbelief at what she was saying. It was Monica who had given him back so much of himself, Monica who had taught him how to care for Ann again, Monica who was giving him everything. "Ann told me all about Anastasia," he said.

"Oh, *no,*" she said, laughing. Then he was laughing, too, as he looked tenderly down at her, and she wanted to cry out for all the joy that brought her—just laughing with him and seeing him look that way. Their hushed voices blended in the quiet office like instruments in an orchestra.

At long last he quit laughing. He was still gazing down at her as if she were rare and splendid. "You're funny," he said. "Funny and wonderful."

She stopped laughing, too.

He took one step closer.

"Richard. No."

His eyes were dark and shining, like obsidian. "I love Ann," he said, his voice rough with passion. "I love her more than I love myself. But I've needed someone like you in my life for a long time, Moni. I've needed to fall in love for a long time."

Monica shook her head. In her mind she was backing

257

away. In reality she was standing in the center of the room, in anguish, unmoving. All she wanted to do was hold him. "I will not stand between you and your daughter."

It was as if her words ignited him, like a match lighting an explosive. His face contorted with pain as his words lashed out at her. "You stick like putty to Joy Martin's rules. Because that's the only way to make this easy—to hide from it, to say it's impossible. . . ."

Her mouth twisted with anger. "There is nothing about this—nothing about this!—that is *easy,* Richard Small. Don't make me take the blame. Not after we've both been so strong . . . tried so hard. . . ."

"And so . . . And so . . ." Each time he said it, his voice grew quieter, as if he was trying to control the volume of his words the same way he was trying to control his resolve. "If we aren't looking for the easy way out, what are we looking for? What are we both so afraid of?"

She was furious at him for even wanting to chance it. "Ann hasn't even accepted *herself* yet. You can't expect her to accept *this.* You don't seem to remember. We are here to help her, to be stable for her, to take her through some of the most dramatic choices she will ever have to make in her life."

"Know what I think?" he snarled at her. The pain was snaking through him, coiling, striking him over and over again, slowly annihilating him as it had been for the past months. "I think you are afraid to test how much she really loves you, Monica. I think *you* don't have faith in her yet. I think somewhere deep down inside you think Ann might not really come through when you need her the most."

"How dare you say that? How *dare* you say that?"

"Tell me I'm wrong."

"She is only a child, Richard. I am here to strengthen her for what she has to go through. And you are, too. You can't expect her to just change her thinking and be there to support us."

He slammed his fist against his desktop. Everything on it jumped an inch off the surface. Pencils scattered. The old green lamp shuddered as if there had been an earthquake, the shade trembling, sending wavering light back and forth across the room.

"You resent her for this, don't you?" Monica continued. "You're blaming Ann for all this even though you're trying to blame me."

"Don't . . . accuse me of that." But he was staring at her, desperate again, and furious at her for coming so close to the truth. "Why would you accuse me of that?"

"That's it, isn't it?"

He eyed her warily. Then his face crumpled as he admitted it. "Yes. All right, Monica, yes. I do resent her. I resent what I've had to give up because I love her. Is it worth it? Will it be worth it in three years when she's gone and I'm alone? In my mind, I'm losing her again. It's my own fault again. But it's your fault, too. *You* are the one who's making me feel this way, Monica. She's standing in the way of everything I could have with you. It isn't a choice of one of you over the other any longer. Can you see it? I am losing everything because of it. *Everything.*"

"Yes," she said softly, taking one step toward him. Her eyes filled with tears again, tears of compassion for him, and tears of love. "I can see it."

His voice grew softer, too. His resolve grew weaker. "I stand to lose everything because I am trying to *protect* everything."

"Ann is worth protecting."

His eyes reached out to her when his arms didn't, drawing her in. They became beacons along a perilous shore. "And so are you."

For one long second, Monica considered flinging her fears and her safeguards aside. Then she thought of Joy Martin's trust in her, of the faith the caseworker had placed in her by matching her with Ann. "No," she whispered at last. "I love her too much to risk it."

"You talk all the time about loving Ann," he said slowly as his eyes burned into her. "But what about me?"

She met his gaze head on. She didn't acknowledge his question. He was a stubborn man. She loved him for that, too. "My first commitment is to your daughter," she told him, "no matter how costly that commitment is to me, or to you."

It took him three steps to cross the room, three steps to reach her, three steps to be close enough to reach out with his hands and grip her shoulders. He held her immobile, his fingers pressing into her flesh with a glorious fire and pain. "How much do we have to sacrifice?"

Her physical response to his touch, not his words, rocked the wall that Monica had shored up against him.

"Everything," she whispered. "We have to sacrifice everything."

As she railed against him, Richard moved closer to her. He rested the huge circle of his hand against the delicate curve of her spine. No matter how wildly she fought, she loved the feel of his hand, loved the idea that, no matter what she said, he would guide her now with the simple pressure of his palm against her skin.

Beloved, said a voice that seemed to come from the rattle of the train tracks and the echo of the building and the gentle whir of the ventilation system. *Even here my hand will guide you, my right hand will hold you fast.*

"I am so tired of fighting this," Richard said. He bent nearer to her, their faces, their lips, only a breath apart. "I am tired of listening to reason. I'm not a teenager, Monica."

"Neither," she said pointedly, "am I."

"Do you know how many nights I've lain awake? Like a fifteen-year-old myself? Wondering what it would feel like to kiss you?"

"Me, too. It's crazy, isn't it?" Suddenly, irrevocably, a great twist of fear plunged through her. *What if we never have the chance for this? What if I do nothing except imagine this for the rest of my life?*

He was looking down at her, his face a gentle mask of regret and sorrow. "Just once, Monica. Don't make me turn away. We've both waited for this for so long."

She was shaking her head. *Ann. All that matters is Ann. Your daughter. My little sister.*

"No matter what we decide later, let me kiss you

261

tonight. So we'll know what it might have felt like, what it *might* have been."

She had no awareness any longer, no sense of his arms around her or of the tears brimming in her eyes. All of her attention was centered in one place, on her lips, in her heart. Somewhere, in another world, she was aware that she was still shaking her head at him.

"You asked me to pray to God one time, Monica. Is this what He is like? Someone who would give a promise of something that is unattainable?"

"Some things," she said, "are only attainable by trusting Him."

"You meant it when you said you thought we had to sacrifice everything."

"Yes."

Frustration burned in his eyes.

"Is that what you are doing, then?" Richard asked. "Letting go of us?"

This time, instead of shaking her head, she bit her lip and nodded.

"And so you've prayed about us?"

She nodded, tears threatening again. "All the time. Constantly. I'm praying now."

"Or maybe," he said pointedly, "you're just too scared to try."

She rested her forehead against his chin as he held her. Monica lifted her head and raised her eyes again. *Yes,* her expression told him. *That, too.*

Richard knew, as he gathered Monica's face in his hands and her shimmering blond hair bowed out around her head and wound into his fingers, that this

262

one kiss would have to last them a lifetime. "Monica," he whispered down at her, his eyes blazing with the truth of how much he had come to treasure her. Ever so slowly, while his heart beat a rapid cadence of restraint, he lowered his mouth to hers and completed the caress with his lips.

"Thanks for the ride, Danny." Ann leaned back inside the car and grinned at him. "It's so neat you got your license. I can't wait to get mine."

"It was a good chance to see you," he told her.

"I'll talk to you later, okay?"

"Sure thing." He gave her a little salute. "Call me if you need anything."

"I will."

"See ya, Ann."

After Danny drove off, Ann turned and started up the steps of Denver Union Terminal. As she tramped up the old stairway, she passed Tyler Hill coming down.

"Hi, Mr. Hill." Her voice rang out in the vastness of the huge, hollow terminal. "Is my dad in his office? I'm looking for him."

"I think so. The last train pulled out about an hour or so ago. He was out on the platform then. I know he had waybills to deal with."

She wrinkled her nose. "He's probably up there then. I spent the night with a friend last night. I haven't seen him since yesterday. I just came by to say hi."

"It's good to see you, young lady." Tyler smiled fondly at her. He had known her ever since Richard had first come to the station. It was too bad about the baby, though. What an incredible burden for such a young child to carry. "Take it easy on these stairs, you hear. In your condition, I mean."

She shot him a timid smile. "I will."

She went on up then, each one of her steps making little slaps against the tile as she climbed.

When she reached his door, she grinned proudly to herself. He was going to be surprised to see her. She had never ventured to the station before.

Chapter Sixteen

The door was standing slightly ajar.

"Dad?" Ann called out softly. She didn't want to interrupt him if he was busy, and he always was. She pushed the door open a little further. She stood for a moment, confused and disoriented, when she saw Monica was there, too.

It took long seconds for the jumbled signals to reach Ann's brain.

What was happening?

For one agonizing, slow-motion minute she stood there stunned, silent, frozen.

His arms were tangled around Monica.

Monica's head was nestled against his shoulder.

They were sort of hugging . . . they were together . . . as if they were lovers. . . . But she couldn't fathom it . . . couldn't think of it. . . .

Monica saw her, looked right at her and, horrified, pulled away from him. That, too, took long, punishing seconds, they were wrapped together so tightly. But when Ann saw the expression on Monica's face, she knew for certain . . . knew she was right.

The little pink purse she was carrying clattered to the floor.

"Ann," Richard shouted.

Everything was happening to Ann in slow motion, every frame caught and held in her mind like snapshots viewed through her camera lens.

Her dad was coming toward her. "Ann."

"What are you doing?" she shrieked. "What are you doing with Monica?"

"Nothing . . ." He was still coming toward her. The distance across the room could have been ten miles. "We were trying . . . nothing at all . . . just kissing . . . oh, Moni . . ."

The emotions coursed through Ann's body so quickly she couldn't even identify them. At the core of it all, at the lowest, most primitive level, came her fear.

Next came jealousy.

She was losing her father one more time. This time it was Monica's fault.

Ann turned her eyes on her Big Sister. "Why are you doing this with my father?" And her next words, when they came, were very sharp. "I hate you. I hate you."

Monica's face went ashen, the color of gray in a storming sky. "Ann. Don't say that. Please."

"What are you doing?" she screamed at both of them. "Why are you together like this?"

"Annie . . . little one . . ." Richard was pleading with her. But he already knew there was no use. He could tell by the astonishment in her eyes that she had never thought of this before, had never even considered the possibility. "We just . . ." He had moved toward her. Now standing just in front of her in the doorway, he could have reached out and grabbed her. But he didn't. He stopped short. He had come all the way across the room and he couldn't finish it with her, couldn't explain it to her; didn't know how to tell her.

Ann looked from her father to Monica and then back again. Emotion closed over her like water in a pool. She was thrashing her way up through it but she couldn't find the surface to reach air. She felt totally, completely, left out. They were the two people who mattered the most to her in the entire world. The two of them had reached for one another, had carried on their lives with one another all this time, without including her.

"How long have you been doing this?" she shouted at them.

"We haven't . . ." her father said. But she could see. Yes, she could see.

In a few moments, everything that was stable and right in Ann's life came smashing down upon her.

They don't need me anymore. They have each other.

She spun around and ran. She ran up the hallway and down the stairs. She could hear them calling from behind her, Monica's voice and her father's, too, pleading with her. "Ann," she heard Richard call out just as she reached the bottom of the stairway. "You've got to stop. You've got to listen to us."

But she couldn't stop. She couldn't listen. She couldn't even think. She wanted only to be away from them, to find a place where she would be alone. She didn't know what to do, or who she was, or if they wanted her.

Another train had pulled into the station and there were hordes of people milling around. She wove her way among them, almost running. She didn't need to run. If Richard came close, she could duck away from him behind five or six passengers.

Besides, she couldn't run anymore. She was exhausted and she could barely breathe because of the baby. And now there was a trickle of water coming down the inside of her jeans.

The baby must've been jostling up against my kidneys again, she reasoned. But it was strange. She didn't need to go to the bathroom. She couldn't think of that, however; not now. There wasn't time. She had to get away.

A frantic Richard grabbed Tyler's forearm. "Ty. Have you seen Ann?"

"Yeah. Sure did. Just about ten minutes ago. She was looking for you."

"No. She found me then. Later. Have you seen her since then?"

"No. I guess I haven't."

"Will you help me look for her? We had a . . . a confrontation. She ran off. I don't know how she got here. I don't know if she's gone. Monica's looking for her in the women's restroom."

"Monica came with her, too?" Ty asked.

"No," Richard sighed. "She was with me . . . in my

office." He looked at his friend with sheer desperation in his eyes. "I have to find her, Ty. She's upset. She was running down the stairs at almost eight months pregnant. There's no telling where she'll go."

"We'll find her," Tyler reassured him. He shook his head. "It's too bad this train had to pull in right now. I just hope she didn't get out of the terminal."

"I know."

Monica came hurrying up beside them. Her face was still the color of gray stone. "No luck, Richard. She wasn't there."

After that they separated. Each of them combed the terminal. Tyler even checked inside the janitor's storage closet, but Ann was nowhere to be found.

"I'm sorry," he muttered, uncertain of what else to say when they all met back in Richard's office about thirty minutes later. "I wish I could have done something more."

"It's okay, Ty." Richard lay a large hand on Tyler's shoulder.

"If you think of anything else I can do . . ."

Richard was shaking his head. "No. There's nothing more I can think of . . . other than covering for me here. I may go home and wait for her there."

But Monica had already called his home. There had been no answer. When she called Danny, he told her that he had dropped Ann off at the station but that he hadn't seen her since. The boy was worried now, too. He was calling Ann's other friends to see if anyone had seen her. But Monica wasn't hopeful. Since everyone found out about the baby, Danny and

Monica had been just about her only friends.

"If you think of anything, ring me downstairs," Tyler instructed. Richard nodded silently and shook his hand. Tyler left them, closing the door quietly behind him.

Richard turned to Monica. She shook her head at him. She couldn't cry, couldn't touch him. Remorse and guilt had sprung alive within her, chortling at her like demons. "It's too late."

"I don't think I realized what that was going to do to her until I saw the look in her eyes. It was as if she couldn't comprehend it—as if we'd betrayed her."

"I know," she said. "I know."

He gazed at her in absolute suffering. "I was wrong, wasn't I?"

Monica nodded. "We both were, Richard."

"But you were right. You've told me for weeks and weeks how much it could hurt her. I should never have let myself want this."

She couldn't answer him. Instead she just stood there, wanting to cry out from the agony she was feeling. She loved him. She loved them both. She had lost herself and she had lost them, too. But it didn't matter to her, nothing did—only the disbelief she had seen flaring in Ann's eyes like a flame.

She had hurt her Little Sister.

She couldn't bear it.

"We cannot let ourselves want this again," Richard said to her as she stood helpless and devastated before him. "It was the biggest mistake I've ever made in my life."

"I know," she whispered back and, when she did, she

saw him flinch. This was as difficult for him as it was for her and she knew it.

"We'll end it then," he said. "It's been decided."

"It already was." Her eyes met his, crying out to him with words she could not say. "Already decided."

"I'm going home," he said.

She looked up at him, her eyes huge. She didn't say anything more.

He opened the door, picked up the little purse Ann had dropped, and walked away.

And finally, left alone, Monica buried her face in her hands and cried.

"Mrs. Martin?" The door to Joy's office pushed open and the caseworker recognized Ann Small. Joy could tell she had been crying. "I hope you don't mind that I came here. I need to talk to somebody. I don't know what to do."

"Come in, Ann." Joy hurried to find her a chair. "Sit down, child. What is the matter?"

"I don't know what to do," Ann said. "I went to my dad's office today. Monica was there and they were all tangled up with each other like they'd been kissing." She started sobbing again.

Joy looked at the crying girl. The very thing she had warned Monica and Richard about had obviously happened. "I'm glad you came to me," Joy said, moving around the table to gather the girl in her arms. Despite her anger, Joy knew she had no right to make judgmental calls against Ann's father and Monica Albright. Instead, she held herself in check and encouraged Ann to talk her way through it. "Tell me what you are feeling right now, Ann. I'm trying to imagine it."

"I don't know," Ann lamented. "I'm feeling so many things I can't even name them. I feel angry the most, I think. Really mad."

"That's okay," Joy said calmly. "You know it's okay to be mad sometimes, don't you?"

Ann nodded. "Yes."

"Are you jealous of them?"

"Yes," Ann told her venomously. "I feel like they were hiding from me and they didn't want me and they got together without me. Didn't they think I would even *care*?"

"I'm sure they knew you'd care," Joy said. "They probably thought they had to be careful because of you."

"But he's supposed to love me. Not her. Things were just starting to be okay between us."

"Things were starting to be good, weren't they?"

"Yes." Ann scrubbed her eyes with her fists, trying to dry her tears. She looked no older than a six-year-old.

Joy shrugged her shoulders nonchalantly. "Do you think, maybe now that your father is learning to express his love to you, he might be learning to love other people, too? That he might be learning to love Monica?"

"I haven't thought about it that way."

"Did you think it might be because of you that your father's life is becoming full again?"

"But it makes me mad about Monica," Ann cried. "She's supposed to be my Big Sister. She's supposed to be my best friend. I really need her right now. And they were looking at each other like . . . like . . ."

"It's okay to be angry at her, Ann. It's fine. And it's fair."

Ann wiped her face once more with the back of her hand. Joy smiled. The six-year-old again. But also a young lady who was deeply troubled and had every right to be. "Do you need a tissue?" She handed her a box from the file cabinet beside her desk. "Every so often I get to needing these in here."

"Yeah," Ann said, smiling a little. "Thanks." She stood to reach for the box, but when she did, a great gush of water splattered on the chair. It was horrible. She didn't know what it was. She started to cry again as Joy hurried around the desk to help her.

"I don't know what's wrong," she said. "It started in the train station but I was running away from Dad and I couldn't stop to go to the bathroom. I didn't need to go, anyway. It's been just a little bit of water until now."

"Ann . . . little Ann . . ." Joy was doing her best to remain calm and to reassure her. Ann had been so upset, she hadn't been thinking of the baby. "I'll bring you a towel so you can dry off. I want you to think about the childbirth classes you've been to. Think of the things they told you, ways you might know you are going into labor."

Ann's eyes widened. "But it's too soon, Mrs. Martin. I still have at least a month to go. It can't be the . . ." But as she said it, she felt a tightness grip her stomach. It didn't hurt really, it was just a cramping that started in her back and then reached all the way around her belly like a belt. She gasped.

"A month isn't too early, not really," Joy said. "But it is a surprise."

"It's my water, isn't it?" Ann gasped again. "My water's broken." And all of a sudden, despite all the classes she had taken and everything she knew, she was scared to death. "Oh, no. . . ."

"It's okay." Joy moved to comfort her but she was worried, too. It was all very well to reassure the girl that everything was going to be okay. But now she had to take action. She hurried to get the towel from the bathroom. She sat the girl back down in the chair and helped her pat her legs dry. "I'm going to call your father now," she told Ann confidently. And, secretly, she was praying he would be home.

"I don't even know where he is," Ann wailed. "He was at the office but I said horrible things to him and I know I made him mad and now the baby's coming and I need him." She was sobbing again, frightened racking cries that made Joy Martin ache for her. It was a horrible time to be alone.

"I'll find him, Ann," the caseworker promised. "What's your doctor's name? I'll phone him, too." Joy was careful to hide all the apprehension and the uncertainty she was feeling on Ann's behalf. She smiled reassuringly. "I'll have them both meet us at the hospital."

Richard gripped the Dodge steering wheel the way he would grip a lifeline. He wove the big truck in and out of the traffic on Sixth Avenue, heaving exasperated sighs every time a car darted out in front of him.

Colorado General Hospital was still three miles away, and he felt as if he was never going to get there. Joy Martin's words reverberated in his head. "We think Ann is having her baby . . . going into labor . . . her water's broken . . . she's alone . . . you've got to come. . . ."

Annie. I'm on my way. You've got to know that I'm on my way.

It seemed like an eternity before he found a parking space and even longer before he found the way in. He had to wait in line to see an admitting clerk who could tell him where to find her. "Ann Small," he barked at the clerk. "In the baby department." The clerk was smiling, amused at him. "My daughter. I'm her father. Ann Small."

"In obstetrics." Another woman leaned over the clerk and searched a list on the computer screen with her finger. "Small?" She looked for another long minute while his raspy, hurried breathing seemed to fill the corridor. They couldn't know what it was like, with everything that had happened today, and being her father. She depended on him. And look where that had left her. "Here she is. She's one of Dr. McCord's patients."

They gave him the room number and he was off and running before he realized he had no idea what direction he should be running in. He went back to the desk to ask for directions. They told him to take the elevator to the second floor.

Once he was on the second floor, it was easy to find the right door. When he slammed through it, he saw her there, propped up on the bed with pillows. She looked like a little barrel with a huge belt of black gadgets strapped around her middle. The baby's heart monitor chirped regularly from a station of instruments just beside her. And she looked so brave and so small and so beautiful, he felt his heart swelling with pride for her, pride and so much love.

He rushed to her side and took her hand. "Annie. I made it. I'm here."

"Daddy." She reached up and touched his shirtsleeve as if she needed to touch him to make certain he was really there. "Daddy . . . I *need* you. . . ."

"I'm here."

Joy Martin had been waiting with her until he arrived. She stood. "I'll go now."

He followed her to the door. "I'm so glad she came to you," he said.

"Yes," Joy said carefully. "We had some things we needed to discuss." She glanced back at Ann to make certain the girl wasn't listening. "She was very upset."

"I can imagine," he told her. "I'll call you. We'll talk."

"Please do. I'll be in to visit her later, Mr. Small. To see the baby perhaps."

"Yes . . . fine . . . do. . . ." But Richard was thinking of nothing except Ann and of how much she needed him. He saw the caseworker out the door and went back to the bed. He stroked Ann's dark curls back up over her forehead. She looked up at him and it was the first time in a long time she let him see how very vulnerable she was. "Daddy. I'm scared."

"Are you?" he asked. He had to give her a little smile. "If I could have brought Abraham to keep you company, I would have."

She gave him a weak smile back. "I'm glad you didn't do that."

"He would have had something new to chew on. Yum, yum. Doctors."

"Dad."

"Sorry," he said, but his eyes were sparkling and she knew that he wasn't. "I'm sort of scared, too. But I'm going to be brave enough to get you through this. I promise."

"Good. Then I'll be brave, too. I'll promise, too."

He stayed with her then and talked to Dr. McCord when he came into the room. The doctor examined her and told them both it could still be a long time yet.

"She's in very early stages of labor," he told Richard. "If her contractions don't start coming strongly in the next three hours, we'll have to induce. We'll give her Pitocin to really start things up. We don't like to wait for babies too long after the water's broken."

Richard didn't know what Pitocin was.

"I don't want that," Ann told him. "It's supposed to make everything worse. I can't do that." She had learned about inducement with everything else in childbirth class. She hadn't worried about it, or even thought of it yet, since labor should have been so far away.

"Calm her down, please," Dr. McCord told him

276

brusquely. "Are you her coach?"

"Her what?"

"Her coach. She's so young. She took the classes, didn't she?"

"Yeah. She went to those classes."

Ann's voice, when she spoke, was very small and sad. She had reached up and grabbed hold of her father's shirtsleeve again. "Monica's my coach," she said quietly and then she turned to the doctor to explain. "I have a Big Sister. My Big Sister took the classes with me."

"Then why isn't she here?"

Ann looked up at her father. "I don't really know."

Richard gripped Ann's hand. He was frantic now for anything that would help her. Even so, he could hardly say the words. "Do you want her, Ann? Do you want her to come?"

Slowly, she nodded up at him. "I do." She squeezed his hand back. "I think I'm going to need both of you."

"Okay," he said, matter-of-fact as ever now. "Okay." They had to have this baby one way or the other. If they concentrated on one thing at a time . . . they had to do it . . . to rally around Ann . . . and, for this, Ann wanted them both. "Consider it done. She's coming."

He hurried into the hallway to use the phone at the nurses' station. He had no idea if he could even find her. He tried the museum but she was out for the day. He tried her house but she wasn't there, either. Finally he found her at the Albrights'.

"Hello? Richard? Did you find Ann?"

"We did. She went to Joy Martin's office." Before he

told her more, he had a horrible premonition that this would be too much for her. He knew without a doubt she would do anything to help Ann. But he and his daughter had both asked so much of Moni already. What he was asking her to do now was go through emotional torture for both of them.

"Is she okay? How did she get there?"

"I think she hitchhiked. Moni . . . listen. There's more. I don't have a right to ask you after everything—"

"What? What is it?"

"We're at the hospital. Ann is in the early stages of labor. She needs—" his voice broke as he tried to say it "—both of us. She needs her coach."

She didn't even hesitate. He knew he should have expected no less of her. She had sacrificed so much for Ann. They both had. He felt the pain needling his heart again as he listened to the determination in her voice.

"I'm coming right now. Tell her I'm coming right now. What's her room number? Tell her to remember her relaxation breathing. You can help her by putting a cool rag on her forehead. Tell her . . ." She hesitated at last, as if she had just remembered everything that had passed between them in this one day. "Tell her how much I love her."

"I will." If it had been hours ago, he would have told her he loved her, too. But it seemed like a lifetime had gone by during the afternoon. Their boundaries had been set and there was no moving past them. "Come quickly."

He went back to Ann then and tried to remember all the things Monica had told him. He couldn't remember any of it except for one thing. He told Ann how much Monica loved her.

Ann nodded up at him with tears in her eyes as she started into a new contraction, and this time, he could see on the monitor that it was stronger.

When Monica knocked on the door and Richard answered it, their eyes met and held in rapport.

"She's doing good," he whispered to her. "You'll be proud. Come on in."

"So," Monica said, grinning reassuringly as she walked toward the bed. "Are we going to have a baby yet?"

"Not yet," Ann said. "But we're trying."

She could feel him standing behind her.

It was crazy. They had both known Ann would have to go through this, but for a long time it hadn't seemed real or Ann hadn't seemed ready. Now they stood together, quietly absorbing strength from each other, the strength they needed to take her through.

"Tell me what's happening, Ann," she said calmly.

"Dr. McCord just checked me again. I'm at four centimeters."

"Good." Monica took her hand. "Remember in class when they said it usually goes really fast once you get past three?"

"Oh, yeah. I do remember."

"Well," she said flippantly. "You're already there."

The nurse came in to question Ann and examine her chart and Richard pulled Monica aside. "The contractions are getting worse."

She looked up at him again. She wanted just to hug

him, to tell him everything would be fine, to hold him, but she couldn't. It was all so impossible now.

From the bed, Ann let out a little sob. Monica pressed past Richard in time to see how tense she was and she knew Ann must be having another one. "How close are they?"

"About every five minutes."

"Okay." She took a deep breath and then gazed back at Richard for one stolen moment. She needed him, would always need him. And from the expression in his eyes, she knew he understood.

She turned her attention to her Little Sister. Ann's mouth was a round circle. She was trying to breathe right, but even the muscles in her fingers weren't relaxing. "You in the middle of one?"

Ann nodded.

"Okay. Just concentrate. Just wait until you're done with this one and we'll talk, okay?"

Ann nodded.

Richard joined them, too, his face full of concern. "You're doing great, kid," he said. He kissed her. "I'm proud of you."

Even if I can't be a part of this family, Monica thought, *I've given him this.*

Ann relaxed. She wasn't fighting a contraction anymore. She reached both hands toward Monica. "Moni. Thank you for coming."

"I wouldn't have missed it for anything."

"But I was so awful—"

"Hush," Monica stopped her. "Don't even say it, okay? Let's work on your breathing."

Dr. McCord examined her two hours later. She had only progressed to five centimeters. He smiled at them wryly. "May be a long night for all of you."

As the hours wore on, they stuck by her. At midnight the night nurse gave her something to take an edge off the pain. And by 3:00 a.m. Ann's contractions were so close together Monica scarcely had time in between to coach her through her cleansing breath. "Come on, Annie," she told her over and over again. "Let the air relax your cheeks and your lips. Go slow and concentrate on it. One . . . two . . . three . . . four . . ."

When the nurse checked her again at 3:15 a.m., she was stuck at eight centimeters.

"How's the baby taking all this?" Dr. McCord asked.

"Good." The nurse checked the heart monitor. "A good, strong 140."

"Let's watch it. If it goes down any, let me know. We may have to think about a C-section." The doctor lay his fingers against her upper arm while Richard wet another cool rag and gave it to her so she could suck it. She was thirsty after her long hours of working. She was much, much too young to be experiencing any of this. "We'll give you thirty more minutes, Ann."

She nodded mutely. "If you haven't made more progress, we'll consider surgery."

Richard and Monica's eyes met over the bed. Neither of them was certain she could hold out even that long.

Richard went to her and wet the rag again, and this time, as she breathed, he raked her hair back with his hand and let cool droplets of water roll into her hair and down her forehead. Monica stood on the other side watching him, loving him for what he was doing, loving them both.

"I don't like this. I feel funny all of a sudden," Ann cried. "Like I need to push."

"Let me see," the nurse said. And this time, she clapped her hands and said. "You've made it! You've made it! We're going to have a little one. Get Dr. McCord in here. Great job, Ann."

Dr. McCord rushed in. "Okay, here we go. Let's get it out of there."

"I can't do this, Daddy," she hollered. "I just can't do this. I'm scared."

"You can do it. I know you can. It will be worth everything. You'll see." There were tears in Richard's eyes as he coaxed her along. "It was exactly that way with your mother and me."

Richard's earnest, caring words spurred Ann on. He supported her shoulders while she strained.

"I'm trying . . . so hard . . . it hurts . . . help me . . ." she screamed.

"Come on, little one. Come right on." Monica gripped her other shoulder, holding her up and cheering for her, too. "You can do it, Ann."

"We've got the head. Here we go," Dr. McCord was excited now, too. "One more shove and we'll have a baby."

This time when Ann moaned and struggled, and as everyone shouted for her, a tiny, dark head was born. Then another push and she collapsed, she was free of it, as the baby's shoulders rotated out. Then out came his tiny rump.

"A boy," Dr. McCord shouted. "We've got ourselves a boy!"

"Oh," Ann sobbed. "Oh. Let me see him."

He handed her the baby before he even cut the cord. Then the nurses took him and dressed him and swaddled him and brought him back again. They were covering Ann with warm blankets now, and her legs were shaking and she was crying, but so was her dad.

Ann touched the baby's tiny nose. "Look at *this.*" It was impossible to absorb all the beauty she saw in his tiny perfection. He had a tiny cowlick and his eyes were sea-blue. He was small—just an ounce below six pounds. And he was looking up at her with eyes so alert it was like he was trying to focus on all of life in her face.

"Dad," she said happily, and Monica felt her heart wrench inside of her. Ann had forgotten she was even there. "Look at his fingernails. They're like crescent moons." She pointed to one thumb. "That one even needs cutting already."

"He looks a little like you did," Richard said softly.

"Does he?"

Richard bent to hug his daughter as Monica smeared tears away from her eyes with her arm. "Your mother would have been so proud of you, Annie. I wish she could have seen you."

Ann turned tender eyes up toward her father. "I love you, Dad. Thanks for being here."

"Thanks for asking me."

They were lost in each other and in the baby. Monica took the opportunity to move back from them. She

283

stepped back, out through the doorway, just as an O.B. nurse came in to do something for the baby.

She peered back in through the window. "How I love you, Richard Small," she whispered. "How I will always love all *three* of you."

But they couldn't hear her. It broke her heart watching them through the little glass window. They were just as they should be—Richard only had eyes for his daughter and the boy she had borne; their arms were intertwined just the way their lives would be. The pride in Richard's eyes and the love in Ann's was picture perfect as Monica forced herself to let them go.

"Good-bye," she whispered to no one.

And then she turned away.

Chapter Seventeen

Danny held out his arms and carefully jostled them so the baby would be in position.

"You sure you've got him?" Ann asked before she pulled her hands away.

"I think so. He feels secure." Danny had never held a baby before. This was certainly a new experience.

Ann turned her tired, pixie face up toward his. "Well. What do you think? Tell me what you think."

Danny's arms were stiff, still half extended from his body. His head was cocked sideways, against one shoulder, as he stared down at the tiny boy. "Oh, Ann . . . I don't know what to say. Just look at him."

"Here." She guided him by touching the crook of his elbow where it was supposed to bend. "Hold him like this. Bend your arms in." And when he did, Danny finally held the baby close.

"Did the nurse show you how to hold him?" he asked, wide-eyed.

"No." Ann gave him a little smile, a timeless smile. She just sort of knew what to do. *I guess that's what having a baby is like. You just sort of end up knowing things. But, still, there are about a million things I don't know.*

The nurse hadn't shown her how to hold him. But she had shown her how to fold him inside his little blanket and how to put his little knit cap on his head so he would stay warm. And the nurse had shown her how to handle the mucus that came up in his throat, to suck it away with a little bulb, and she had done it several times although it scared her.

"I want to hear what you think, Danny," she grinned at him proudly. "You're being awfully quiet. Did I do an okay job?"

"I should say so."

She let out a little peal of laughter. "Tell me over and over again. I need to hear it."

"It's amazing, isn't it?" he asked. He was still staring down as if this was the first baby he had ever seen. "Here is somebody . . . somebody who's going to be a person . . . who wouldn't be here if it wasn't for you and me."

"I know. It's kinda weird."

"Does he look like one of us? Like you, maybe?" Danny asked. "I think he sorta does."

"Dad thinks so," she answered softly, craning to see

285

the baby again. It was hard to keep her eyes off of him. "I think he looks like a little old man. He's all wrinkled and he's almost bald except for around his cowlick and he looks up at me like he knows everything."

"Maybe he does. That's a neat thought. Maybe babies come into the world to teach us to be. . . ." He handed the baby back to Ann. "Mom wants to come up and see him tomorrow. Is that okay? She says she's really proud of us. It might be sort of hard for you to talk to her."

Ann was smiling serenely again. "Not too much of this has been easy, Danny."

"Da-dum!" Richard sang out as he pushed open the door with his backside and carried Ann's tray into the room. "Dinner is served. I just happened to run into the gourmet cook outside and he said I could deliver it."

Ann lay the baby down in his little cradle and kissed Danny good-bye. Richard sat in the chair at the foot of the bed, his elbows propped against his knees, and looked at her.

"Are you okay?" he asked her abruptly. "Are you really okay?"

She laid down the fork she had just picked up. "I'm okay." But tears came to her eyes when she said it. She was awfully emotional now, but the nurse had told her she would be. "I really am."

They sat in silence for a moment, just looking at each other, loving each other, before Ann found the courage to ask what was on her mind.

"Where did Moni go?"

He looked at her for a long time before he answered. "I don't know."

"Did you know when she left?"

He nodded. "Yeah." Ann hadn't seen her but he had. He hadn't spoken to her much but even at the end, when things had been so intense and the baby had been coming, he had known her every move. "I know when she left."

There were tears in Ann's eyes now as she spoke. "I meant what I said to both of you, Dad," she said gently, knowing she owed him her honesty. She was feeling so many things. In her heart, just now, she couldn't make it right for them. "I'm sorry. I can't help it."

"I know that," he said, smiling sadly. "Feelings have a way of just running away with us sometimes. We can't always stop what they do to us."

"So . . ." She asked it tentatively and he knew, by the way she said it, she was afraid of his answer. "Are you in love with her?"

"Does it matter?"

". . . maybe . . . yes . . ."

He moved close and stroked her hair back from her forehead in a movement that had become almost second nature to him during the past hours. "I am in love with her, Ann. I just—" He did his best to put it into words now, how all of it had happened to them, over time. "I've spent the past months learning how to open up my heart. It became a whole new way of thinking and, as I saw the way she was caring for you, giving you things I couldn't give you, I began to care for her, too."

"So. Are you two gonna get married?" Ann asked

somberly. She steeled herself for his answer. She hated the idea. She felt more left out than ever and she hadn't even had time to think about it.

"No," he told her. "That isn't in the plan."

She hated herself for it but a crushing weight seemed to rise from her chest. "Why not?"

"It isn't an option, Ann. We haven't discussed it. What we have discussed, over and over again, are our loyalties to *you*."

She lay her head back against the pillow. She felt awfully guilty suddenly and she wasn't even certain why.

"You and I . . . we've just gotten close again. . . . Monica says . . ." he was fumbling for words again, trying to say the right thing ". . . you'd feel like she was trying to take me away . . . that it wasn't fair . . . that you'd feel left out if we got together." It was exactly what Joy Martin had said so many times. But Monica had said it first. He wanted to give her the credit in Ann's eyes. She deserved that and much, much more.

Ann closed her eyes as huge teardrops squeezed out and plopped on her hospital gown. "I certainly didn't make it easy for you, Dad. I just . . . didn't know."

He took her hand and held it. "Monica and I aren't going to see each other anymore. It isn't worth it to either of us to hurt you." His words were just what she needed to hear. "It was hard for us being together on your birthday. Monica came yesterday because I called her. We both needed to talk about things we were feeling."

"You weren't talking when I saw you." She couldn't help her accusing tone any more than he could help the pain in his eyes. She was aching for them but she thought her heart might break, too. He didn't know it but she needed Richard for herself so desperately now because of the decision she was reaching about the baby.

"I know," he said quietly. "That was my fault, too."

"Dad," she said, just barely whispering it, as he moved to her side and gathered her against him. "I really do love you, you know."

"I know," he whispered back to her.

August 5
Dear Diary,
I have so much to say and I don't really even know where to start. Me and this kid are staying in the hospital a few extra days. Me, the doctor says, because I'm just fifteen. And the baby, the doctor says, because he's still small. (He was almost six pounds but he's lost a little since he was born.) But everybody says he really is okay. Everybody says he's beautiful. (And I think so, too.)

I guess I've just realized these past days how much my dad loves me. You know what? He loved Monica, too. He told me he isn't going to marry her because he wants to be with me. That makes me feel funny and wonderful and sad at the same time.

I keep thinking about how unselfish that is. My dad is so wonderful. I don't think I can ever be as good as he is now that I know him again. Sitting here thinking about it sure makes me want to try, though.

I keep thinking about the baby. I want to love him just as much as my dad loves me. I know Monica knows how much her real mom loved her. She loved her enough to give her to Sarah and to Mr. and Mrs. Albright so they could be her family instead.

I think that is what I want to do.

The social worker has a list of families who want babies. Last time I was at Dr. McCord's office, they said I could even pick which family I wanted him to go to. There are lots of neat families (good families, not just clean ones) that I can pick from for him. I could go back to school. I could take photography classes and be on the yearbook staff maybe. Danny wouldn't have to worry anymore. And the baby, my first, precious little boy, would be good, too.

If anything makes me sad, it's thinking that we wouldn't be a part of each other's lives anymore. Except we'll always be a part of each other. Because we are a part of each other. I'll always be his momma in my heart. We'll always just belong.

More later, I promise.

Love,
Ann Leidy Small
(Age 15)

Ann stuck her pen inside the nightstand beside her bed. She shrugged into her robe and stuffed her diary into her suitcase. It felt good to be up. She strolled leisurely up the hallway where she could see the other babies.

As she rounded the corner, she came upon a tall woman with her face pressed against the glass. "Hi," Ann said politely.

"Hello," the woman answered.

Just then, from around the corner, came a man who had to be her husband. He was loaded down with a mass of baby equipment—a diaper bag and bottles, a little quilted pink bunting, a video camera and a huge mauve teddy bear. The lady, who had left a little smudge on the nursery window right where her forehead had been, laughed at him.

"Darling. You didn't have to bring *everything*."

"I didn't," he snorted. "I didn't bring the baby seat. I left that in the car."

Her forehead was back on the glass again. "You ready?"

"Any time you are."

"Okay." But she couldn't seem to tear her eyes away from a tiny child wrapped in pink blankets lying in a bed beside the window.

"I'll get the nurse," he offered.

"Are you taking your baby home today?" Ann asked tentatively.

The woman looked surprised. Then she looked pleased. "Why, yes. Yes, we are."

"You look really nice for just getting out of the hospital."

The woman started. Then a broad, slow smile crossed her face. "I haven't been in the hospital. We're adopting her. We've tried for eleven years. She's such a little miracle, isn't she?"

A nurse appeared, carrying the baby, with the new father right behind them, doing his best to videotape everything. "Here she is," the nurse said as she handed the baby over. "The papers are all in order."

The woman had forgotten Ann entirely as she crooned down at her new little daughter. "Hello, Ciara. Hel-*lo*. Are you ready to go home? We have a bit of a drive but we have a room all ready for you that looks just like a pink cloud. We have dresses and dolls and you will have a kitty and a puppy . . ."

Her voice faded out as they walked down the hallway, but for a long time, Ann could still hear her words.

It's such a miracle . . . We've tried for eleven years . . . Hello, Ciara . . . hel-lo. . . .

She heard her father's words, too, as he spoke of Monica.

It became a whole new way of thinking . . . after I saw the way she was caring for you . . . giving you things I couldn't give you. . . .

And even her own words prodded her.

We'll always be a part of each other. Because we are a part of each other. God tied us together once and now we belong.

Ann closed her eyes for a fraction of a second, then drew her robe closer around her. She hugged herself with her own arms. She had to go back to the room now and call Danny. Because, now, she was certain of it; she knew exactly what it was she was going to do.

"I didn't want to do anything before I talked to you,"

she told Danny as he stood at the foot of her bed, gazing at the baby. "It's your decision, too. He's as much yours as he is mine."

"You know," he said, "if it had been up to me a long time ago, I wouldn't have even wanted you to have the baby. And I'm so glad you did, Ann. It seems so special now." He was feeling a myriad of conflicting emotions. Hope. Sadness. Relief. He was doing his best to sort them all out. "When did you change your mind?"

"I've been changing my mind all along, I think," she told him. "And I didn't know how much I was going to love him until now. I didn't know how I was going to feel about him."

Danny was astounded. "Really?"

"I want him to have so much, Danny. I want him to have a little blue bicycle and swimming lessons every summer and his own room with funny posters on the walls. I want him to grow up and go to school and have a mom and a dad who can spend lots of time with him. I want him to have more than just me, more than just us, just kids who don't know anything yet."

Danny moved to the side of the bed, took his friend's face in his hands and held it. "Listen to me. You know plenty. You've taught *me* plenty. You've had to do so much."

"But it was worth it, don't you think? All of it. Just to see his little face and to know I've given him a *life?* I know I'll always love him even after I'm grown up."

"But you *are* grown up."

Ann was shaking her head at him. "No. No . . . not nearly enough."

• • •

Monica shut off the lights in the toy museum and went to get her purse.

She felt as if the lights had been shut off in her soul, too, she felt so alone and so . . . She struggled to come up with the right word.

Finished.

Everything in her life was finished.

But she knew that wasn't really true. She knew that someday, a long time away, there was the possibility she might feel alive again. But first there would be hundreds of desolate days stretching out before her. The recovery would be slow.

Monica thought back to her last view of Richard and Ann together with the baby, intertwined, as they should be. Perhaps, just perhaps, she could take a bit of the credit for bringing them together, for helping Richard express everything he was feeling.

That thought brought a small smile to her face.

It had been three days since Ann had delivered the baby. Three days since she had been with them . . . a part of them. They had been a family of sorts.

Three days since Richard had held her, kissed her and told her he loved her.

She was mourning the loss of him now, mourning the loss of them all. She moved through each day as if she had lead weights on every limb, pulling her down . . . down . . . until she was unable to stand. . . .

As she started to lock the door, she remembered one thing she still needed to do. She went back inside the office, flipped on her desk lamp and pulled up the

Word program on her computer.

She typed and, as she did, she felt as if her heart was rending in two.

Dear Mrs. Martin,

I regret to inform you that I do not think it suitable for me to serve as a Big Sister any longer. As you know, I care deeply for Ann Small. However, my unfortunate relationship with her father has been detrimental to her. I think it best at this time to step out of their lives entirely. Now that Ann has delivered her baby, I trust you will find another Big Sister to stand beside her in my stead. Thank you.

She couldn't sign her name to it. She sat there, pen poised and ready, but she couldn't do it. She couldn't absolve herself of the responsibilities she had taken on and had failed to fulfill.

Do it, she told herself bitterly. *It's the only way you can help Ann now.*

She raised the pen and this time she did it, scrawling her name across the bottom of the page in her elaborate script.

Monica Elaine Albright.

She stared at the page for a moment, read it over once and then creased it into thirds. The letter ended a possibility, a promise, that could have made her life very, very different.

She couldn't cry. Her emotions ran too deep for that, like a deep dry river, hollowing her out, draining her.

Monica slipped the letter into the envelope and

sealed it. Then, secluded in the semidarkness of the room that had been built especially for her—with one chair, one desk, one light—she buried her face in both hands and rocked back and forth, dry eyed, while her grief engulfed her.

"I wish I had a better case or something for him to take his things in," Ann told the nurse as she folded the receiving blankets and the little yellow sleeper into a paper grocery sack. "I have some other things at home, too." Really, she was talking to herself even though the nurse was in the room helping her. "I should send them." But that was crazy. The things she had to offer him were so meager and he was going to a home where they had probably waited for him for years.

He would have everything. She loved him enough to want him to have everything.

She stuck a little rocking horse rattle in the bag. Danny had brought it to him the day he was born. She wanted him to have that, too.

"Know what I think?" the nurse asked. "I think you're sending him several special things. That's good. But you ought to save the things you've got at home. You can use them when you have a baby of your own."

You can use them when you have a baby of your own.

Already it was as if he didn't belong to her any more, as if he was expelled from her body and now expelled from her life. She knew he was going to a much, much better place.

Ann had picked the family herself. The dad was a master electrician and the mom worked at a pharmacy.

She had already decided to quit and stay home when they got a baby. The social worker showed her pictures of their pretty little house and of the horse they kept. And the application said they went to a little Baptist church.

She couldn't think of anything better for him.

His new family was coming from Wyoming to see him today. They would take him home tomorrow. Ann was going home today and she was taking an envelope full of remembrances of him—a beaded, blue and white bracelet that said "Small" on it, a tiny snip of his dark hair. She also had a picture of him; the nurses always took one the day before babies left the hospital. This morning the nurse had taken two of him, one for Ann and one for his new mother. Ann was going to keep it in her locket, close to her heart, for always.

There came a knock at the door, and this time it was another nurse, bringing in the baby. "I heard you wanted to spend some time with this little guy today."

"Yeah." Ann reached for him lovingly. "I do." Then she sat on the bed with him and cooed and clucked at her son as she cuddled him. He lay in her arms, looking up at her with a celestial brightness in his eyes, studying her, as if he was absorbing her, as if he would never forget the features on her face.

After a while the door opened slightly and Richard stuck his head inside. "Can I come in?"

"Yes," she answered. But she never took her eyes from the baby.

"Thought I'd like to see him one more time. Ann, it isn't too late," he said abruptly. He hated that she was doing this so quickly and he hated to think he might have forced her decision. "You haven't signed the relinquishment papers yet. You can still change your mind."

She gazed up at him and he could see the peace in her eyes. "I know that," she said quietly. "But I won't change it."

"You're sure?"

"Don't worry," she said as she smiled sadly up at him. "I'm sure. I'm doing it for him and for nobody else."

"Okay, Pumpkin," Richard said slowly as he gingerly stuck out one index finger and touched the baby's nose. "But I want you to know one thing, okay?"

"What is that?"

"How proud I am of you."

She nuzzled the baby again to hide the tears that were forever springing to her eyes. "Thanks, Dad," she told him. "Knowing you feel that way . . . it helps a lot. . . ."

"You want me to stay with you until it's time to leave?" He asked it almost wistfully. The minutes were ticking by relentlessly and it was going to be hard for him, too.

But Ann was shaking her head. "No. I just really want to be alone with him for a while, if it's okay." The morning had gone by too fast for her, too. She had thought it would last forever and, really, it was the hardest morning she had ever lived through. Danny and his mother had come by to see the baby again and to sign the papers. Tyler Hill had come, too. Ann had been busy filling out forms and talking to the nurses and packing for him, and now she knew she had only minutes with him left.

"It's okay with me," he said with tears in his eyes. He knew he had to choke back his emotions. This was hard enough for his daughter without her having to see him breaking down. He believed Ann was doing the right thing. Still it broke his heart to know he would never see this precious little fellow again. "I'll give you some time with him."

"Thanks, Dad."

He couldn't hold his tears at bay any longer. They dripped down his leathery cheeks as, one last time, he cupped his big hand over his grandson's head. "Goodbye, you little guy. Have a *good* life. Be happy."

And, with that, he kissed the baby's fuzzy hair and left the room.

August 9
Dear Diary,
I think today, after I write this, I will read this thing one more time and put it away for a while. I think I'm getting too old to write in a diary anymore. Besides, I guess I am finished. And I think I am satisfied.

I kept this diary so when I have a teenaged daughter I can look at it and remember how all this feels.

But it will be a long time before I need it again. Because I had my little baby, a little boy, and I gave him away to a new mom three days ago.

It's been hard putting away the little things I got

for him. But I didn't have much. Just some booties and two gowns and a sleeper. I'm not going to get rid of all that stuff. I'm going to keep it and sometime I'll get it out again. I know I'll have another baby someday. I know I'll be a good mom then just the way my mom was good to me.

I cannot write and make anybody understand how much I loved him. But, when I told Dad that, he just smiled and said, "So now you know how much I love you." Isn't that amazing? Wonderful?

No matter what place my baby grows up in, he'll always belong a little bit to me. Dad says he felt like that when I was a baby, too.

The phone rang in the kitchen and Ann stopped writing for a moment to listen. When she heard her father coming up the hallway to find her, she stuffed the diary beneath her pillow so he wouldn't see it.

"The phone's for you," he told her. "It's Mrs. Martin. She says she needs to talk to you so you can make some decisions together." He frowned when he saw her perched on the bed next to the box of baby things. She had been thinking about the baby again. Richard knew she needed to do it, needed to grieve for him, but still he was worried about how incredibly hard it was for her.

"I'm coming," she said softly, then she went to the phone while he watched her. He was glad he had taken time off from the station so he could be here. He sensed how desperately she needed him.

"Hello?" he heard her say.

"Ann. This is Joy Martin. How are you feeling?"

"Okay," she answered. Then she paused. "I'm getting better."

"I'm glad to hear that," Joy said gently. Then, carefully, she continued, because she knew that if Big Sisters was still going to help Ann, the two of them had to talk. "I got a letter from Monica Albright several days ago, Ann. She feels that it is in your best interest for you to have another Big Sister—"

"Oh, *no,*" Ann said. She wasn't thinking of anything else, not even of seeing Monica and her dad together, when she said it. She hadn't thought of losing Monica. "Why?"

On her end, Joy smiled. "Because she loved you, I think. Now. Tell me what we do. Do we accept her resignation? Do we find you another Big Sister? Do we tell her we don't accept her resignation? What are you feeling?"

"I don't know . . . I mean . . ." She was stumbling. "Yes . . . I mean no. . . ." She stopped and collected herself and then she smiled as Richard walked into the kitchen. "I think I know what I want to do. But there are some other people I need to talk to first. And I want to talk to her, too, if you don't mind. This should be between us, I think. . . ."

"Ann," Joy said. "That sounds just fine." She crossed her fingers on her end of the phone. She could hear a hint of enthusiasm in Ann's voice again. And she was hoping . . . hoping . . . "Phone me."

"I will," Ann answered.

After she hung up the phone, Ann went back to her

room and pulled out her diary again. She flipped through the pages once more, skimming them.

I sounded so young when I wrote some of this stuff. I guess I've grown a lot since I started this.

Her eyes paused on an entry she had written long ago. Maybe it's okay to question. And I'm a little scared sometimes but I'm thinking that being scared is okay, too. Maybe I'm feeling secure enough to carry on with the choices I make.

"Oh, Monica," she said aloud. "Maybe what you told me a long time ago was wrong. Maybe a tree can be stronger if it's willing to bend."

She flipped to the last page in the book, the page she had just finished writing. She didn't add anything more. She signed her name with a hasty flourish.

> *See ya,*
> *Ann Leidy Small*
> *(Age 15)*

Then, proudly, she slapped the little book shut and stuffed it into the box of baby things. She smiled, contented. It would be there, waiting for her, when she needed it.

Chapter Eighteen

"Daddy?" Ann called out to him tentatively. And then her reservation gave way to excitement now that she knew what she was strong enough to give them. "Da-ad," she hollered in a singsong voice. "Come in here, please. We need to have a conference."

He pushed open the door and eyed her. She was sitting cross-legged on the bed with her new high school photography book open beside her. She had already told him she was taking one more class before she applied to work for the yearbook. He was glad for her now. It had been months since he had heard joy in her voice the way he heard it now. "A conference about what?"

She bounced on the bed. She felt tiny and she had plenty of energy, and already she was wearing her old jeans again. "Come sit down."

He was carrying Abraham and stroking the little dog's fur. He had stayed with her for days now because of the baby and he had told her missing the baby made him sad, but Ann knew his melancholy ran deeper. He wandered around the house or played with the dog and he always looked lost and alone. He wouldn't say it, but Ann guessed it was much, much more than just the baby. She guessed that his life had changed, too, that it was hard for him now, without hope, without Monica.

He sat down beside her and she took his hand.

"What is this about?" And then he wrinkled his nose at her and chuckled because she was looking so proud of herself.

"I am making a formal presentation," she said, patting his hand just like a grandmother would. It was a loving, possessive gesture and it made him smile.

He began to laugh in spite of himself. Smiling felt good. It had been a long, long time since he had felt like smiling. "I don't know if I can wait for this or not," he said, looking curious.

"You can't," she said softly. "Trust me. You've

already waited for this one for too long."

"I have?"

"I've learned a lot these past few weeks, Dad." Her eyes teared again. "I loved that little baby so much, just in the few days I knew him. . . ." She gulped, stumbling on her own emotions again. She knew that part of it was going to be difficult for a long time to come. She knew now what it felt like to love something unconditionally, utterly selflessly, like a parent's love, or God's. She wanted her father to know she could give him that much, too.

He saw her struggling and he pulled her to him. He wanted to hug her but she drew away. She wasn't finished.

"When I gave him away, the only thing that made it possible was the fact that I loved him enough to want him to have everything in his little life."

"I know that, Pumpkin." He was struggling, too. This was hard for him as well. And he didn't know where she was leading. "I know that."

She turned her pixie face up toward his. "I love you that much, too, Dad. I love you enough to want you to have everything, too."

I know that.

But he didn't say it aloud. He was just staring at her again, the confusion rumbling around in his mind as he tried to figure out what it was she was saying.

When Ann finally got to it, she said it so softly he could scarcely hear her.

"I love you enough to want you to have Monica."

She was watching him carefully to see his expression, to see what he would say, what he was feeling, how he would accept the gift that she was giving him. It was a gift he had deserved to have a long time before now. She knew that.

I want you to have Monica.

The first thing Richard felt was surprise. The second was sheer disbelief. And finally, finally, Ann saw what she wanted to see on his face—raw elation, joy in its purest form. Beneath that, he thought: *Monica was right to trust God. My daughter, giving us her blessing, in a way that gives her joy. I could trust a God who works this way.* "You really mean that?" he asked and his voice was gruff with emotion. "You really mean that?"

"Yeah." And she nodded. "I really do." She kissed him. "Furthermore," she added, "I think you and I need to jump in the truck and drive up there together, to tell her together, so she'll know we're serious about this."

I could trust a God who works this way, Richard thought. *Monica will show me how to bring Him into my life, too.*

"Oh, Annie." He pulled her next to him and hugged her so tightly he took her breath away. "If it's really okay . . . if it's what you want . . . let's do it, oh, Annie . . ." His eyes were sparkling and he wanted to laugh with merriment but he was crying, too. "Let's do it."

"Good," she said, still grinning. "I was hoping you'd say that."

She pulled the keys to the old Dodge out from behind her back and dangled them in front of his nose.

"I just wanted to talk to you a little bit," Ann said as she stood beside Monica. Monica was running the trains for a tour group that had come in from Texas.

Richard quietly joined the tour so Monica wouldn't see him.

She beckoned to Sylvia and asked her assistant if she would finish the demonstration for her. Monica and Ann stood side by side for a while, silently watching the little train go around before the tourists moved on to the next exhibit.

"I'm glad to see you, Ann," Monica said quietly, trying her best to push away the pain that seeing Ann again brought forth. "Although I don't know what we have to talk about."

"We have to talk about everything."

"Everything?"

"Well . . ." Ann chose her words carefully. She wanted to be kind and she wanted to say the right things. She knew her father had mingled in with the tour and was waiting. "I think we need to talk about you being my Big Sister."

Monica flinched. She had hoped so hard to avoid this, to avoid hurting Ann anymore. "But I thought . . . I wrote . . . Joy Martin should have told you . . . I don't . . ."

She couldn't finish it.

Another group had stepped up to the trains and Sylvia was running them again. The little train chugged merrily along beside them . . . through a tunnel . . . over a trestle . . . around the bend.

"Joy called me," Ann said evenly. "She told me what you were trying to do." Ann touched her Big Sister's arm and Monica met her eyes. As she did so she had the oddest feeling, as if she wasn't looking at Ann at all but at someone else instead. Someone who had changed and grown. "I thank you for that, for not wanting to hurt me . . ."

"Oh, Ann," Monica whispered. "We tried so hard not to."

"I know. Dad told me. And that's why I decided . . . what I decided. . . ."

Monica's heart was breaking. She was sorry Joy Martin had given Ann a choice. If only the caseworker had just told the girl what Monica had decided, it would have made it easier for her. That's what Monica had wanted all along.

"I decided I don't want you to be my Big Sister anymore," Ann said carefully as Monica felt her knees try to buckle beneath her. How she cared about this young lady. "I want you to be much, much more than that. And so does my dad."

Monica stared at her.

A lanky, dark-haired man left the tour group and came to stand beside them. "Yeah," Richard said, grinning. He looked boyishly handsome and expectant. "Only we decided Ann needed to be the one to tell you. Now—" he reached for the train controls that Sylvia had set back on the little platform "—can I drive this thing? I've been waiting for my turn all this time."

"Richard?" He was acting so oddly, but she was so glad to see him and so glad to see Ann, too. She didn't understand it all yet. She knew Ann had seen them together, knew Ann understood how they cared about one another, yet here she was, with him, smiling mischievously.

She felt her heart catch in her throat, not because she was hoping for anything, but because of the joy it brought forth in her, just seeing them together and seeing them happy.

"What we came here to tell you . . ." Ann went on jovially, as Richard concentrated on the miniature engine beside her. Monica was standing shoulder to shoulder with him, and even now the physical effects of his nearness were overtaking her. She had to smile a little bit despite her bewilderment. She couldn't see his face but he was pushing the train harder, making it go faster . . . faster. . . .

Richard was gritting his teeth. There was no way to turn back now and he wouldn't have wanted to. It had been years since he had proposed to Carolyn. And this was so different. He and Monica were both so much older and, by teaching each other, by standing beside each other, they had already given each other so very, very much.

He thought of how soft her hair had felt beneath his palms. He felt like a kid again. He wanted her so badly. He had almost lost her once. Now he was scared. Scared to death.

"What we came here to tell you," Ann repeated, "is . . ." He and Ann had worked this out together in the car and, with his daughter sitting beside him, giggling and plotting, he had been so certain it would work. Now all of a sudden his nerve was gone. His heart was beating like a snare drum.

What if she said no?
What if she wouldn't do it?

"What we're trying to tell you," Ann said again, "is that we love you. We both love you. And since we both love you, you don't really need to be my Big Sister anymore. Because I really won't need a Big Sister anymore . . . because I'll have you . . . if you'll just . . . do what we want you to do . . . and *marry* us."

It couldn't be. It was impossible and perfect and Monica just stood there stunned while Ann held her breath beside him and Richard turned to take both of her hands.

When Monica didn't answer immediately, Ann added more to it. She and Richard hadn't planned this part in the car. But so much had happened that Monica didn't know about. Ann knew, if there were questions in Monica's mind, it would help her to know just this one thing. "I know how much my dad loves me, Moni," she said gingerly. "I know how much he wants to love you, too."

Finally, as Monica began to understand it all, she found herself laughing, laughing so hard she was almost weeping. It was crazy and wonderful and perfect. Ann had just proposed to her for both of them. It was incredible. She had wanted this for so long and now they wanted her to be a part of their family, too.

Monica winked at her Little Sister. She had no way of knowing how frightened Richard was. She stood there for what seemed to him like ages, just basking in all the happiness she was feeling. But all of a sudden he was shaking, he was so frantic she would say no.

He gripped her shoulders. And even though he was frightened and almost desperate, his words were tender as he gave up his pride and began pleading with her. "Oh, man. Oh, Moni. You've got to say yes. I'll die if you don't. Ann and I have it all planned out and we'll . . ."

That's when he looked down at her and saw all the answers he needed written across her face. Her eyes were brilliant with hope and happiness.

He hugged her and picked her up, lifted her right off the ground and spun her around.

All of the love she was feeling poured forth from her eyes as she cupped his wild curls in her hands and held his face, surveying his features. "You seem awfully serious about this," she teased him. Then she bent forward once more and kissed him full on the lips. It was glorious. They didn't have to hide it or deny what they were feeling or worry any longer. "Yes," she whispered down to him as he held her tiny frame high above him. "Yes. Yes. Yes. Yes. And, in case you don't quite get it yet . . . *yes*."

It was Richard's turn to believe in fairy tales and happy endings as he clutched her to him and spun her around. "You mean it?"

She nodded. "Every word." And then she grinned. "That means Ann will officially be cousins with Patrick and Kaylen. Can you handle that, kid?" She looked around for Ann, waiting for her answer, and that's when they both realized she wasn't there. "Where did she go?"

Richard raised an eyebrow at her. "She's a good kid.

She's pretty sneaky, though. She must have figured we needed some time on our own in here." With that, he released her ever so slightly, just enough for her to slide down the length of his torso, and then he circled her with his arms again. He held her so tightly it felt like he would never let her go. And, just then, he knew it: he never, never would. "She must have figured we needed a little more of this," he whispered, grinning wildly, before he met her waiting lips with his own, working them in a delicious rhythm against her skin as she clung to him joyously, full up against his body.

For the next few minutes they were oblivious to everything —the time, the place, even the tour group leaving on the bus—as they tasted the future that lay before them. But just as it seemed like everything around them was a watercolor painting, blurred and running together, Ann cleared her throat behind them.

She was standing in the doorway, her arms crossed as she stood on one leg and balanced against the door jamb. Richard shot her a victorious grin.

"From what I can see," she said mischievously, "it isn't hard to guess what her answer was."

"Nope," Richard said. He winked down at the slip of a woman who meant so much to him, who was going to turn his family into a trio. "It isn't hard to guess at all."

"I don't know, though," Monica said with a glint of mischief in her eye. She couldn't resist teasing him. "I can't keep from wondering if he just wants to marry me so he can play with my trains."

"You crazy lady." He hugged her to him again. "I'm

marrying you because I love you, not because I want your model railroad."

"You're sure?"

He nodded. "Maybe I'll call Mother. Maybe I'll see if she can't drag out Dad's old set." He trailed off. Slowly, as their eyes met, they realized there would be a myriad of possibilities to share together over the years.

"Maybe so. We've got time for everything. We'll just have to try things out, one by one . . ."

They had so many things to plan now and so many things to talk about and decide. But they both knew that would come with time before the wedding and for a lifetime afterward. Right now it was enough that the three of them just belonged as they came together, their arms tangled, into a three-way hug.

Richard knew they might have some hardships to overcome. Monica still didn't know about the baby, and telling her would be bittersweet. But of all the decisions they faced in forever, they had already made the most important one. They had made the decision to be together, and to trust their faith.

It was brilliant, autumn morning in Evergreen. The sky shone as clear blue as a sapphire. The sun beamed down through the leaves of the quaking aspens and shone on the group of family and friends gathered together in Heritage Grove.

Monica stepped out, her hand resting firmly in the crook of Cohen Albright's elbow, her eyes on the lean, good-looking man who waited for her in the grove of trees.

As she walked forward, she moved from beneath the huge ponderosa pines into the aspens, from shadow into sunlight, and it was as if that was what had happened in her life, too. Loving Richard. Loving Ann. She had everything now, all of her happy endings bundled into one.

As Richard stood before her, between the pastor and Tyler Hill, his soul was reeling inside.

She loves me. She loves me enough to dive headfirst into my life with me.

And he had told her all along that it wasn't going to be easy.

He had never loved anyone more than he loved Monica just then, as she came to him, accepting him. She gave him her tiny hand. He could see the tears and all her commitment glittering in her eyes like pearls as she gazed up at him.

"Here we go, Moni," he mouthed down to her.

"I'm with you all the way," she said, searching his face and grinning.

Then, together, they stepped forward, hand in hand, to take their vows of marriage before a Heavenly Father who loved them. When it was time for Richard to place the gold band on her finger, she gave him a little smile as she tugged off her gloves and handed them and the Bible to Ann, her new daughter, her Little Sister, who stood beside her.

"By the authority vested in me by the State of Colorado," the pastor proclaimed, "I now pronounce you man and wife." Then he grinned crazily at Richard. "You may now kiss the bride."

313

Richard did kiss her, a long, languishing, lazy kiss that set everybody in the audience tittering. It was such a priceless moment and a priceless gift, to be kissing her this way for all the world to see. He wanted the kiss to last forever, but at last the pastor cleared his throat and said pointedly, "May I now present to you Mr. and Mrs. Richard Small." Richard pulled back finally, his eyes gleaming with mischief as the applause began. And Ann was the first to hug them.

After that, everybody came to congratulate them, family and friends who had supported them, who had helped them weather the past months together. For long minutes everything was bedlam. Abraham ran by, barking. Ann had brought him and even dressed him for the wedding, with a huge, white satin bow around his neck and a brand-new bone for the occasion.

"What's a dog doing at a wedding?" somebody called out.

"He had to come," Richard answered the crowd. "He's a very special member of our family."

"What you two need are real babies," someone else shouted in jest. "When are there going to be babies in the Small family?"

Monica and Ann's eyes locked and held. They would never forget the tiny little boy who had been so much a part of their lives. Even as Ann's eyes teared a little, Monica was smiling and answering. "It'll be a while. We have a long time to grow up, grow together and make things right."

Sarah and David stood next in line for hugs. They had just returned from a trip to Belize and they were happy, relaxed and tanned. "Love you, Sis," Sarah whispered in her ear. "I hope you're *so* happy."

"We are," Monica whispered back.

Kaylen flung her arms around Monica's knees. "Aunt *Monica*," she shrieked happily. "I thought that man was going to kiss you *forever.*"

Monica laughed, and the sound of her laughter was like a melody. It hung in the air around them like music before she stooped to give her niece a big smack on the lips. Then she stood and took Richard's hand again, and as she gazed up at her new, beloved husband, her eyes were full of happiness. Deep in her heart she valued this man, because she had seen him begin to trust Jesus, because she had already sampled the strength they could share, because she knew he would grow to be a man of the Lord.

When she spoke this time, she was speaking to Kaylen but her words were directed at the staunch, solid man who stood beside her. "You're right, kid. I thought he was going to kiss me forever, too. And you know what?"

"What?" Kaylen asked.

Monica's eyes were twinkling as she grinned. "Just between you and me, I can't help hoping that he does."

AUTHOR NOTE

I offer many thanks to the Colorado Big Brothers/Big Sisters agency for their hospitality and for answering numerous questions and phone calls during the writing of this book.

It is with joy and gratitude that I offer this story to you. *Just Between Us* was first published several years ago while I was following a star in the secular publishing world. The word that I can best use to describe my secular writing career is *beguiling*. While I was writing stories to please the world, I often included mention of Jesus Christ and God. In every case, these spiritual overtones were never edited out or changed. But something else was happening in my life. I had always thought that to be spiritual and religious, I had to act a certain way around people. If I had feelings or thoughts that didn't honor the Father, I squashed them deep and went about my life paying attention to "looking spiritual" on the outside. Only the Heavenly Father knew the things I was hiding inside.

I have always been a people pleaser; I care way too much about what people think. And, because I cared so much, I let myself be tossed in different directions when people told me what to believe about God. On the way home one Sunday, I broke down. Driving home, I could barely see the road. I cried out to the Father with all of my heart. I will never forget the words: "I am *sick* of other people telling me what to believe about You! I want You to show me who You are. I don't want to hear human voices telling me what to believe anymore. I want to hear Your voice."

How can I describe the changes that came in my life those next few months? Above all things, I found out that I didn't have to *try.* He just wanted to be there, loving me. He wanted me to be honest and real; He wanted to love me as I am. For me to try to earn anything from Him was to negate the power of the cross. There wasn't anything I could do to make the Father love me any more than He already loved me, and there wasn't anything I could do to make Him love me any less. My tired, thirsty heart could just . . . rest.

Our church service the next week was based on 2 Samuel:23, the tale of three fighting men who fought beside King David. That Sunday as I sat in the pew, my pastor made one point that went over my head. He made another point, and my attention was elsewhere. But just before Pastor Mike began the third point of his message, it seemed as if a friend draped his arm across my shoulder and whispered, "Deb, listen. This one is for you."

The story was about a man named Shamah who stood in the middle of a lentil field and fought against the Philistines. My pastor held up a Ball jar filled with lentils so we could see how small they were. As the story went, not a lentil was lost in the battlefield, and the Scripture said, "Great was the victory for the Lord that day."

This was the first moment I understood what I'd been doing. I had been giving away lentils in the Lord's battlefield every time I wrote a book that included both my faith and physical love scenes that I wrote because I thought they would please the world.

And so my life and my career have both come to a new, amazing place.

When Joan Marlow Golan, Executive Editor at Steeple Hill, offered me the opportunity to rewrite *Just Between Us* and three more of my early books, I could only see it as an honor and a gift from my Father. I have been given the opportunity to edit my own words and offer this again, the work of my hands, for His glory! This book is a physical example of how humorous and personal and creative His forgiveness can be. Thank you for blessing me by purchasing this book and journeying down this new path at my side. I offer this to you, in His name, with all my joy.

—Deborah Bedford

Center Point Publishing
600 Brooks Road ● PO Box 1
Thorndike ME 04986-0001 USA

(207) 568-3717

US & Canada:
1 800 929-9108